ASSASSINS IN LOVE

KRIS DeLAKE

sourcebooks
casablanca

Published by Sourcebooks Casablanca, an imprint of Sourcebooks, Inc.
P.O. Box 4410, Naperville, Illinois 60567-4410
(630) 961-3900
FAX: (630) 961-2168
www.sourcebooks.com

Printed and bound in Canada
WC 10 9 8 7 6 5 4 3 2 1

*For my husband, who inspires me
more than he will ever know*

PART 1

Chapter 1

HANDS FUMBLING, FINGERS SHAKING, HEAD ACHING, Rikki leaned one shoulder against the wall, blocking the view of the airlock controls from the corridor. Elio Testrial leaned against the wall at her feet. She hoped he looked drunk.

Things hadn't gone as planned. Things never went as planned—she should have learned that a long time ago. But she kept thinking she'd get better with each job.

She completed each job. That was a victory, or at least, that felt like one right now.

The corridor was wide and relatively straight, like every other corridor on this stupid ship. Every floor looked like the last, which had caused problems earlier, and all were painted white, as if that was a design feature. She didn't find it a design feature. In fact, it was a problem feature. Because any dirt showed, and blood, well, they said blood trailed for a reason. It did.

So far, though, she'd managed to avoid a blood trail. Of course, she'd thought about avoiding it, back when Testrial really was drunk. And because she thought about avoiding it, she had.

But there was no avoiding this damn airlock.

Her heart pounded, her breath came in short gasps. If she couldn't get a deep lungful of air, her fingers would keep shaking, not that it made any difference.

Why weren't spaceships built to a universal standard?

Why couldn't she just follow the same moves with every piece of equipment that had the same name? Instead, she had to study old specs, which were always wrong, and then she had to improvise, which was always dicey, and then she had to worry that somehow, with one little flick of a fingernail, she'd touch something which would set off an alarm, which would bring the security guards running.

High-end ships like this one always had security guards, and the damn guards always thought they were some kind of cop which, she supposed, in the vast emptiness that was space, they were.

Someone had fused the alarm to the computer control for the airlock doors, which meant that unless she could figure out a way to unfuse it, this stupid airlock was useless to her. Which meant she had to haul Testrial to yet another airlock on a different deck, one that wouldn't be as private as this one, and it would be just her luck that the airlock controls one deck up (or one deck down) would be just as screwy as the controls on this deck.

She cursed. Next spaceport—the big kind with every damn thing in the universe plus a dozen other damn things she hadn't even thought of—she would sign up for some kind of maintenance course, one that specialized in space cruisers, since she found herself on so many of them, or maybe even some university course in mechanics or design or systems analysis, so that she wouldn't waste precious minutes trying to pry open something that didn't want to get pried.

She cursed again, and then a third time for good measure, but the words weren't helping. She poked at that little fused bit inside the control, and felt her fingernail rip, which caused her to suck in a breath—no curse words for that kind of pain, sharp and tiny, the kind that could cause her (if she were a little less cautious) to pull back and stick the offending nail inside her mouth.

She'd done that once, setting off a timer for an explosive device she'd been working on, and just managed to dive behind the blast shield (she estimated) fifteen seconds before the stupid thing blew.

So she had her little reflexes under control.

It was the big reflexes that worried her.

"Need help?" Male voice. Deep. Authoritative.

She didn't jump. She didn't even flinch. But she did freeze in place for a half second, which she knew was a giveaway, one of those moments little kids had when they got caught doing something wrong.

"I'm fine, thanks," she said without turning around. No sense in letting him see her face.

"Your friend doesn't look fine." He had just a bit of an accent, something that told her Standard wasn't his native language.

"He's drunk," she said.

"Looks dead to me," he said.

She turned, assessing her options as she did. One knife. (People were afraid of knives, which was good. But knives were messy, hard to clean up the blood, which was bad.) Two laser pistols. (One tiny, against her ankle, hard to reach. The other on her hip, obvious, but laser blasts in a corridor—dangerous. They'd bounce off the walls, might hit her.) Fists. (Might break a bone, hands already shaking. Didn't need the additional risk.)

Then stopped assessing when she saw him.

He wasn't what she expected. Tall, white-blond hair, the kind that got noticed (funny, she hadn't noticed him, but then there were two thousand passengers on this damn ship). Broad shoulders, strong bones—not a spacer then. Blue eyes with long lashes, like a girl's almost, but he didn't look girly, not with that aquiline nose and those high cheekbones. Thin lips twisted into a slight smile, a *knowing* smile, as if he understood what she was doing.

He wore gray pants and an ivory shirt without a single stain on it. No rings, no tattoos, no visible scars—and no uniform.

Not security, then. Or at least, not security that happened to be on duty.

"He's drunk," she said again, hoping Testrial's face was turned slightly. She'd managed to close his eyes, but he had that pallor the newly dead sometimes acquired. Blood wasn't flowing; it was pooling, and that leached all the color from his skin.

"So he's drunk, and you're messing with the airlock controls, because you want to get him, what? Some fresh air?" The man's eyes twinkled.

He was disgustingly handsome, and he knew it. She hated men like that, and thought longingly of her knife. One slash across the cheek. That would teach him.

"Guess I've had a little too much to drink myself," she said.

"Oh, for God's sake," the man said as he approached her.

She reached for the knife, but he caught her wrist with one hand. He smelled faintly of sandalwood, and that, for some reason, made her breath catch.

He slammed the airlock controls with his free fist. The damn alarm went off and the first of the double doors opened.

"What the hell?" she snapped.

He sighed, as if she were the dumbest person he had ever met, then let her go. She did reach for the knife as he bent at the waist and picked up Testrial with one easy move.

She knew that move wasn't easy. She'd used an over-the-shoulder carry to get the bastard down here, after having rigged the corridor cameras to show footage from two hours before. Not that that did any good now that this asshole had set off the alarm.

He tossed Testrial into the airlock itself, then reached inside and triggered the outer door. He barely got his hand back into the corridor before the inner door closed, protecting them from the vacuum of space.

"What the hell?" she asked again.

The man gave her a withering glance. "He was dead, you were going to toss him out, and then you were going to go about your business as if nothing happened. I just helped you along a little."

"And now every security agent on the ship will come down here," she snapped.

"Yeah," he said. "But it won't be a problem."

"It won't be a problem?" she asked.

But he already had his arm tightly around her shoulder, and he dragged her forward. The movement felt familiar, as if someone had done this to her before.

Except no one had ever done this to her before.

"C'mon," he said. "Stagger a little."

"What?" she asked, letting him pull her along. Her hand was still on her knife, but she didn't close her fist around the hilt. Not yet.

"Do you know any drinking songs?" he asked.

"Know any… what?"

"*Stagger*," he said, and she did without much effort, since he was half-carrying her, not allowing her feet to find a rhythm.

They stepped onto the between-decks platform, which she loathed because it was open, not a true elevator at all, and he said, "Down," and the stupid thing jerked before it went down, and suddenly she was on corridor cameras.

"Do you know any drinking songs?" he asked again.

"No," she said, ready with an answer this time. "I don't drink."

"No wonder you lack creativity," he said and added, "Stop," as they passed their third deck. He dragged her down the corridor to the airlock, and slammed it with his fist.

Another alarm went off as the inner door opened, and he reached inside, triggering the outer door.

"What the hell are you doing?" she asked again.

"Is that the only question you know?" he asked.

"Just answer me," she said as he turned her around and headed back toward the between-decks platform.

"Weren't you ever a teenager?" he asked.

"Of course I was," she said.

"Then you should know what I'm doing," he said.

"Well color me clueless," she said, "because I don't."

His eyebrows went up as he looked at her. "Color you clueless? What kind of phrase is that?"

"The kind of phrase you say when someone won't tell you what the hell they're doing."

"Watch and learn, babe," he said. "Watch and learn."

He took them to the platform again, and as it lurched

downward, he pulled her toward him using just his arm and the hand clutching her shoulder. A practiced move, and a strong one, considering how much resistance she was putting up.

He held her in a viselike grip, and then, before she could move away, kissed her. She was so startled, she didn't pull back.

At least, that was what she told herself when he did let go and she realized that her lips were bruised, her hand had fallen away from the hilt of her knife, her heart was pounding rapidly.

That was a hell of a kiss, short but—good God, had she ever been kissed like that? Mouth to mouth, open, warm but not sloppy, his tongue sampling hers and hers, traitor that it was, responding.

"Yum," he said, as if she had been particularly tasty, and then he grinned. He was unbelievably handsome when he smiled, and she didn't like that either, but before her addled brain figured out what to do, he added, "Stop," as they reached one of the lowest decks.

He propelled her forward with that mighty arm of his, and she tripped stepping from the platform into the corridor, which was a good thing, since a male passenger stood near the platform, looking confused.

The passenger, middle-aged, overweight, tired, like most everyone else on week three of an interstellar cruise, peered at them.

The man beside her grinned, said, "Is this the way to the lounge?" and then kept going.

The male passenger said, "What lounge?" but they were already too far away to answer him.

They reached yet another airlock and the handsome

man still holding her hit the controls with his fist, setting off yet another alarm and doing his little trick with the doors.

This time he kept going straight, swaying a little, knocking her off balance.

"Too bad you don't know any drinking songs," he said. "But then, you don't smell like booze. Enhancer, maybe? Too many mood elevators? No, that doesn't work. You're not smiling."

They rounded a corner, and came face to face with three terrified security guards, standing in three-point formation, laser rifles drawn.

"Stop!" one of them, a man as middle-aged and heavyset as that passenger, yelled. He didn't sound nearly as in control as Rikki's companion had when he told the platforms to stop. In fact this guy, this so-called guard, sounded dangerously close to panicking.

Rikki stopped, but the man didn't and neither did his arm, so he nearly shoved her forward, but she'd faced laser rifles before, and had even been shot with one, and she'd never forget how the stupid thing burned, and she wasn't going to get shot again.

"Ah, jeez, Rik," the man said, and she jolted. The bastard knew her name. Not the name she was using on this cruise. Her *real* name. "Let's go."

"I said stop," the guard repeated.

"*You*," the man said, turning to the guard, and slurring his words just slightly, "are too tense. C'mon with us. We're heading to the lounge."

"What lounge?" the female guard asked. Not only was she the sole female, but she was the only one in what Rikki would consider regulation shape. Trim, sharp, but terrified too. Her rifle vibrated, probably because she wasn't bracing it right.

Amateurs.

"I dunno what lounge," the man holding Rikki said. "The *closest* lounge."

He grinned as if he had discovered some kind of prize, and if she didn't know better, she would've thought he was on something.

"You've gotta be kidding me," the third guard said. "Is that what this is all about?"

"I dunno," the man said, "but you sure got a lotta doors leading to nothing around here. Where's the damn lounge? I paid good money to have a lounge on each floor and I been to—what, hon? Three floors? Four—"

He looked at Rikki as he said that and pinched the nerve on her outer arm at the same time. She squeaked and hopped just a little as he continued.

"—and we ain't found no damn lounge anywhere. I wanna drink. I wanna enhancer. I wanna burger. Real meat. You got real meat on this crappy ship?"

The first security guard sighed, then lowered his rifle. The other man did the same, but the woman didn't.

"Oh for God's sake," the female security guard said to the guard in front. "You gonna let them get away with this just because they're drunk?"

"I'm not drunk," Rikki said, and the man pulled her close again so that she had to put a hand against his waist to steady herself.

He tried to kiss her again, but she moved her face away. "She's not drunk," he said rather grumpily, "because we can't find the damn lounge."

The front guard shook his head.

"They opened three airlocks," the female guard said.

"They're *passengers*," the male guard hissed at her.

"Reckless ones," the female guard said.

"What's your room?" the guard asked.

"Um…" the man said, his hand so tight around Rikki's upper arm that he was cutting off circulation. "B Deck, Something-something, 15A?"

"If you're on B Deck, it would be 15B," the female guard said.

The man extended his free hand. "'S on here," he said, and to Rikki's surprise, let them scan the back of his hand to get the code upscale passengers had embedded into the skin so they didn't have to carry identification.

"B Deck," the female guard said to the others, "Section 690, 15B."

"Suite," the male guard hissed again. "Expensive."

Rikki tried not to raise her own eyebrows. She had a cabin, K Deck, without a view. Cheap.

"We'll take you to a lounge," the male guard said to the man holding Rikki, "but we're going to have to fine you."

"For taking me to a lounge?" He sounded indignant. "Jus' tell me where to go."

"I'd love to," the female guard said.

"No," the male guard said. "We'll fine you for the airlocks."

"Not interested in a damn airlock," the man said. "Wanna lounge."

The second male guard shook his head. "I need a new job," he said softly to the woman.

"Good luck with that," she said back to him.

"I've got your information," the male guard said to

the man holding Rikki. "I'll be adding 6,000 credits to
your account. Two for each airlock you opened."

"Didn't open no damn airlock," the man said.

"We'll talk about it when you're sober," the male
guard said.

"Don't plan to be sober anymore this entire trip. Too
damn dull." The man glared at him. "You said lounge.
Where's the damn lounge?"

"This way," the guard said and headed off the down
the corridor.

The man holding Rikki lurched after him, dragging
Rikki along. She tripped again, this time because her toe
caught the man's heel. He was doing that on purpose,
but she didn't argue. She was slightly breathless from
the strangeness of it all, and from the way he held her.

The other two guards followed a good distance behind, clearly arguing.

The first guard led them to an actual elevator, in the
main section of the ship. Four other passengers stood
inside, three women, one man, all older than Rikki, all
better dressed. They eyed her as if she lowered their net
worth by factors of ten.

The man holding her grinned at them. It was a silly,
sloppy grin, and it made him seem harmless. "You goin'
to the lounge too?" he asked.

She realized as he continued to slur his words, all
trace of that accent was gone.

The four passengers leaned against the walls and
looked away, wanting nothing to do with him.

They got off on the main level, but the guard led
Rikki and the man to B Deck and took them to the B
Deck-only lounge.

"It's exclusive," he said to the man. "Just touch the door with your fist, like you did with the airlocks."

She stiffened. The man holding her had ID embedded in his hand. They had known who he was from the moment he hit the first airlock.

That was why she stayed below decks. Cheaper. No identification required.

He grinned at the guard and gave him a mock salute. "You need a favor, friend, I'm there for you," he said, then slapped his palm against the door to the B Deck lounge.

The guard nodded, almost smiling himself. "You won't say that tomorrow when you look at your accounts."

"Hell, I got enough. Should tip you, really," the man said.

"No, you shouldn't." The guard was smiling now. "Enjoy your evening, sir."

The guard stepped back as the door slid open. The man staggered inside, pulling Rikki along. The noise startled her—conversation and music, live music, and a view. The entire wall was clear, showing the exterior of the ship, darkness, pinpoints of light, patterns she didn't recognize.

Full tables, filled with overdressed passengers, laughing, talking, a few waving drinks. Some people at a roulette wheel to the left, others at a card table to the right, some sitting on couches, leaning against each other, listening to the music.

No one noticed as Rikki and the man holding her entered.

"Thanks," Rikki said, starting to pull away, but he held her tighter.

"Not yet, babe," he said as if he had the right to call her "babe." He pulled her to the bar, slammed his fist on it as if it were an airlock control, and said, "*Dos cervezas, por favor*," and the accent was back, thick and wrong. He clearly didn't speak Spanish either, at least not like a native, so he wasn't from Earth, not that Earthers were common this far out.

The bartender—a real person, male, wearing a blousy shirt with tight sleeves, matching pants and some kind of decorative apron—poured two amber-colored beers with an expression of distaste. The foam flowed down the side of both glasses.

Rikki fumbled for her credit slip, but the man caught her hand. "On me, sweets," he said.

Then he grabbed his beer, still holding her, and started for a table, stopping suddenly and nearly spilling.

"You need your drink," he said with the mock seriousness only the really drunk seemed to have.

He backed up, but didn't turn around, so she had to move slightly to grab her beer. The glass was cool and wet beneath her fingers, the foam yeasty, like real beer, not the stuff they served below decks.

His grip on her wasn't as strong, and she knew she could shake him off. But she wasn't quite ready to now.

She let him lead her to an empty love seat near the clear wall. The material between her and space itself looked thin and unreliable, even though she knew it wasn't. It made her dizzy, especially when she realized she could see herself reflected against the view.

She did look out of it, hair messed, shirt askew, pants stained along one thigh. Shadows under her eyes, hollow-cheeked, too thin by half, but muscled. Hard to miss the muscles, even with the shirt twisted.

He kept his arm around her shoulder until they reached the love seat. Then he slid his hand up to her clavicle, and shoved hard, so that she either toppled sideways or sat down.

She sat, without spilling a drop. Apparently her shaking had left her long ago.

"Do you always manhandle people you've just met?" she asked as he sat beside her.

His smile was different now, slightly feral, revealing a perfect row of teeth. "How do you know we just met?"

Her pulse increased. She studied him again. White-blond, blue-eyed, naturally pale skin, not the pasty stuff that came from living in space. Midthirties, maybe younger, stronger than she was, which was saying something, and—oh, yeah—he knew her name.

"What was all that?" she asked.

"Just me saving your ass," he said.

"I don't need saving," she said softly.

"Oh, honey, yes you do." He sipped the beer, made a satisfied sound and leaned back on the love seat.

"Well," she said and set her glass down, resisting the urge to wipe her soggy hand on her pants. "Let me thank you for the beer and the grand adventure, but—"

"No," he said, catching her arm. "You're not leaving."

"Why?"

"Because the entire crew of this ship thinks we're here to drink, so we're going to drink. We're going to get roaring drunk. We're going to dance and laugh, and come close to screwing right here in the lounge. Someone'll tell us to go to our room, which we'll do, and then we'll look mighty sick when we come out twenty-four hours later. Hungover and queasy because we forgot to take something before we decided to get drunk. Might help if you can puke on cue. Can you puke on cue?"

"Are you kidding?" she asked.

"Just hoping," he said and sipped his beer again. "So drink up, milady. It's gonna be a long night."

Chapter 2

LONG NIGHT. NO KIDDING. REALLY LONG NIGHT. LONG and strange.

She'd never been in this ship's first-class lounge before. The glasses seemed like the real thing, but she didn't know how there could be glass on a space cruiser, even a high-end one. The beer was exceptionally tasty, and the clothes—she'd kill for clothes like that.

Well, she wouldn't really. She didn't just randomly kill. She killed for work. It was a *job*, for heaven's sake, but still. She'd love to dress like everyone else, the high-end stuff, natural fibers, glittery jewels worth more than the cost of her crappy room on this ship—hell, worth more than the cost of his expensive suite, if indeed, he really did have a suite and not just someone's stolen identification chip embedded under his skin.

His lovely, lovely skin. Men shouldn't have skin like that, smooth and pale and perfect. And if they did have skin like that, then it should blush when his mood changed and show every single emotion. And she wasn't seeing emotions.

When she was looking, that is. She gawked like a tourist at the view—pinpoints of light, sure, but really, stars that she couldn't see from her crappy room; windows showing just how black space really was and just how much energy this ship was using because it positively *glowed*, and reflected in the windows, and

sent notice out to other ships—if there were other ships
nearby, which she doubted—that this stupid cruiser,
whose pretentious name she always forgot was right
here, right now, heading somewhere special with the
beautiful people on board.

Beautiful people like this man, this handsome, handsome man. Too handsome for her. She'd never been
near a man this attractive before. She always shied
away because they were highly visible. Women and gay
men noticed them—she noticed them, and if she noticed
them, then she wasn't safe around them.

She wasn't safe around him.

He hadn't even told her his name, not that she'd
asked, and it bothered her that he knew hers. But she
didn't ask him about that either, because he kept giving
her these little signals—*Drink. Drink more. More!*—and
she tried. But she wasn't a drinker, even though her head
was spinning, which she wanted to blame on his near-
ness, not on the alcohol content of that beer that he kept
encouraging the stupid bartender to bring her.

She could hear herself laughing, really laughing, because everything he said was funny or it seemed funny
or maybe it seemed funny among the beautiful people
with the pinpoints of light and the blackness of space
behind him.

Somewhere—fifteen minutes in? Twenty? Two
hours?—he ordered food and told her to eat some.
Burgers. Real meat. Real potatoes, fried up. Real bread.
Real. Wow. And the smell of it all made her queasy.

Or maybe she already was queasy, because she was a
little dizzy too, and dizzy came with queasy, right? She
wasn't sure.

"Eat something," he said, sounding normal, sounding not drunk, that damn elusive accent back. "It'll help the queasy."

How did he know about the queasy? Was she green? Oh, she hoped she wasn't green. That would go so well with her mousy brown hair (dyed rich chestnut for this job, she had to remember, she had almost forgotten how she looked—with the special-ordered bright green eye tint as well, hiding her baby browns, the only thing unusual about her). So the green would match her eyes, a thought that made her giggle and made him frown.

"Eat," he said again, and she was going to ask him about that accent, but he took a fried potato and she watched his long fingers caress the food, and she thought about those fingers on her—how they had been on her, and even though he had held her tightly, he hadn't hurt her, he had actually felt good. That kiss had felt good. It had tasted good—

"I mean it," he said. "Eat."

So she did. And he was right; it settled the queasy. She was just hungry after all. But she still felt weird and slightly out of control and wow, she wanted to take him to bed. She hadn't felt like this in a long, long time, unable to think about anything except him. Naked. Inside her. And—

This was why she didn't drink on the job. She was on the job. Really she was.

The thought sent a chill through her and didn't make her sober, but made her pretend to be sober, or try to be sober or wish she was sober. His gaze changed a little, a slight frown formed on his forehead, and before she could stop him, he reached out, grabbed her hand, and pulled her onto the dance floor with the beautiful people.

She didn't have a gown. She had stained pants and a twisted shirt and a knife on her hip for God's sake—or did he take the knife? She wasn't sure. She patted it, realized the shirt was over it, and he cupped her hand as if he knew what she was doing, then he pulled her close.

That sandalwood smell and something decidedly him. His body was hard and muscled, stronger than he looked, and he pressed against her, moving with the music, and she realized with surprise that he was as aroused as she was. She pushed against him, rubbing a little, and damn if she didn't get a blush or a flush or *something*, just a bit of blood under that pale skin in his cheeks, making his blue eyes so bright that they seemed as powerful as the lights on the outside of the ship.

She could just eat him up, and this—this was why she never drank. Not on the job, not off the job. She hated this out-of-control feeling. Or she usually did. Right now, she was swimming in it, in the want and the lust and the desire for him.

Whatever the hell his name was.

She couldn't sleep with a man if she didn't know his name. She'd made that a rule after a disastrous night when she'd slept with a guy she'd been assigned to kill, and that, *that* had been one of the worst moments of her entire life, when she looked at him and realized—

This man, this nameless handsome man, slipped his hand down her back and into the top of her pants, his fingers just playing with the firm flesh near her hip. She wanted to shift, to move his hand downward.

He pulled her closer and she remembered she had no

idea who he was and she couldn't take it, so she whispered that in his ear, his right ear, and he swayed with her, his hand dipped down, cupping her bottom, and as it did, his mouth moved over hers.

He tasted of beer and burgers and something so good, something she had to have, something she'd been missing her whole life. She pressed against him, wanting more, and he wanted more, she could feel it against her thighs, hard and urgent, and she slipped her hands against his flat stomach with just a trace of hair, erotic, that's what the hair was, and she couldn't breathe.

He was kissing her so hard she couldn't breathe, or maybe she was kissing him that hard. It didn't matter because she didn't want to breathe, not ever again, not when she could lose herself in him—

God, that thought stopped her. Like ice water.

She didn't know him. She had no idea what his name was, but he knew her, and he didn't mind that she had killed someone, the only person she was assigned to kill on this trip, thank you very much, so she wouldn't have to kill him, but what about the future? Or what if he was after her? She couldn't trust anyone. That was her training. Do not trust. Do not let your guard down. Do. Not...

She tried to pull away, but he brought one hand up and placed it on the back of her head. "Not so fast," he whispered in his not-drunk voice. "Information has a price. You buy it, one kiss at a time."

Then he kissed her again, and she didn't fight—she really didn't want to fight, if she told herself the truth. He was a good kisser, the best she'd ever kissed on the job or off, and she decided it wouldn't be a hardship to back him against the wall, peel off his clothes and take him right here in the lounge, the *exclusive* lounge, here on B Deck.

But, part of her brain told her—the rational, always-in-control part—that she really was drunk or at least tipsy (hell, no, drunk) and the desire to screw him brainless probably came from the alcohol. Still, he was handsome, he tasted good, he smelled good, and he was as aroused as she was, so she reached inside his shirt, and he said,

"Room. Need to go to the room."

And the voice sounded drunk again. He'd been sober before, telling her—what? Something about information. He put his hand around her again, only this time reached inside her shirt, and tweaked her nipple and it felt damn good, and someone said something about leaving and he said they were and could they have one for the road? And the bartender gave them an amber bottle.

They staggered out into the corridor—and she really was staggering this time—and the door closed, the air cooler, smelling fresher, and she felt—oh, still dizzy, but she didn't care—and he took her hand, pulling her along, *much better this way*, she thought, not being forced to move with him, but moving because she wanted to, through all the corridors down to the end of the hall and big double doors that opened as he approached into one of the largest suites she'd ever seen. The living room alone was four times the size of her room.

The doors closed, he held up a hand, and took out something—some kind of zap-it that disrupted audio—and set it down, and then said something about names.

She didn't give a good goddamn about names, and

said so, muttered "Bed," and he laughed, taking her up a curving flight of stairs (Stairs! On a ship!) into a room with a bed the size of her first apartment, and she was the one who pulled him onto it, she was the one who tore off his clothes, and then she stopped.

He was beautiful, truly beautiful, with rippled muscles down his chest, gorgeous legs with strong muscles of a kind men didn't have in space, the kind they got when they exercised in gravity, muscles tapering into firm ankles, and great feet, and she was only looking at his feet because his penis pointed at her, ready, waiting, slightly moist at the tip.

She took it in her hand, and he moaned and arched into her, which made her blink in surprise—why had she thought he was in control of his arousal?—and then he grabbed her shirt and ripped it off her. One movement. One quick movement, and her breasts bounced free.

His hands cupped them, his mouth drank from them. Foreplay. When was the last time a man had attempted foreplay? And she didn't even care about it.

With one hand, she unzipped her pants, but she couldn't slip out of them, not with one hand, and he didn't seem to care, he was still cupping her breasts and drinking them, worshipping them, so she shoved him backward against the bed (big, soft, wow again), and then she moved down, so that his mouth couldn't reach her any longer.

Her mouth found him. He tasted as good here as he had tasted when they kissed, maybe better, and she sucked, trying to get more of him, and that was when his hands cupped her face, tugging just a little, trying to move her away, because he was getting harder, and she knew he was going to come if she kept doing this and she didn't care.

But he did or his brain did or something did, because even as he arched into her mouth, his fingers kept pleading *stop, let's slow down*, he didn't stop, and she didn't want to slow down.

Her mouth was busy, but her hands weren't. She finally managed to pull off those pants, and the moment she was free, she moved as fast as she could, head up like he wanted. She was wet and she had made him wet and she slid onto him as if they were made for each other, and they pushed into each other.

He filled her, and she hadn't realized she had been empty. It felt so good. So damn good.

She bounced twice, and his eyelashes fluttered, a flush working its way down his chest almost to his navel, and there was no more control—or so she thought until suddenly he grabbed her, flipped her, and thrust, hard fast perfect, *perfect*, she kept muttering *perfect*, and then he kissed her and as he did, she pulsed, pulsed and pulsed and shattered—

And he came with her, holding her tight. She could feel him, every bit of him—she had never been so attune to her body in her life—and they arched into each other, and for a moment, just the briefest of moments, they had achieve something she had never thought possible, something explosive.

Something perfect.

Something right.

Chapter 3

IT HAD BEEN A LONG, SPECTACULAR NIGHT.

Or at least it had seemed that way when she was drunk.

But the next morning she woke up sober, sprawled naked and sore on the bed of a man she didn't know, in a room that had to cost as much as she earned in an entire year.

She remembered the bed—how could anyone forget this bed? It was the softest, warmest, most luxurious bed she had ever been in, with smooth covers, sheets that didn't scratch, and a mattress (or something mattressy) that cradled her body.

The room itself looked familiar only in outline. She remembered the carpet because it surprised her (and scratched her bare back at one point), but she hadn't noticed that it was the palest of blues. She remembered the windows because she saw herself reflected naked in them, and she hadn't cared at the time.

Now she cared, and fortunately, the windows overlooked only the blackness of space. Unless a ship had pulled up right next to these windows, no one had seen her and—what the hell was his name? Jeez. She had done things with him she had never done with another human being, *willingly* done them (and she still tingled remembering them)—and she had no idea who he was.

He wasn't in bed next to her. He was standing near the bathroom door, knee bent, one bare foot against the wall,

and a smile on his face. He wore brown pants that clung
to his magnificent legs, a half-buttoned, billowy white
shirt, showing those abs that rippled all the way down.

With his clothes on, he looked slight, which was
deceptive. He wasn't slight at all. He wasn't slight *anywhere*, particularly in the places (place) it counted.

At least he was as handsome as she remembered.
Those high cheekbones, that perfect nose, those startling
blue eyes. And the white-blond hair? It was his natural
color. She had found that natural color nested between
his legs, and she had found that unbelievably erotic too.

She still did, which disturbed her. Because as
crummy as her head felt, she shouldn't find anything
erotic. She had clearly had too much to drink last night.
He made things worse by holding up a glass of something foamy, which reminded her of the beer and made
her stomach lurch.

"Misha," he said.

"What?" The word came out mushy. God, how much
had she had to drink? Her mouth tasted like dirty socks.

"My name," he said. "It's Misha. I figured you earned
that much."

Earned it. She didn't like the idea of earned, as if
she'd paid for it with sex. A lot of sex. Damn. How
many times had they—

"And yes, we met," he said, "but I doubt you remember."

It was as if they were having a conversation she didn't
remember either. Her head hurt, and she brought a hand
to her eyes. They felt gummy and sore. Everything was
sore. And she had bruises on her wrist. Had he done that?

"Here," he said and handed her the foamy liquid.
"Drink it fast and try not to taste it."

She glanced at him through her splayed fingers. He looked serious, and younger than she remembered. Hadn't she thought him midthirties? His body was midthirties—flat abdomen, visible muscles, and at least half a dozen scars—but his face was maybe fifteen, at least at the moment. He had shadows under his eyes, and his mouth turned downward, as if a frown were his natural expression.

The sadness caught her—if indeed it was sadness and not something else. That, and the scars. She had been so involved (*involved*, what a euphemism) that she hadn't even noticed. How could she have missed all those scars?

She had no idea who he was. Misha? She didn't remember a Misha, even though he said they had met before.

She shouldn't take the drink from him. God knew what was in it. But if he were going to hurt her, he would have done it last night, while she slept.

Jeez, she'd trusted him more than anyone in recent memory. She had slept with him, actually slept, her guard all the way down. He could have done anything to her. He could have killed her or kidnapped her (although, in all fairness, where could he have taken her on this ship?) or given her to the authorities. He could have had his way with her—in ways she would never have agreed to, not in the way that she had.

She sat up, the sheet falling away. Her skin had finger marks, bruises, love bites, scratches. She remembered each one, so she hadn't been that drunk. Just the thought of his teeth grazing the tender skin above her breast made her shiver.

He leaned forward, handing her the glass as if he didn't want their fingers to touch. A bit of the stuff overflowed onto her hand, warm and foamy. Her stomach lurched again, so she took the glass from him and downed the stuff.

It tasted like carbonated bile with a touch of dog hair, but she managed to swallow it all without getting sick.

Her stomach settled the minute the crap touched it, and slowly her headache eased.

"What was that?" she asked.

"A couple of alcohol antidotes mixed with an emergency scrubber that I always carry," he said. "Works, even if it tastes like day-old vomit."

She grimaced, then wiped her mouth with the back of her hand. She no longer felt hungover, although she did feel wrung out.

"What happened last night?" she asked.

He smiled and looked pointedly at her breasts. "If you don't remember—"

"I mean…" she said, not wanting him to continue. She wasn't sure if she was embarrassed or not. She certainly hadn't been herself. At least, any kind of self she recognized. She'd been insatiable.

She'd never been insatiable in her entire life.

She cleared her throat. "What were you doing? Following me?"

"Of course I was following you," he said.

She sat rigidly, her fingers still cupped around the glass. Her heart rate increased.

She hadn't even seen him follow her. She hadn't noticed him at all on this ship, and given her physical response to him last night (this morning too, dammit), she should have noticed him from the moment she had come on board.

Her mouth had gone dry.

He hovered close to her. He had bite marks, too, and scratches and bruises, as well as the mark of her teeth on the very pale skin of his neck.

She had given as good as she had gotten, at least.

"Who trained you?" he asked.

Whatever she had expected him to ask, it hadn't been that. She licked her bottom lip, and noted with some satisfaction, that his eyes tracked the movement.

"Why do you care?" she asked. She'd been responding to his question on training, but she could have been asking about herself. Why had he cared about her?

His gaze dropped to her naked breasts. He visibly swallowed, then moved back to the wall.

Suddenly she understood the distance. He still wanted to touch her.

"Your training," he said, his voice flat.

She would have thought him completely in control if it weren't for his eyes. They moved toward her breasts, then her stomach, and her hips, buried under the covers. Then, as if he had to use the force of his own will, his gaze moved up to meet hers.

His expression stayed flat, as if he didn't care.

But she was paid to observe people, and she could see him. Of course, he could see her. Her nipples were hard, and she couldn't blame the temperature in the room. It was balmy in here, much warmer than her room down on K Deck had ever been.

She needed to get out of here. He was making her nervous, and she had no idea what he was about.

So she gave him her sultriest smile. "My training?" She stroked her breasts as if she had just noticed they were bare. Her fingers lingered on her nipples, then she shifted slightly, so the covers fell away from her hips and pooled between her legs.

His gaze dropped, and she had to work to keep her smile from growing.

Then his gaze rose again.

"Not that kind of training," he said in the same flat voice.

"Oh?" she asked, sliding out of bed. She crossed the distance between them in just a few seconds, and as she did, she slid her hand down the front of his pants. He was hard and hot, just like he had been the night before. "My mistake."

He put his hands on her shoulders, as if he was trying to hold her back. He was trembling. For one moment, he didn't move, and then he pulled her toward him.

The kiss was rough. She leaned into it, letting her breasts rub against his naked chest. His hands still held her shoulders, fingers tightening. She slid her thumb along his penis and he groaned against her mouth.

Finally he pushed her back just enough to separate their mouths. She kept moving her thumb, though, and his cheeks flushed.

"No," he said, his voice as rough as that kiss. "No. I'll die if I don't eat something."

"Ah," she said, leaning into him. "*Mais c'est la petite mort.*"

"No," he said. "I mean a real death."

Then his flush grew darker. He seemed surprised at himself, as if he hadn't expected to reveal his knowledge of yet another language.

Or maybe he was just surprised at the way his voice shook.

She continued to move her thumb. His whole body vibrated. She could feel it. With her free hand, she unbuckled him, and then she slid onto him.

He half closed his eyes, made a sound of surrender, and grabbed her buttocks, lifting her so that he could thrust. She wrapped her arms around his neck, pulled him as close as she could, and kissed him, moving her mouth to the rhythm of their bodies, surprising herself. She had thought she was done with this—too sore, too tired, too achy.

And not drunk.

But he felt good, the movement perfect (that word again) and she tilted her head back, let him devour her neck, let him slide in and out of her, until his legs buckled. He sank to the floor, bringing her with him, and as he did, she could feel him pulsating inside her.

His eyes had rolled back for just a moment, then they opened all the way, and she saw unguarded surprise. And a vulnerability she hadn't expected. And maybe just a bit of fear.

"See?" she said. "Just a little death."

"It wasn't little," he said. "It wasn't little at all."

Chapter 4

WHAT THE HELL WAS THE MATTER WITH HIM? HE HAD never reacted to a woman like this, not once in his life. Oh, he'd slept with them, and he'd enjoyed them, but he never got so aroused with just a touch, or if he was honest, just a look.

He had to get away from her.

Mikael Yurinovich Orlinski, Misha to his friends, put his hands on her shoulders and held her in place as he separated himself from her. Slipping out of her warm body felt like a loss, and he lowered his eyelids for just a moment, so that she would not see the emotion.

He couldn't hide it from her, any more than he could hide her effect on him. He wanted to. He had never lost control like this, not once in his adult life.

He stood, knees still shaking from their inability to hold him a few minutes ago, and he looked down on her.

Her cheeks were flushed, her long hair mussed, her lips swollen because of him. She looked like she'd been thoroughly fucked, which she had, only it hadn't felt like fucking.

It had felt more personal than that.

His heart raced. He was still wearing his shirt, but nothing else. He didn't reach for his pants—that would be an admission of a loss of control. Instead, he grabbed the clothes package from the bedside table. He thrust the package toward her, and was momentarily gratified to see her confusion.

"What's that?" Her voice was husky and it sent a wave of desire through him. If he didn't know better, he would have thought someone slipped an aphrodisiac into his food in the last twenty-four hours.

But even the most powerful aphrodisiac wouldn't have done this. Oh, he'd have screwed her and she'd have responded, but by morning, they would have repelled each other. That was the first and best sign of outside-induced lust. First the incredible attraction, and then the almost sickening moment when they looked at each other and realized they loathed each other. They wouldn't have done either normally, but it seemed that aphrodisiacs created two reactions: first the lust, then the loathing.

He felt no loathing. In fact, he wanted her again, even though his body was spent. He doubted he could do anything right now.

Even though he had doubted that about twenty minutes ago, and then he had responded to that thumb gently caressing him as if he were nineteen years old and able to rebound with a single thought.

Which he was doing now. He could feel himself hardening, again.

Fortunately, she hadn't noticed. She was still looking at his hand. He wanted to take that clothes package and put it in front of him, hiding his growing arousal.

But he didn't.

Instead, he said, "Clothes for you."

He was amazed he could sound so calm. He sounded disinterested. If he was dressed, he could have convinced her of his disinterest, although he had tried that before and it hadn't worked.

"My clothes are over there," she said, waving her hand toward the window.

He shook his head. "I sent them into the ship's disposal. Your pants were stained."

He didn't add, *It looked like blood*, even though it did.

"So?" she said.

"So, no need to incriminate yourself."

"I'm not," she snapped, grabbing the package from his hand. "It seems like you're doing a good enough job for me."

Then she got up, and walked to the bathroom. He watched her. Not a roll of fat on her. Her body was all muscle, but not like his. Feminine muscle, covered by firm flesh that had felt so good under his hands.

She slammed the bathroom door shut, and then he heard the shower turn on. She didn't say a word about the water, although he half-expected her to. Only luxury suites had unlimited water for bathing.

He wanted to go in there and get in the shower with her, to slide soap over that perfectly formed body—

He shook his head. He wasn't going to do that. Instead, he grabbed a different set of clothes for himself, and walked to the other side of the suite to the other bathroom. He pulled off his shirt and its rich scent of her, and dropped it on the floor. He turned on the second shower, knowing he would be charged double water usage, and not caring. He stepped inside the heat, and scrubbed her off him as best he could.

It was just an attraction, combined with too much to drink, and the fact that she was more energetic than he expected. He had expected her to fight him, not jump him. If she had fought him—

He still would have found it arousing.

He leaned his forehead against the tiled shower wall and let the water fall on his back. He hadn't planned for this. He was good because he was calm and he wasn't vulnerable and he was always in control.

You have passion, his mother used to say. *If you harness it, you can use it. If you let it consume you, it will destroy you.*

He shook that thought from his mind. His mother, cold and frightening, often looked at him like he was some subspecies of bug. His mother, who had trained him, registered him, and somehow kept him alive in all those early years.

She would have laughed at this. She would have said, *How like your father you are. He had passion as well.* But she wouldn't have said that with affection or even a momentary pang of loss. She would have said it as the fact it was, and nothing more.

Misha got out of the shower and stood on the drying platform, letting the hot air touch him where Rikki had touched him not half an hour ago. He hadn't expected her to be so beautiful. Or so passionate.

Or so right.

He had noticed her beauty when he had noticed her, that first night as the ship left port. She wore a slight black dress that clung to her large breasts and narrow waist. He could have done without the chestnut hair and the emerald green eyes, although he knew why she changed them. He preferred the light brown hair she had had as a girl, and the way that her brown eyes matched exactly.

He had noticed that much about her back then, thinking she would be a striking woman someday, in that idle way that people did when they observed something from afar. She had been too young to notice as anything but a particularly pretty child. He had been twenty, obsessed with girls his own age and women much older. She had been twelve and serious and so damaged that it made his heart break, even then. He hadn't even thought then that she would someday become a woman, let alone a woman who could make him lose his precious control with a single touch.

He had to stop thinking like that. He made himself take a deep breath and clear his mind, using old techniques, things he had learned in his teens when his passions, as his mother called them, threatened to destroy them both. She had found him training so that he could learn control, because she had realized early on that she couldn't give him that herself.

Some of his passion had been directed at his mother. He had grown to hate her within a few short weeks of their meeting, and the hatred had become a live thing. Misha had hated his mother more than anyone else ever—except, of course, for the man who had murdered his father. That man had been the first person Misha had ever killed, and the only death that had actually felt good.

Justified.

Misha pulled on his clothes, willing them to be his armor against the woman in his suite. He had to think of her as the problem she was, not as the first person who had ever made him crave her.

And the only way he could do that was to forbid those thoughts.

He felt like he had a bit of control as he pulled open the bathroom door. He walked down the stairs to the suite's main living area with its two couches, three entertainment units, full dining table, and comfortable chairs. Then he saw her, sneaking to the front door.

He reached her as she grabbed the lock. His fingers closed around her wrist, and he wanted to pull her against him again, kiss her until she was senseless.

Instead, he clutched that wrist against his chest in a hold that if he put a slightly different amount of torque on it, might actually break a bone.

It didn't hurt her, but she knew what he was doing. She looked up at him with those beautifully shaped eyes. The green was too bright. He wanted to tell her to remove it, to look like she used to.

Hell, he wanted to feather her face with kisses, make her moan the way she had made him moan.

Instead, he said, "Where are you going?"

"I'm going to get us breakfast," she lied.

He nodded, deciding to play along. "No need. I ordered some a while ago."

Her face shifted. He couldn't tell if she knew he was playing her or not. He kept a hand on her wrist, but loosened his grip, and led her to the large table.

When he got there, he tapped the top. The food he had ordered before she woke up slid through the system into the release window beneath the table. The smell of coffee and fresh baked bread filled the room.

Using just her wrist, he eased her into an upholstered chair. She looked gorgeous in the clothes he had gotten for her. The pale pink blouse was open, showing just a little cleavage. The tan pants fit snugly, leaving nothing to his imagination—not that he needed to imagine.

His heart started racing. He made himself focus on the food instead.

He grabbed it out of the automatic delivery tray, and set plate after plate on the table. Then he lifted off the covers, revealing steaming eggs and real bacon, and fruit so fresh that it made his mouth water. The entire platter of pastries alone could have fed the two of them for a week.

She was staring at the pastries as if she had never seen anything like them. Maybe she hadn't. She seemed to be doing everything on the cheap and apparently had for some time.

"You think of everything," she said. "Clothes, food…"

Her voice trailed off, but they both knew what she had left off.

"The clothes look good." He had ordered those as well through the ship's boutiques, and had them sent through the same system that sent the food. At the luxury level, he paid for any kind of service he wanted. He didn't have to leave the suite for the entire trip if that suited him, which it did not. But he was taking advantage of that this morning.

She ran her hands along the blouse. She stopped at her breasts, again, knowing that aroused him. She was trying to distract him so—what? she could bolt out that door?—and it was working. Indeed, the slight movement made him think that the color of her nipples matched the blouse. He wondered if that was what made him order it.

He made himself look away.

"We made it clear last night that we were going to

spend the next twenty-four hours with each other," he said. "It hasn't been sixteen yet."

She shrugged. "People get sick of each other. I'm sure the staff here knows that."

He moved to the other side of the table. "I'm sure they do. But we have to keep up our little charade just a bit longer, so they don't notice what you did last night."

She raised her eyes to him. Her hands fell to the table top. Her expression was flat now. "If they notice, it'll be because of you. I set the cameras so that they looped. No one would have realized I even opened the airlock if you had given me just a few more minutes."

He shook his head. This was why she was getting into trouble. She thought short-term, not long-term.

"They would notice," he said. "Not on the trip, but shortly thereafter. You didn't think this through—"

"The schematics were different—"

"Not that," he said. "The consequences."

"No consequences," she said. "I would be gone before they realized he was missing."

"That's not how it's done," he said.

She frowned. "Not how what's done?"

"The job," he said. "The key isn't to let them slowly realize that something had gone wrong. The key is to make the death seem natural."

She looked at him. "Who *are* you?"

He had already told her, but he did so again. "My name is Misha."

He paused for just a moment, wondering why it was so important she know his real name, why he hoped she remembered him. Before she woke up, he had planned to tell her the name he traveled under in this sector, but when her eyes opened, he had blurted his real name. His heart name. The name only people who cared for him used.

She hadn't understood him, which should have given him a reprieve, but some part of him wanted to hear that husky voice of hers murmur his name as if it meant something to her.

"Misha," she said, frowning. Was she trying to place the name or had she finally figured out who he was? "You said that when I woke up."

He felt an odd surge of disappointment. "Yes, I did."

"And you know who I am," she said.

"Of course I do," he said. "Since I'm the one who hired you."

Chapter 5

"YOU WHAT?" SHE ASKED. WHATEVER SHE HAD EXPECTED him to say, it hadn't been that. Her hands fell to her sides, and she felt cold even though the suite's environmental controls were set slightly warm.

"I hired you," he repeated, as if it was the most natural thing in the world.

For what? she wanted to ask, but stopped herself just in time. She wasn't sure she wanted the answer. The room, the clothes, the food, everything made more for a seduction than for a murder.

But he had helped her with Testrial, so he wasn't talking about the sex. Not that she hired out for sex. She hired out for assassination, but never sex.

"What did you have against Elio Testrial?" she asked.

Misha's smile was cool, faint, the smile of the man she had met in the corridor, not the man she had touched with such abandon a half an hour before. "He was a bad guy."

"So you knew him?" she asked.

"No," he said.

"Then why the hell did you want me to kill him?" she asked.

Misha leaned back slightly. He rested one elbow on the back of the chair. From this angle, she could see his muscular torso, the power in his body. He didn't look slender now. He looked like a man who built for speed and danger, a man who could move across the table, grabbing a butter knife as he did so, and plunge it into the vulnerable base of her neck without a single thought.

"I hired you to kill him because I wanted to see you work."

Her breath caught. "You wasted a man's life for that?"

"*I* wasted?" he asked. "I'm not the one who killed him."

She rose out of her chair. "You bastard."

He hadn't moved. Apparently, he didn't perceive her as a threat. "Actually, I'm not a bastard. I'm legitimate in more ways than you are."

That caught her. "What do you mean?"

He shrugged a single shoulder. "I am licensed. You're not."

"I don't need a license to operate in the NetherRealm." Which was true. This ship had to fly through the NetherRealm—an area of space between two organized governments, an area that no one claimed. She had waited to kill Testrial until the ship reached the NetherRealm.

"Technically, that's true," Misha said, "but this is what I mean by short-term versus long-term thinking. You hid your crime from security so that no one would stop you—"

"I didn't commit a crime," she said. "I was on the job."

Throughout this part of the galaxy, assassination was a crime only for the person who hired it done, not the person who actually carried out the work. And assassination wasn't always considered a crime, if the person who ordered the death could prove justification.

Technically, Misha was the one guilty of a crime if he couldn't prove that Testrial's death was justified.

Misha, because he hired her.

"You didn't let me finish," Misha said softly. That voice brooked no disagreement. It made him seem as dangerous (more dangerous?) than his posture did.

She waved a hand at him, pretending a calm she didn't feel. "By all means. Finish. After all, you hired me."

His gaze met hers. He clearly knew what she was implying, that the crime here was his.

"It's illegal to take a job as an assassin in both Litaera and Sygn Sectors if you don't have a license," he said.

"And the NetherRealm is between them," she said. "So?"

"So," he said with a bit of heat in his voice. "This ship will dock in Litaera. That's when the authorities will discover that Testrial is no longer on board."

"I'll be long gone." She knew that because she'd used this very method before. No one had caught her then. No one would catch her now.

"You'll be long gone and wanted," he said. "Because there will be no proof when Testrial died. And when there's no proof, then governments decide that they can charge someone with a crime."

"Well," she said. "You gave them proof with your stupid airlock stunt."

"I gave them a possibility," he said. "One they'll ignore. They'll decide that he went into the disposal system or into one of the engines or into the recycling system, something that would have also left no trace."

He was starting to make her angry now. He had screwed up her job. She had killed Testrial right on schedule. Then she would have dumped him out of the airlock and left no trace. The only way anyone would know he was gone was when the ship's purser figured out that the number of passengers who left was one shy of the number that originally boarded. The crew would search to see who hadn't checked out, find Testrial's name, and then conduct a ship-wide search for him. The search would take hours. And when they didn't find him, they would have to review exit footage to see if he just forgot to scan his pass.

When they realized he hadn't done that, then they would examine his credit slips to see when he ate his last meal. Then they would figure out that he hadn't done anything for half of the trip—since the NetherRealm. That would be when they would start searching for evidence of foul play.

By then, she would be deep in Litaera Sector, enjoying a few days off before searching for her next job. No one would connect her to him. No one ever connected her jobs to her.

Until Misha.

"I really don't understand what your problem is," she said. "I was doing my job just fine. I'm good at it. And you're the one who screwed it up."

He shook his head as if she was the one being difficult.

"*And*," she said with a bit of emphasis in case he wanted to talk over her, "you seem perfectly capable of doing the job yourself. In fact, if I can believe you, you're *licensed*. So you could have finished the job in Sygn Sector or in Litaera Sector or in the NetherRealm, giving you a lot more opportunity than me. You didn't need to hire me. And if you were worried about Testrial recognizing you or something, then you took a really big risk because you were on board anyway. So seriously, Misha—or whatever the hell your name is—"

He winced. The movement was so slight she almost didn't see it. However, she did, and it didn't stop her. She continued, "You're the one with the problem. Me, I just did a job, and I would have done a better job without your little drunk act."

His entire body tensed. "My little drunk act? My little drunk act probably saved your career if not your life."

She snorted. "I don't need saving."

He slowly leaned forward, his arm dropping at his side. "Really? Because those security guards were on their way when I found you. If I hadn't helped, they would have found you fiddling with that airlock door, a dead body beside you, and you would have been arrested."

She crossed her arms. "I would not. They found us on a different floor."

"It doesn't matter," Misha said. "You don't think that the moment a passenger touches the airlock controls that someone notices?"

"I would have made the notice look like a glitch," she said.

"With what?" he asked. "Your magic powers?"

She let out a small breath. She wasn't going to argue that point with him. Once she had figured out the changes in the airlock controls, she would have made the changes.

"They weren't going to arrest me," she finally said, knowing it sounded a bit lame.

"Yes, they would have. The moment they saw Testrial's body. Then, if you told them you'd been hired, they would have asked for proof, and you don't have proof because I never gave you any."

"Except the initial order for the job," she said.

"Which isn't enough for Litaera Sector."

"Fortunately, if they had found me with a dead body in that corridor, then they would have known I killed him in the NetherRealm. Tell me, who would have prosecuted me? In case you've forgotten, there's no government in that realm, and the ship's passenger instructions clearly state that the ship has no responsibility for crimes committed on board. The ship gives those instructions to cover its ass, in case thieves work the ship, to make sure there's no liability. But it works the other way. The ship has security guards, sure, but they have no way to prosecute criminals."

"Right," Misha said. He was leaning even closer, his blue eyes flat. "They give anyone they catch to the local government when they land."

"And the local government prosecutes if they have jurisdiction. But they have no jurisdiction in the NetherRealm." She stood up. "I've done this before. A lot. And no matter what you think of me, I know my job."

"If you knew your job, you wouldn't be causing so many goddamn problems."

She raised her eyebrows. He looked a bit stunned, as if he hadn't expected those words to come out of his mouth. Or maybe that was just an act.

"Problems?" she asked softly.

"I've been arrested three times for your kills," he said. "I've had to prove that I had nothing to do with them."

"Really?" she asked. Then she smiled. "Thanks for the confirmation."

His eyes narrowed. "Of what?"

She grinned at him. "That my method works."

Then, wrapping her hand in a cloth napkin, she grabbed the biggest, gooiest pastry. She waved at him with the other.

"Thanks for the great night. It always feels good to not only scratch an itch, but get some free clothes and food in the bargain." She walked across the room.

This time, he didn't try to stop her. She got to the door before he even stood up. Then she waved two fingers, said, "See ya," and let herself out.

But before she closed the door, she leaned back in.

"Oh," she said as if she had just remembered something. "Since you saw my work, you know that I completed the job. You owe me the balance. Might as well pay now, since the final balance was due on notification of completion."

Then she pulled the door closed and headed down the hall.

She wished she felt as jaunty as she had sounded. Instead, she was off balance and a bit confused.

He had hired her? Why? Because she annoyed him?

Or because he had planned for her to get caught, so he could prove that she was the one responsible for whatever killings he'd been arrested for?

She stopped when that thought hit. The bastard planned to turn her into the authorities.

Which was why he kept her in his room. The good sex, for him, was just a bonus.

Suddenly she felt dirty. And angry. And used. If she was an impulsive woman—which she usually was not (last night's proof to the contrary)—she would go back into that room and give him what for.

But it was better to stay away from him.

No matter how much she wanted to go back in there and kick his (really sexy) ass.

Chapter 6

MISHA STARED AT THE DOOR. HE SHOULDN'T HAVE LET her go. For her own good, he shouldn't have let her go.

But he couldn't move. He still sat at the large table, eggs cooling in front of him, bacon looking soggy, a slight frown making his forehead ache. She was willing to let someone else take the blame for her work. And it apparently didn't matter who.

So someone, some innocent someone, who didn't have an assassin's card or a proof of hire or even a partial justification, might actually go to prison because of someone she killed.

And some of the prisons in this sector—hell, in most sectors—were horrible places.

He stood up. He was shaking, and not because he needed to eat. He did, though. He was spent and tired and a bit achy, but in a tingly way—and he wrenched that thought out of his head. He couldn't think like that. He couldn't think about *her* like that, particularly now, now that all of his fears had been confirmed.

She really did have no ethics. She didn't care about anyone else. Just like he had suspected when he started tracking her down.

Last night, he had thought she would be different. Last night, he had known she was different.

Naive, he told himself.

Confused.

Incompetent.

He'd even thought she was funny, the way she staggered under Elio Testrial's weight, the curses she uttered as she tried to open that airlock.

Naive, confused, incompetent, *funny*—and beautiful.

He had found her attractive the moment he saw her on this ship, noting how she moved when he followed her, watching her laugh in the ship's casino, watching her flirt in one of the ship's bars.

And then he had touched her. At that moment, he had stopped thinking. He had gotten her out of her terrible little mess—which he had thought so cute. *Amazing*— he had thought, his arm around her shoulder, her body pressed against his, that scent of hers filling his nostrils— *how someone so incompetent had managed to complete so many jobs.*

He had actually thought she had bungled her way toward success, and as he led her from corridor to corridor, airlock to airlock, controlling her every move, he had two concurrent thoughts: first that she would be grateful he had rescued her, and second that she would beg him to teach her how to do the job right.

Beg him. Yeah, that had worked. He hadn't expected the mad, no matter how it made her eyes flash and animated her face. He hadn't expected her utter ruthlessness.

He hadn't expected that passionate, passionate woman he had touched the night before to be so very cold.

He made himself sit back down. He took the eggs and shoved them into the heater behind the table. He put the bacon into the recycler, and made himself eat some of the fresh fruit while he was waiting for the eggs to warm.

Assassins Guild Rule Number 65: An assassin's body is

his first weapon. Therefore it must be in the best possible condition at all times.

He believed in the Guild. He believed in the rules. They had kept him alive. They had kept the other assassins alive. Assassins, like any other profession, formed a community. They had gotten most of the organized sector governments to agree, allowing the profession to proceed with honor. Ethics were a big part of that honor. Ethics made certain that random people didn't die unnecessarily, that civilians didn't get accused of a crime for which they would have no defense, that everyone— from the assassin to the client to the victim—understood the rules, even in the abstract.

The profession was an old one. It had existed as long as human societies had existed, and was sometimes legal and sometimes not. Throughout this galaxy, the legality of the profession varied. But in the sectors where Misha worked, the Assassins Guild held sway.

He had joined at the urging of his mother, so that he could stay out of the situation she had found herself in. She had been an assassin for a particular government, and had been unable to tell anyone, including her husband, Misha's father. When she refused to do a job so heinous that it even got through her shady ethics and then she rigged things so that no one could ever do that job, her own government hired an assassin to take her out.

Only the assassin had decided to go one step further: he also targeted her family. Misha and his father were on a vacation cruise on a much smaller ship than this one when that assassin opened fire, killing everyone except Misha. The assassin left Misha gravely wounded but alive, then made sure the ship docked at the space station where his mother was hiding out. She found Misha and saved him, and she was the one who realized all of those deaths were a warning to her and other assassins to always do their job.

She tracked down that assassin, but Misha killed him. Barely thirteen, he had managed—through anger and sheer adrenaline—to take down a man three times his size. That was when his mother realized she had a talent on her hands. That was when she realized that together, she and he could hire out for difficult jobs.

She took him to a more civilized part of the galaxy, joined the Assassins Guild, and sent him to their training. He had taken to their rules—she once said—as if she had sent him to a religious school. He never returned to the area of his birth, and except for traveling through places like the NetherRealm, he never left Assassins Guild territory.

He worked legally or not at all.

But Rikki didn't. Apparently she was as amoral as the man who killed Misha's father. Apparently she didn't care who got hurt when she performed her job.

She finished, got paid, and then left the mess for someone else.

And lately that someone else had been him.

But no longer.

Now he would stop her. If she didn't want to join the Guild, then her career would have to end.

One way or another.

Chapter 7

AFTER SPENDING THE NIGHT IN MISHA'S SUITE, RIKKI found her room to be so small she wondered how she had managed to stay there for the first part of the trip. When the door opened, it brushed against the bed. The bed itself barely fit her, and it was uncomfortable as hell.

Uncomfortable probably wasn't the right word. Torturous would be better.

It had no mattress, not really. It was some kind of pad that supposedly remembered her sleeping position and lulled her into some kind of deep sleep. She had slept well here before she had gone to Misha's room—where she *hadn't* slept, thank you very much, or slept much, as the case might be.

She would never ever ever get that mattress out of her mind. (That night, really. The best night of her life. The morning after—not so good [well, it started out great]— but the night, the night was spectacular.)

She sat on the edge of her horrible bed, thinking that it did her no good. The mattress (or whatever the hell it was) remembered her sleeping position when what she really wanted was a place to sit. And the bed didn't remember her sitting position. She looked at the room's only chair. It was some metal thing with no padding that was more uncomfortable than the bed. She certainly couldn't work on that chair, and the room wasn't big enough for a table.

Hell, it wasn't big enough for a real closet either, but that hadn't bothered her until—

She shook her head, trying to get that suite out of her mind. She had to concentrate.

She ate the last bite of the most sinfully delicious pastry she had ever had, wished for real coffee, regretted that she hadn't poured herself a cup when she had been in Misha's suite, then ordered up a cup from the little servo unit on the wall.

The servo unit had been specific when she arrived. If she wanted high-end anything, she had to leave the room and go to the high-end restaurants, bars, or lounges. She could only get the things included in her tab here. And real coffee—the kind made from beans and not some reconstituted fake-o garbage—was not included in her tab.

Nothing fresh was. She got bread that had clearly been stored in some kind of container, cheese that tasted like plastic, meat that actually said on its little patty that it was made from vegetable and animal by-product (whatever that meant), and pastries that tasted like they had been made on Earth before the first spaceships took off back at the dawn of time.

Her room was designed to keep her out of it, in the shopping areas and restaurants spending money. Misha's room—well, Misha's room had been designed for exactly what they had done in it.

And more.

She shook her head again, and willed him out of her mind. Which was hard to do, considering how her nipples were still sensitive so that every time she moved her arms, her shirt brushed them and reminded her of him. Her lips were swollen, her neck covered with so many love bites that she was going to have to wear the only high-collared dress she had purchased later that evening.

Getting him out of her mind was, in fact, easier than getting his imprint off her body. And the weird thing was, she still craved him.

Even though she had figured out he was using her.

She leaned over the non-networked tablet she had brought with her. She had it flat on the bed. Her tablet didn't have all of her information on it—she knew better than that—but she had downloaded most of the research materials she needed so that she had easy access to it without going through the ship's systems.

She had learned long ago that she was better off not leaving a computer trail—and that was hard to do.

Before she had gotten on this ship, she had down-loaded its passenger manifest. The man in the room she had left was not named Misha. Or at least, he wasn't traveling under that name. He was traveling as Rafael de Brovnik, a man with incredible financials and a history marked *private*. She had learned long ago that anyone who spent enough money at these places got all kinds of preferential treatment, no questions asked.

She had been required to fill out all kinds of details about her fake identity's financial situation. She had nearly three dozen identities, all of them airtight, and so far she had used none of them twice.

Instead of using her real name, Rikki Bastogne, on this ship, she was Rachel Carter, a recently divorced woman who was using her settlement to take the trip of a lifetime. She had learned that "recently divorced" was code for "willing to party in excess," and that ships like this loved passengers like Rachel. Even though the room was crappy, she had gotten it at the last minute at half price, partly because the ship wanted to fill every berth and partly because it wanted to fill every berth with the kind of passenger who encouraged other passengers to have fun.

Supposedly Rachel was that passenger. She had certainly played the role with Elio Testrial, flirting, laughing, eating meals with him, letting him think she was interested. Then when they got back to his suite—which wasn't nearly as nice as Misha's—she had killed him after, of course, she had recited a list of his crimes that the client (which apparently was Misha) had instructed her to recite.

Testrial had listened the entire time while she held his face between her hands. Then she had asked if he understood, and when he nodded, she finished the job.

Which Misha hadn't finished paying her for, even though she had reminded him as she left the suite. She doubted he would ever pay her now. The last part of the payment and the expenses were probably never going to arrive in her account.

Good thing she always overcharged.

The job was technically done, all except for the escape. Normally, she wouldn't be worried about that, but this morning (last night) meant that nothing was normal. Misha might try to have her arrested, and she wasn't sure how she would survive that, since he—as Rafael de Brovnik, the filthy rich trustworthy suite-renter—could swear that she had committed the crime in front of him.

He would automatically have more cachet with any authorities than she would.

Unless she could prove Rafael de Brovnik a fraud.

She supposed she could do that—she supposed she needed to do that—but she wasn't doing that. In fact, she wasn't sure why she was doing what she was doing because she'd been over this ground before.

She was researching Elio Testrial.

Unlike what she had implied to Misha (or whatever the hell his name was), she actually did have standards. She didn't kill nice people. She didn't kill heirs to thrones or political rivals. She didn't kill business partners, no matter how legal it was, or widows who stumbled into a fortune after two years of marriage, no matter how bitchy they were.

She prided herself on one thing: she killed bad guys.

And, yeah, occasionally her definition of bad was a bit eccentric, which if anyone had asked her (and no one ever had) she would have blamed on her horrific childhood. But mostly, her definition of bad was the universe's definition.

She killed folks who continually preyed on the innocent, the weak, and the impoverished. She killed folks who stole billions and caused suicides; she killed folks who ordered mass murder and helped carry it out; she killed real long-term dictators and child molesters and illegal weapons traffickers. She killed people who left a trail of destruction behind them—and not the kind she left. She killed people who would not be missed, not because no one ever noticed them but because no one would mourn them.

And she made sure all the information she had was correct.

She never took the client's word. She always spent weeks researching the target. And then she hired a service (a different one each time) to do similar research, because she knew her favorite databases could be tampered with.

Sometimes she found serious discrepancies. Sometimes the client was the bad guy and the target was the innocent victim. She turned down those cases, and a few times, she had even warned the target.

But mostly, she accepted a few jobs a year, which kept her in cash. She wasn't in it for the money. She did the work because she was good at it, and because it provided a challenge, and because she felt the need to wipe the scum off the universe's metaphorical shoe.

She could never be any kind of law-enforcement official. Their worlds were too narrow. Plus they were bound by all kinds of strange laws, some of which made prosecution difficult or actually protected the really bad guys.

She liked working without rules.

Which was why she avoided the Assassins Guild, sanctimonious bastards that they were. A "license" was required. "Rules" had to be followed. "Hands" couldn't be dirtied, or there would be some kind of review.

She had looked at the Guild early on, when she realized she had a talent for these things, saw the list of one thousand rules and twenty-five hundred guidelines, and realized that the organization was not for her.

Mostly she tried to stay out of their territory—or at least, that had been her plan until she realized that other territories were a lot less friendly to assassins. So she stayed on the fringes, accepted only jobs that could be done away from the main population centers, and kept her prices low. Yes, she undercut most members of the

Guild, but she didn't have to give 20 percent of her earnings in dues every year.

Amazing what kind of money that saved over time.

Maybe that was why this Misha had hired her. Not so much for Testrial, but to get her out of the Guild's territory. To shut her down.

She sighed, got up, and nearly hit her head on the ceiling. She grabbed her so-called coffee, took a sip, and winced. At least the stuff had caffeine, or some kind of stimulant. And at least it wiped out the taste of that pastry, because the sinfully good taste of that pastry reminded her of Misha, and that suite, and that bed, and the way his eyes softened when his hand cupped her—

She shook her head for—what was it? The third time? Five hundredth? She had no idea. She wished there was some kind of drug that selectively wiped the memory because she would use it now. She needed to forget that fantastic night so she could properly hate the man without her hormones getting in the way.

She went back to the bed, and stared at the tablet. Everything she had on Elio Testrial from both sources—hers and the service she hired under yet another name—made it clear that this man had bilked thousands of people of their life savings, then destroyed their ability to work. He had savaged them financially and emotionally, and when their families had come to him, begging for refunds, for mercy, for *help*, he had turned them away.

Which sadly hadn't been enough for Rikki to kill him—not in cold blood. Although she might have trained one or two of those family members to do so if she had known about Testrial during that period.

Nope. What convinced Rikki was this: he decided to "help" the families. If they had a family member who met certain physical specifications, he would not only abolish the family's debts, but he would restore their finances—with interest—so long as that family member worked for him.

It all sounded well and good until it became clear that the new employee wouldn't survive the year. Testrial sent people into mines that couldn't be mechanized. Nothing human beings invented could work inside those mines for long. Neither could humans. But the human body was resilient and survived longer than anything with cogs and wheels and drives and bits. Not a lot longer, but long enough to actually do some valuable work. Besides, paying those families their lost funds was cheaper than building an android with the same specifications as the humans who ventured into the mines.

It was icky, it was gross, and it was entirely legal, because Testrial's string of mines were in Yhgred Sector, where human life was generally not valued like it was elsewhere in the galaxy. The laws were lax there, so lax that she never traveled into that sector, not even for a job.

If Testrial hadn't had business in Litaera Sector, she would never have taken this job in the first place.

She sighed. Thousands and thousands of families destroyed by Testrial. If she searched for a Misha among them or a Rafael or a slender blond man, she would find thousands of them.

This wasn't the way to figure out who he was. Or if he had lied to her.

Because she wasn't sure about that either.

Maybe he wasn't a licensed assassin. Maybe he worked for Testrial or Testrial's cohorts. Or maybe he was after her for a different reason.

She stretched, and shut off the tablet, setting it back in the tiny excuse for a closet.

She should just get off at the next port. Or, if things got really bad, steal an escape pod.

And maybe she would do those things.

But not yet. So far, no one had knocked on her door and demanded her identification. No one had accused her of unjustly killing Testrial.

Probably no one except this Misha guy even knew that Testrial was dead.

The problem with leaving now was that Misha—or whoever the hell he was—would still be tracking her. She wouldn't know how to get him off her back or even why he had been interested in her.

If she wanted answers, she needed to stay. For a while, anyway.

At least until Misha gave her a few answers—whether he wanted to or not.

Chapter 8

RIKKI WORKED BEST WHEN SHE HAD A COURSE OF ACTION, even if she abandoned it later. After much pacing inside her little cabin, she decided on a plan. ("Pacing" being a hopeful, delusional word. "Pivoting" would have been more accurate.)

What she needed to do first was figure out if Misha was actually a member of the Assassins Guild or if he had lied about that to put her on the defensive. And there was an easy way to figure it out: Guild members had DNA on file. If she put his DNA into the right database, then she would find out not only if he was a member of the Guild, but what his real (or at least his admitted) name was.

Her plan was to get his DNA—which was stupid. Because if she had thought of this plan earlier, she would have had a much easier time of it. After all, he had given of his DNA freely—and frequently—last night.

If she was half a step dumber, she would go back to his suite, rip his shirt off, slide her hands down his pants, and have her way with him.

The problem was, she wasn't sure if she could get out of that suite again. Not because of the sex. She could control herself enough to stop after one go. (She hoped.)

No, she figured he might try to keep her in that suite for good, especially now that she had left. She had surprised him at that breakfast table. He had thought she was some kind of sex-crazed bimbo, and while she had done a reasonable impression of one (or at least, had let the sex-crazed bimbo side of her personality have sway over the rest of her [much more reasonable] personality), she really wasn't one.

She was smart and competent, and she had survived a long time because of it. He finally realized that.

So if he thought she was a threat before, he really had to think she was a threat now.

Her only option, then, was to find him in a public place. She knew he didn't spend his evenings in the ship's casino, because Testrial had, and she had been with Testrial every night as his "good luck charm." (Heh. That hadn't turned out well for him.) She hadn't seen Misha at all—and she doubted she would have missed him.

Although she had missed him up until last night, and he made it sound like he had been following her. Still, if he had been in the casino, she would have seen him. She had made a point of sizing everyone up, including the people who were trying not to get noticed.

So, assuming he wouldn't be there and assuming he would be out of his gorgeous suite—which, she had to admit, was a hell of an assumption given how damn comfortable that suite was—then he would either be in the pubs, the restaurants, or the ballroom.

She would haunt them all until she saw him again. Then she would get just a bit of DNA, and figure out a way to get it to the Assassins Guild's database.

Civilians didn't have access to that database, but she would solve that problem after she had solved the others.

She slipped a DNA holder on the tip of her little finger. The holder looked like a part of her, but if she flicked it on and then swiped, she would get a few skin cells or a tiny strand of hair. That would be all she needed.

The DNA holder was the easy part of her wardrobe. She stood in front of her tiny closet for what seemed like eternity while she figured out what to wear for the evening.

She had brought along a variety of fancy dresses, all but one of them revealing a lot of skin. The one that didn't had seduced her with its material. It was made of a watery silk, and had cost more than she usually made at her highest paying job. It was black and silver, with long sleeves and a high neckline, both of which she needed on this night. It had no slit along the side, so her legs didn't show at all.

She wore it with pointy-toed silver heels that made her taller, and she wound her chestnut hair around the top of her head. She looked expensive and a lot more seductive than she planned. The silk was thin and the silver panels looked more like white skin peeking through the black.

Only up close did the material appear as what it was: a soft silver, as smooth to the touch as the black silk itself.

The dress made her feel beautiful, and she needed that after her humiliation in front of Misha that morning. She wouldn't have needed it at all if she hadn't thought that his passion was based in more than lust, but his words had convinced her otherwise. He was probably one of those sexually insatiable men, the kind who could perform no matter who the woman (or the man or the android) was.

The very thought made her cheeks heat up.

She took one last glance at herself in the room's full-length mirror. Then she took a deep breath and headed into the corridor.

She would find him, get his DNA, and figure out exactly what to do next.

Chapter 9

MISHA INITIALLY FOUND HER THROUGH THE IDENTI-card the ship had given her when she booked her room. The card listed her name as Rachel Carter. When he first found her, he wasn't sure that Rachel Carter was the woman he wanted. He had a list of four that he was keeping an eye on.

He had followed the down payment he had sent her for the job, and had watched as she transferred the funds from place to place. By the time she paid for her cruise, he had the amount and the ship's name, but not her name. She had used some kind of trick to book her passage, a trick he couldn't quite follow.

So he had to go through the difficult task of eliminating the other passengers. He managed to eliminate all of the wrong gender and the wrong age, but that left him with four single women. He had had to eyeball all of them.

And he had been surprised when he realized who Rachel Carter really was.

Then he switched out her identi-card so that he could follow her. That had taken some work and some planning. If she had a more expensive passage, she would have had a subcutaneous chip like he did. Those expensive identi-chips made it possible for the very wealthy to visit all parts of the ship. The chips got read as the passenger went from deck to deck, lounge to lounge, even if the passenger didn't touch an identi-circuit.

He liked cruise ships for that very reason. They had to keep track of passengers, and they used a short-term tracking system that he could easily access. He had been doing it for years, and he had become so good at it, he could turn his own identi-chip on and off, something he hadn't told Rikki when he'd been slamming his fist against the airlock circuitry.

But identi-cards didn't allow the easy passage throughout the ship. Any identi-card user had to scan the card as she went from section to section. Rikki had altered her card enough to give her access to the parts of the ship she had frequented with Elio Testrial, but she never would have gotten into the B Deck lounge (for example) without Misha.

She couldn't have done a lot without Misha.

She seemed to think she had completed her job well. She didn't realize that he had saved her ass, and part of the way he had done so was with his own identi-chip.

When he hit that airlock with his fist, the circuitry had identified him as Low-Level Maintenance Staff, a designation it used in the first few days of a trip, when the new employees hadn't yet been assigned their exact jobs.

That meant neither he nor she would get caught. Only later, when the security guards would mention seeing them, after someone figured out that Elio Testrial was missing, would the security guards would remember that incident. Then they would find the identi-chip reading and realize that it was suspicious.

Right now, he assumed, the ship's staff considered that a malfunction, and nothing to worry about, since it had only been a pair of drunks messing with the airlock doors. He had identified himself at that airlock, after all, so as far as the ship was concerned, the mistake with the identi-chip was just that: a mistake, a malfunction, not something to worry about.

Of course, he was (theoretically) one of the richest, if not the richest, passenger on this ship. Had Rikki tried a stunt like that, with her lower-level berth and her cheap boarding pass, then the staff would instantly have been suspicious.

He had protected her, and she hadn't realized it.

It still galled him. Everything about her galled him.

She had spent most of the day in her room. That had surprised him. He would have thought that she would go all over the ship, trying to be visible after the kill like so many amateur assassins did.

But she didn't seem to care who saw her—or so he thought until he watched her little identi-card move along the corridor map he had brought up on his wristscreen.

About an hour after the nightly dress ball began, she went into the ballroom.

That surprised him too, since she had spent all of the preceding evenings in the casino.

Apparently the casino had been where Testrial wanted to go, and had nothing to do with her.

Misha had planned to keep a distant eye on her, but he couldn't stay away. He told himself that he needed to watch her, to make sure she didn't pin Testrial's death on some innocent passenger, but he knew that was just an excuse.

He wanted to see her.

He wanted to see if the past twenty-four hours had rattled her as much as they had rattled him.

Chapter 10

MAYBE COMING TO THE BALLROOM HAD BEEN A MISTAKE.

Rikki stood off to one side, holding a champagne flute and watching the dancers. The light was dim to give the illusion of privacy, but there were stage lights on the orchestra in the very center of the cavernous room.

The orchestra was made up of real humans, not some holographic players. She'd been in a dozen different ballrooms over the years and only a few had even bowed to the niceties of a holographic orchestra. Most places simply had music piped in, music the passengers or the dancers or whomever was running the place chose.

This place had more class than she had expected.

Except for the cost. Her stupid identi-card was barely designated for this place. She could get in through a side entrance—no one announced her like they announced the rich and famous guests—and she had to pay for every damn thing.

Like this flute of champagne. She had opted for the cheapest stuff because she didn't want to pay the equivalent of the cost of her room for the good stuff. Not that she was planning to drink it.

She had had more than enough to drink the night before.

She stood near the wide-open staircases that flowed up the second floor, figuring she could see and hear best from this position. She couldn't see all of the entrances, but enough of them were visible. Even if Misha entered through one of those entrances and she didn't see him walk in, she would be able to hear the announcement and glide her way over to him.

Or at least, she would try to glide. She liked to imagine that she could glide in this dress. She knew it looked good because at least a half dozen men (and one quite beautiful woman) had hit on her since she took her position near the steps.

"No, I don't want to dance, thank you so much," she had said repeatedly. Six of them went away murmuring regrets, but one guy had parked himself in front of her. He was a bulldog of a man, with a pugnacious face and a tuxedo one size too small. His muscles bulged out of it.

"If you don't want to dance," he said, "then why the hell are you here?"

Good question, she thought, but didn't say. Maybe that DNA idea wasn't as good as she initially thought. Maybe she should just put the entire encounter with Misha behind her and go on with her plan.

She had an optional ticket, one that allowed her to disembark at any port if she ran out of funds. The limitation was in the small print, and really it was designed for the cruise line so that it could legally toss her off the ship if she ran out of money.

Apparently, back in the early days of the cruise line, too many people paid the starting fee and then never paid for anything else, and the ship couldn't legally toss them off. Instead, the cruise line had to sue for its money, and that never really worked out.

Hence the "new" guidelines, which only existed

on lower-class fares. Upper-class fares, like Misha's, forced the purchaser to pay for everything, including meals, even if the passenger disembarked early.

She had checked on those regulations before she followed Testrial on the ship. She hadn't mentioned that little piece of information to Misha in their fight that morning because she didn't want to tip her hand about when she might be leaving the ship.

But that nice little clause in the cruise line's fare regulations made it even harder for the ship to prove that Testrial didn't just disembark at some earlier port. Eventually they would find out that his identi-chip—the one she had disabled after she killed him—hadn't been found leaving the ship, but it would be an eventual discovery, not a quick up-front one.

"C'mon, honey," that pugnacious bulldog said to her, extending his fat hand. He was dressed well. He clearly had money. Although dancing with him might have been uncomfortable, given that he only came up to her shoulder.

Still, if she hadn't spent the night with Misha, she would have taken this guy up on his offer. He would have been one of her alibis. But she needed him out of the way, in case Misha showed up.

If Misha showed up.

"Thank you," she said, "but I'm not in the mood to dance."

"C'mon," he said, grabbing at her wrist, "just one."

She moved her hand slightly so that he didn't catch her wrist. Instead, he caught her fingers. She gripped his thumb and pushed it backwards enough to hurt him, but not enough to send him to his knees.

"I'm really not a woman you want to mess with," she said.

His eyes widened. His face had grown pale.

"Yes, right, okay," he said. "Just let go, all right?"

She did.

He rubbed his hand, kneading the area near his thumb particularly hard. "You could've just said no, you know," he said.

"I did," she snapped. "You didn't listen."

He nodded and scurried away—if a bulldog could scurry. He looked a bit like a tottering tree stump.

She watched him go. She might have felt sorry for him, if he hadn't been the second man in twenty-four hours who didn't listen to her.

In fact, that was the hallmark of this entire trip, because Testrial had laughed when she started her litany of his crimes. He hadn't gotten serious until he saw how serious she was, and how much she had changed.

She was so intent on watching the bulldog that she almost missed the announcement.

The androgynous voice with the formal tone and upper-class accent said, in its snotty little way, "Rafael de Brovnik."

She turned toward the main doors, and there he was. Her breath caught. She had forgotten in just a few hours how absolutely gorgeous he was.

A diffuse light had fallen on him for just a moment. That was how the entrances of the rich and famous worked in this ballroom—they had everyone's attention, if everyone wanted to give it to them.

Misha looked a bit uncomfortable, like he didn't want to be here. He was wearing a long black coat, a brocade vest, and snug black trousers. The brocade brought out his blond hair and highlighted his boots, which were threaded with what looked like real amber.

The light found amber all over him—cuff links, ear posts, buttons. Amber made him look expensive and softened him a bit.

Or maybe the room softened him a bit.

For the first time ever, he seemed out of his element.

He looked around as if he was searching for her. She slipped behind the staircase. She could still see him, but knew that the shadows here protected her from him.

She wanted to observe him for a few minutes, just to get her breath back.

God, he was beautiful.

God, she wanted him.

Her entire body remembered exactly how his felt. She could almost imagine his hands on her right now, touching her—

She didn't quite shake her head this time, but close. She hated the effect he had on her. Or rather, she wanted to hate it.

She was mad at him, that was it. She was mad and she hated the way he had made her feel, so cheap and used.

She had to remind herself of that because she also loved the way he had made her feel—all night long.

Maybe she could turn into one of those women who didn't care how their lover treated them because the sex was so very good.

Yeah, right. And maybe she could step out of an airlock and breathe without any special equipment.

Speaking of breathing—or thinking of it,

anyway—she made herself take a deep calming breath. She had to get control of herself.

And as she breathed, she had a thought:

How had he known she would be here? Or had he known? Had he been frequenting the ballroom all along?

She doubted that, given the discomfort on his face.

Which meant that he knew she was here.

Which meant that he had been following her from the moment she got on this ship.

The son of a bitch.

She felt the anger slide over her. She grabbed onto it like a lifeline, using it to cancel out the attraction.

Then she squared her shoulders, and walked across the ballroom, keeping to the shadows so he couldn't see her.

For once, she would have the element of surprise.

For once, he wouldn't know what hit him.

And then she would find out who he was, and what he really wanted. Once she knew that, she could make her next move.

She could figure out just how much of a threat this Misha/Rafael de Brovnik really and truly was.

Chapter 11

MISHA HATED DANCING. HE REALLY AND TRULY DID. The very idea of going into the ballroom made him uncomfortable.

But Rikki had gone into the ballroom, and she wasn't leaving. He had watched her icon for a good fifteen minutes before he headed there. He had hoped that she would go elsewhere, a bar or one of the portside pubs. But given her reaction to his suggestions about drinking the night before—and hell, given her reaction to the tiny bit of alcohol she had consumed—he had a hunch that drinking of any sort was low on her priority list.

He usually avoided cruise ship ballrooms. Even on a ship this large—one of the largest in the fleet—the ballroom seemed stuffy. On some ships, the ballroom actually *was* stuffy, but here it couldn't be. The environmental systems and the design of the room wouldn't allow air to overheat or get stale.

Still, it felt that way to him. On the first night, he had gone inside, stared at the room in awe, and then had gotten overwhelmed and left. Most passengers stuck with the awe. The ballroom was one of the largest rooms on the ship, extending upwards three stories, in addition to taking up a space as big as the lower-class dining room.

Maybe he found such places stuffy because he found dancing unnecessary. It was one of those activities he would never pursue if it hadn't been for his job.

But, weirdly, he had to dance a lot for his job. He had become a spectacular dancer. He had become good at a lot of things he never liked or expected to like. He had rather thought he would like dancing, but then he did it, and he loathed it.

It was a complete waste of time.

Tonight, he wouldn't be able to avoid dancing. In fact, he needed to dance.

He wanted to talk to Rikki. He also wanted to touch her, but he didn't want to think about that.

He had set up the tracking program on a small screen he wore on his wrist. The screen was black and the band itself was black flecked with gold. It went with his amber jewelry and his black clothing. Still, he kept his wrist covered so no one realized how much hardware he wore.

Just like no one would know he carried two weapons, one—a small nearly weightless laser pistol—in a pouch built into the seam of his waistband, and the other a knife made of bone that he kept in a specially built part of his boot.

Whenever he wore the boots, he carried the knife.

It was the laser pistol that was unusual, and he wasn't sure why he was carrying it. Apparently he trusted Rikki even less than he had just twenty-four hours ago.

He arrived at the ballroom and stepped into a world of light and shadows, swirling colors, and rich sound. The music overwhelmed in here, as if it was alive. Dancers covered the floor, their clothing whirling with their perfect movements. The air didn't smell stale; it smelled faintly of sweat and perfume and alcohol. It provoked a heady excitement that seemed almost palpable.

Perhaps it was. Some of these ships did put intoxicants into the air, things that enhanced an experience.
Usually, those intoxicants were limited to small doses,
and placed in areas like a dance floor so that people
would think they had enjoyed themselves a bit more
than they actually had.

He adjusted his collar, then brought his hand down.
That movement was a nervous tick, and he shouldn't be
nervous. He was a man on a mission, a man who came to
this ship to travel from one sector to another, true enough,
but also a man who had come to have a good time.

He took a second step inside, passed the place that
the ship's designers had set up as the hesitation point,
and listened as an androgynous voice announced his ar-
rival: "Mister Rafael De Brovnik." The voice sounded
official, but it barely carried over the music. Only the
closest dancers even looked at him. Everyone else continued twirling—*one*, two, three; *one*, two, three.

There had to be two hundred couples on the dance
floor. The music came from an actual orchestra, with
real human players. He hadn't realized this ship actually invested in musicians, not androids, not elaborate
reality constructs.

He scanned the room, and didn't see her. He knew
that a few moments ago, she had been standing to his
left, but he didn't see her there. But "to his left" encom-
passed a lot of room. The ballroom was too big to take
in all at once. He took another step inside.

The main part of the room was given over to dancing. The floor had a permanent shine that no shoe could
scuff. Wide, curving staircases rose on each side, leading to a balcony that bridged across the middle. Some

couples stood up there, looking down at the dancers, enjoying the music and some champagne from above.

Beneath the stairs were private areas that could opaque. If the air had the kind of aphrodisiac that he had worried about from the night before, the area under those stairs would be crowded with mismatched couples, unable to keep their hands off each other.

But he saw no untoward groping on the dance floor, and even though the air had the faint tang of sweat, it didn't carry the starchy, unmistakable smell of semen.

He was greatly relieved. Because he didn't need a mood enhancer to augment his barely controllable lust for Rikki Bastogne. Time to stop fooling himself. It had been a mistake to come here. He wouldn't be able to control his response to her, and he didn't dare risk touching her.

He turned, and as he did, a hand brushed his arm.

"Leaving so soon?"

She stood next to him. Only this wasn't the some-what disheveled, angry woman who had left his suite that morning. This was a goddess.

She wore a black and silver dress that covered every part of her and yet left nothing to the imagination. The silver shoes peeking out from the frothy hem added several inches to her height. That, plus the way that she had swept up her hair, made her taller than he was.

He had to look up at her, which was even more disconcerting.

"I'm not fond of dancing," he managed to say.

"Then what are you doing here?" she asked.

"Looking for you," he said.

"To apologize?" she asked with a slightly wicked smile.

He almost said *Apologize for what?* Then realized that no woman would respond well to that question.

He made himself answer her smile with a smile of his own. Then he extended his right hand. "Dance with me," he said.

She raised her eyebrows. One of them glittered. She had pasted some kind of jewel at the very tip.

"I thought you're not fond of dancing," she said.

"I'm making an exception," he said.

She looked down at his hand. He could feel her reluctance. Then she raised her eyes. Her gaze met his, and he felt a bolt of heat run through him. He wondered if, in this slight darkness, she could see the flush coloring his cheeks.

"I'm mad at you, you know," she said in a pleasant tone. Anyone listening would have thought they were flirting.

They weren't flirting, were they? It felt like flirting. But it also felt more serious than that.

"I figured that out," he said dryly. He felt stupid with his hand extended, but he didn't move it, and he wouldn't move it. Not yet, anyway.

"I shouldn't ever touch you again," she said.

"Wouldn't that be a crime," he said and just barely stopped himself from looking panicked. He hadn't meant to say that.

She laughed and slid her hand into his. "I don't know," she said. "I think in some sectors half of what we did last night was a crime."

Besides killing Elio Testrial and shoving his body out an airlock? Misha wanted to ask, but didn't.

Instead, he focused on the feel of her hand in his,

the way that such a small touch made his skin tingle
with anticipation.

The waltz music continued, and she tilted her head
toward him. "Well?"

He slipped his hand behind her back and pulled her
against him. She put her hand on his shoulder and tried
to add some distance between them.

He wouldn't let her. He liked the added height her
shoes gave her. Her body rubbed against his in an entirely different way than it had the night before.

He led her onto the dance floor, and they whirled
through the couples, moving in concert, as if they had
practiced this dance every day of their lives. The brush
of her thighs against his through the thin material of her
gown, the pressure of her breasts against his torso, made
it hard to think.

"I want to make a deal with you," he said, forcing
himself to concentrate on his words and not the soft
scent of her.

"I figured as much." She didn't look directly at him.
Instead, she was watching the other dancers, as if she
was looking for someone.

"Join the Guild," he said, "and I won't turn you in."

She swiveled her head toward him. "Turn me in
for what?"

"You know what," he said. He wasn't going to say it
on the dance floor. Too many people brushed too close
to them. Their conversation felt private, but it wasn't,
and he wasn't going to risk anything by being explicit
out here.

"I haven't done anything wrong," she said. "Although
you have. You're the one who has no obvious ties to the

man we discussed last night. You're the one who has no justification for all you've done."

He didn't feel cold—he couldn't, not with her so close—but her words did have a chilling effect. It was suddenly much easier to separate himself from his arousal.

He continued to lead her in the dance, but he no longer let himself enjoy it, no longer let himself acknowledge the feel of her body against his.

"You investigated me?" he asked.

She smiled prettily at him. She looked stunning, but her eyes were cold. "Isn't that what you've been doing to me?"

"You're going to blame me for what happened last night?" He couldn't keep the incredulousness from his voice.

"If you blame me," she said. Then she caressed his cheek. The touch felt like a lover's, but her gaze, so hard and distant, belied that touch.

The music shifted without pause to another waltz. Some dancers left the floor. The rest remained, bright swirls of red and blue and green against the darkness of the room itself.

He felt a little dizzy. He wasn't breathing properly.

"I want you to join us," he said and hoped he didn't sound desperate. He hadn't felt desperate until the words came out.

Those eyebrows went up again. Her face was mobile but the expression in her eyes never changed.

He wondered if she hated him.

He was beginning to think that she did.

"You want me to join the Guild?" she asked.

"Yes," he said.

"So that I follow your rules?" she asked.

"Yes," he said.

"Hm." The sound was soft, timed to the music. She moved with him. They hadn't missed a step, and their bodies were still pressed against each other. Only he didn't feel the desire anymore.

Until he thought about it. Then the desire was so powerful, it took his breath away.

He forced himself to breathe, and to think about how cold her words were.

He willed the desire away.

"How do I know you're a member of the Guild?" she asked.

"I told you I am," he said.

"Rafael De Brovnik is not," she said.

He tilted his head just a little, chastising her without saying a word. Of course Rafael De Brovnik wasn't a member. All Guild members used false names. That way, assassins didn't become famous. It allowed them to work in anonymity, where they belonged.

But if he ever got in trouble, all law enforcement had to do was run his DNA and they would discover that he was a member of the Guild. Yes, that might keep him in custody until matters got straightened out (like he had been on those occasions when Rikki had left her mess behind), but it was a small price to pay for the right to work freely.

She shrugged. That pretty smile was back for a moment. He realized then that it was her patronizing smile, one that most people probably never even realized she had in her repertoire.

"How do I know that you're who you say you are?" she asked. "How do I know you're not law enforcement—"

He laughed. He couldn't help himself. "I'm not," he said.

"—or someone who works for Elio Testrial. How do I know you're not a bounty hunter or someone who is after me for another reason?"

"You have a bounty on your head?" he asked.

It was her turn to tilt her head and silently chastise him.

Of course she did. Somewhere. He did too. It was part of the job.

"I belong to the Guild," he said.

She shook her head. "And I'm just supposed to take your word for it?"

"Yes," he said.

"What do you get," she asked, "a commission for every person you recruit?"

He felt offended but he wasn't sure why. He continued to move with her as they danced, his hand clutching hers, probably a bit too tightly. "I'm not recruiting you," he said. "I'm trying to control you."

As soon as the words came out, he knew he had said the wrong thing.

She stopped dancing so suddenly he almost tripped over her. Of course she stopped dancing, he realized, because a waltz was all about control—he had to control her every movement. He had been leading, after all.

"So now we have the truth of it," she said softly.

The other dancers had to dance around them. A few nearly collided with the two of them, standing still in the middle of the dance floor, his hand still on her back, her hand still on his shoulder, their other hands clasped as if they were going to start dancing again.

She leaned into him. "Am I working your territory, then? Am I undercutting the market? Since I got here, are you now hurting for work?"

Her words cut. Just like they were supposed to.

"No," he said.

"Then back off." She let go of his shoulder and his hand, but he kept his hand firmly against her spine, holding her in place.

"What if I don't want to back off?" he asked. He wasn't sure if he was talking about his desire to get her into the Guild or his desire to get her back into his bed.

"Back off," she said quietly, "or I'll scream so loud that the orchestra won't be able to drown me out."

He held her for one moment longer, testing her. She raised her chin, looked toward the stage, and took a deep breath.

Then he let go.

"You should join us," he said.

"I don't join things," she said.

"Your mistake," he said.

"Is that a threat?" she asked.

"Should it be?"

Her eyes narrowed. "You have no idea who I am."

"Oh," he said. "That's really not true."

He thought he saw something—a flash of fear, a bit of concern? He couldn't quite tell. As quickly as it appeared, it was gone.

"Stay away from me," she said. Then she turned and walked off the dance floor, her long skirt swaying around her feet.

Wow, she was beautiful. And boy, did he mishandle that.

He was going to have to keep track of her in a different way. He would have to keep his distance again. And then, when they arrived at their destination, he would make certain the authorities knew about Elio Testrial, so that she would go to jail.

He would get her out. And use that moment to convince her that she needed him.

Or, actually, needed the Guild.

He had meant the Guild.

Even though he knew, deep down, that he hadn't. He wanted her to need him—or, at least, to want him as much as he wanted her.

Chapter 12

SHE WALKED AWAY FROM HIM, HER HEART POUNDING. She had never felt like this. She was furious at him—had been furious at him throughout the entire waltz—and yet she wanted to kiss him, to go under the stairs and pull off that delicious coat he wore, and find the muscles underneath.

The desire between them was rich and fine, as if they hadn't slaked it at all several times the night before.

He had been aroused as well, and hadn't tried to hide it from her. That had made her task even more difficult.

She had used every trick she knew to keep her features impassive, her voice calm, her body under control. She had to concentrate on every word, feel that anger, and separate herself from the situation as if she was watching it from above.

She had to act like she didn't care.

More than that, she had to act like she had on her very first job, when she had realized she was in over her head, that she really and truly had had no idea what she was doing, and it was too late to stop.

After that, she had gotten training. After that, she had learned how to do her job. But that one assignment had been torture—and not exquisite torture like this dance had been.

She shook the memory from her head, and made her way through the crowd of dancers. Some of them flitted by her, almost too fast for her to see. She was amazed no one had crashed into her.

The music seemed louder than it had a moment ago, but she knew that had more to do with her than with the musicians themselves. The orchestra played on a stage in the center of the dance floor. They sat with their backs to each other, facing outward. The director stood behind them, but appeared on the monitors on their music stands. The instruments were old, and probably valuable, without the technical garbage that so many had.

She shook that thought away too. Too much learning for too many jobs, jobs she worked hard at, jobs she spent time thinking about before she did them.

Jobs whose targets often haunted her in her sleep.

She would never tell anyone that, particularly since the targets were such horrible people. Why should she feel guilty about her role in ending their miserable lives?

Dancers continued to move around her. Most of the couples were older, some built solidly. None were as glamorous as this ballroom deserved.

Or as glamorous as she had felt in his arms, moving to the music, wishing circumstances were different.

She made her way off the dance floor, heading for one of the side doors. As she passed part of the stage, one of the male violinists smiled at her. She did not smile back.

They continued to play waltzes, one right after the other without a break. Apparently no one had to stop dancing if they didn't want to.

Part of her hadn't wanted to. But she had been losing her grip on her emotions, so she had to stop.

She had already gotten the DNA. She had caressed

Misha's cheek with her hand, making certain to get skin cells. She probably had gotten them from his hand, but she wanted to be precise.

She needed to be precise for what she was going to do next.

Even if what she was going to do next wasn't ethical. As if she needed to worry about ethical. She *killed* people for a living. But only people who deserved it.

Misha didn't really deserve what she was going to do.

But she couldn't think of any other way to get the information.

Once she got it—the next day or the day after—she would claim she made a mistake. But right now, she would use what she had.

She was just mad enough to do it. *I'm not recruiting you*, he had said. *I'm trying to control you.* Like that was a good thing. Like that was better than recruiting her.

Damn him. Who the hell did he think he was, anyway?

The double doors opened inward and they appeared to be manual, which was extremely annoying. She had to tug them open. They were heavy. She slipped through the slight opening and stepped into the corridor, where she stopped.

It was colder out here, and brighter. The white walls were a shock after the dim lighting inside that ballroom. She adjusted her dress. It felt askew, even though it hadn't been.

His touch just affected her that much.

She looked at her finger. This was the moment of truth. The DNA inside that little pouch would answer some questions. He had told her that he was with the Guild, and part of her wanted to believe him. But she had believed the night before that he was actually concerned about her, that their time together in his suite was something spontaneous, not something he had planned.

She had believed him because she wanted to.

And now she didn't believe him at all.

Control her. Yeah, right.

She took a deep breath, and set her plan into action.

Chapter 13

MISHA STOOD A HALF SECOND TOO LONG IN THE MIDDLE of the dance floor. Several couples had to swerve around him at the last minute. One couple nearly hit him, and the man swore at him, loudly, creatively, and noticeably.

Misha moved.

But he kept his gaze on Rikki. She stalked past the orchestra and didn't even look at them, although at least one of the clarinet players tried to catch her attention. He pointed the instrument at her, leaned in her direction, and she didn't even notice.

Misha had never been close to a real clarinet. He had no idea if they sounded louder when they were pointed at someone than when they weren't.

But the clarinet player wasn't the only person who noticed Rikki. Several other people did as well, mostly men, some of them dancing. They gazed at her over their partners' shoulders, often with longing, as if they wanted to be with her instead of with the woman they were dancing with.

Hell, he still wanted to be with her.

Although he had effectively blown his chance.

What had he been thinking? What was that line about trying to control her? Jeez. No one wanted to hear that even if it was true.

And it was true. But not in the way that it sounded.

He didn't want to control her every move. He had just wanted to make her stop interfering with his life.

The fact that she hadn't been doing it intentionally rankled more than he wanted it to. It rankled a lot.

A couple nearly hit him, then another, and another. He had to get off the dance floor.

He did, keeping his gaze on Rikki. She stopped in front of one of the side exits and put her hands on her hips as if the thing offended her. Then she sighed, grabbed the handles, and pulled.

Apparently the fact that it hadn't been automatic had offended her. That thought made him smile, even though he didn't want to. He liked her, even though he didn't want to. Even though he had learned over the years that for him at least, like and lust were mutually exclusive.

Or as his friend Hazel Sanchez had once told him, every woman he fell for reminded him of his mother—cold, brittle, terrifying, and without a soul. Every woman he liked couldn't get near him.

That comment had made him stay away from Hazel for a while too, even though it had been hard. They'd been in the same class in the Guild, and they usually partnered with each other. But after that comment, he had been afraid that she had been interested in him.

She hadn't been, but it had taken her weeks to convince him. They remained friends, good friends, even though she had hated every single woman he had been involved with.

He wondered what she would have thought of Rikki. Rikki certainly wasn't brittle, and she wasn't terrifying, but her eyes had been cold tonight. Or maybe they had been cold to him, because beneath that chill, he had seen anger.

She was furious at him, and when he had said that stupid thing about control, her eyes had flashed.

His mother's eyes had never flashed. They got flinty when she got angry, and anyone in the vicinity could feel the chill.

He stopped beside a pole in the very center of the room, away from the floor. The pole was clear and allowed anyone to see through it to the floor. He leaned against it, shattering the illusion that it wasn't there.

The ship's employees running the room probably hated that he was doing this, but they couldn't stop him. To them, he was Rafael de Brovnik, a man who made more money than all of them combined would make in their lifetimes.

If only that money were his instead of the Guild's.

He wondered what it would be like to work off the grid, to keep all the money he earned instead of paying a large percentage of it to the Guild. Of course, then he would have to defend himself if he got into legal trouble, handle his own health care, handle the cost of all of his jobs, and deal with any angry colleagues/friends/family of his targets on his own.

That was the biggest problem, in his opinion, anyway. Dealing with the angry people attached to his targets, people who didn't understand that he wasn't the one who ordered the hit, that some client had done so, and that by law in almost every part of this sector, the client was the one responsible, not the assassin himself.

"What did the bitch do to you?"

Misha started at the sound of the male voice on his left. He looked, saw no one, then looked down. For a moment, he felt disconcerted. Not only was the man shorter by a significant amount, but he was square.

And he shouldn't have been able to sneak up on Misha. Misha never lost track of who or what was beside him.

Yet he had in his contemplation of Rikki.

"What?" Misha asked.

The man held out his hand. The thumb was hidden in a mound of flesh and it took Misha a moment to realize that the skin around it was swollen.

"I think she broke my thumb," the man said. "Then she dances with you, and I think, that's why she wasn't interested. She knew she had some pretty guy on the hook."

Misha felt his cheeks heat. Pretty? Really? He wasn't pretty. Or maybe he was in this outfit. His mother had always dressed him down in the early years, telling him that no one would pay attention to a wispy too-thin boy, and that made him a good weapon.

It wasn't until he went to the Guild that he started to dress up, and then not often. Mostly he continued the dressing-down thing.

"But," the guy was saying, "then she gets that look, the one that I swear could have killed you mid-waltz, and stops, and you nearly fall over, and then she stalks off. So I figure that she did something to you too."

He was talking about Rikki. Misha blinked, and managed to focus. Jeez, Rikki wasn't even in the room, and he was having trouble focusing.

"She did that to you?" he asked, indicating the thumb.

"Okay," the guy said. "Granted, I'm not suave or debonair or pretty like you, but I got money, and most women recognize that. So I asked her to dance and reached for her and she bent my thumb back so hard that I heard something crack. And now look at it."

Misha beckoned with his own fingers. The stubby

man held up his hand. The swelling had worked its way down to the wrist. Something was broken.

"She did that?" Misha asked. "Really?"

He wasn't as surprised as he pretended to be. Everyone in the field knew how to bend a thumb backwards to bring a target to his knees.

"She made you get down on your knees?" Misha asked, wondering if the guy was some kind of target.

"Naw," the guy said. "She let go before it hurt that bad, but believe me, I was thinking that I'd better get away. I was heading to security when I saw her hook up with you. I thought I'd watch for a minute, and wow, that was some show. You two know each other, huh?"

Misha's eyes narrowed just slightly. "Not really," he said. "Although we did have a rather surprising time last night."

"Hah," the short guy said. "Thought so. Didn't end so well for the lady, huh?"

"Actually, it didn't end so well for me," Misha said.

"So that's why she was waiting. She wanted you in her clutches again. Well, lucky you. You're better off without her."

His words made Misha's heart clench. And he didn't want his heart to clench. He wanted to nod and sagely agree with this guy, and then forget Rikki ever existed.

"Women like her," the man said. "Dangerous. Wouldn't surprise me if she was some kind of pro. You got money, right?"

For a moment, Misha had forgotten who he was supposed to be. "Yeah," he said a bit too slowly. "I'm comfortable."

Which was what all the rich people said.

"Thought so," the man said. "You were targeted, buddy. Now you're supposed to go after her, and lay some funds on her to make her feel better. If I were you, I'd report her to security."

"For what?" Misha asked coolly. "Abandoning me on the dance floor?"

He almost said that the guy had a better case against Rikki, at least for shipboard security, but Misha didn't want to mention that. He didn't want to call too much attention to her. Attention might lead to the Testrial incident, and ultimately, he was the one liable for that, not her.

"Looks like you should head to medical with that," Misha said.

"Yeah, you're probably right," the guy said. "Who'da thought that just asking some broad to dance would get me a broken hand. I'd rather get it for a good grope, if you know what I mean."

Fortunately, he was trundling away before Misha could come up with a response to that. He watched the man to make sure he didn't trundle out the same door as Rikki.

He didn't.

Misha sighed with relief. Although he wasn't sure why he sighed with relief. He was angry at Rikki, too, wasn't he?

But not quite. He was more confused by her.

And he hadn't been confused by a woman in a long, long time.

Chapter 14

RIKKI STAGGERED FORWARD AS IF SHE WAS INJURED. Adjusting her dress had probably been the proper thing to do, if anyone reviewed the security footage later. She ran a hand over her face and she made certain that hand shook.

Then she stumbled across the corridor as if her eyes were blinded with tears. She walked as if walking hurt until she reached the nearby ladies room, and let herself inside.

The front part of the room was a gigantic lounge, with soft chairs and tables. Individual mirrors lined the wall, with partitioned counters in front of each one, along with a stool, so that a woman could sit down, adjust her makeup, fix her hair, and make certain she still looked beautiful.

Rikki paused in front of one, then sat down hard, almost as though her legs had collapsed beneath her. She peered in the mirror, started at her green eyes like she always did, saw that her skin was paler than usual, and leaned forward.

With a shaking hand, she pulled down the collar of her dress. Yep, the love bites were there, worse than they had been that morning. And yep, they looked like bruises.

That would probably be enough.

She sat for a long moment, then closed her eyes. She

reminded herself that she was trying to find out information; that was all. Security was lax on these ships; they couldn't do much to Misha even if they felt the need to hold him.

And they wouldn't hold him, because he had money. He could be the worst criminal in the universe, and they wouldn't hold him. Not if he could buy his way out.

They'd only hold him if he killed another passenger.

And so far, he hadn't done that.

She had.

She closed her eyes, and took a deep breath. She could back off on this. She wasn't quite sure how much she was doing because she was mad and how much she needed this information.

But if he was lying, if he wasn't connected to the Guild, if he was law enforcement or, worse, one of Testrial's men, then she needed to know. She needed to escape him, and quickly.

God, she was so attracted that she was worried about what would happen to him. And really, she should have been worried about what would happen to her.

She'd manipulated information before to get something; it wasn't like she was doing anything unusual.

This was part of her job.

She had to see it that way. It was just a job. Like she had been a job to him. *I'm trying to control you.*

Well, screw that, buddy. She'd show him what control was like.

She pulled just a few random strands loose from her hairdo, then adjusted her dress again. She left the collar bunched on one side, as if she had forgotten it.

Then she made her way back to the corridor.

Security was on the main passenger deck. The big area, which also included medical facilities, took up a large portion of the middle of the ship. There were corridors and rooms on the outside—no sense wasting exterior portals on a part of the ship that few passengers saw—but those were considered lower class accommodations just because they were in the center of things.

She knew because she had had a choice between those and a room in the lowest deck on the ship. She had taken the lower deck, even though the room was just a bit smaller. She hadn't wanted to be noticed.

That was her usual M.O. She never wanted to be noticed.

And here she was, about to be noticed.

But sometimes, she had to alter the plan.

She lurched toward security, hoping she wouldn't turn an ankle in these shoes. She took the lift with relief, because that way she wouldn't have to walk for a few minutes.

Then she got off the lift on the main deck, used a hand to steady herself, and silently cursed that no one seemed to notice she was having trouble. Misha had noticed the night before.

Of course, that had been suspicious behavior on his part: she had to remember that. He had been following her. He had hired her to kill Testrial so that he could keep track of her, capture her, and have his way with her.

Um, she meant, do away with her.

Um, oh, never mind.

She let the confusion happen, because she knew it would add to her story in security. She pushed open the ivory colored door, with security written on it in half a dozen languages, and stepped into a utilitarian space.

Most of the places on the ship—at least the ones she had been in—had either been highly decorated or extremely opulent. But this wasn't an area that catered to passengers. Here the walls were unadorned, the chairs looked as uncomfortable as the one in her cabin, and in the distance, she could see cubicles marked off by the same ivory colored material that covered the door.

A man in a green uniform sat on a clear plastic chair. Five screens floated around him, and he ignored all of them. Instead, he stared at her.

"Yes?" he said in a tone that almost made her regret coming here.

She licked her lower lip. "Security, right?"

"Yes, ma'am. Can I help you?"

"I think I got myself in some pretty serious trouble." She made sure her voice broke. She raised one shaking hand to her neck and pulled down her collar as far as it would go without ripping. "See what he did to me?"

To his credit, the guard didn't stand. Instead, he sent a small round drone about the size of her fist to examine her skin. The drone flew just under her chin and hovered. She could hear it whir.

"Who did this, ma'am?" the guard asked, his voice not quite as calm as it had been.

"He says his name is Rafael," she said. "But I don't believe him. He—knew things—no rich guy should know. Last night, he gave me something."

"Besides the bruises?" the guard asked, and Rikki silently thanked him. She had made a deliberately misleading statement and he had gone with the safest question. Although she knew his mind had silently asked a dirtier one. *He gave you what, ma'am?*

A woman came out of one of the cubicles. The male security guard looked relieved to see her.

"Why don't you come talk to me?" the woman said.

She wasn't the guard Rikki had seen the night before. This woman was in shape as well, but older, her face lined as if she was permanently tired. Her name badge read *Bess Windham*.

Rikki followed her past the main guard, into the hallway formed by the cubicle walls. Most of the doors into those cubicles were open, but no one sat inside. She didn't know if that meant security was understaffed or if they were all out on assignment.

She rubbed a damp palm on the side of her dress. She didn't have to pretend to be nervous. She was nervous. She hated being anywhere run by authority figures.

Windham's cubicle was at the very back, and it was larger than the others. The sign on her door read *Passenger Relations*, but the words were in a holographic font. Rikki wondered if they got changed for each crisis that someone reported.

This cubicle actually had a desk, and several comfortable-looking chairs around it. The cubicle looked friendly enough, but Rikki recognized some of the displays above her: they were made of tiny lenses, so that everything could be recorded multiple times.

Normally, she would care. But she didn't here. She wanted this interview to get recorded.

"How may I help you, Miss—?"

"Carter," Rikki said as if she didn't know that the woman already knew her name. "I'm Rachel Carter."

"Miss Carter." Windham had a gentle voice. "What's happened to you?"

Rikki ran her hands along her sleeves. She made her eyes as big and vulnerable as possible. Then she swallowed hard.

"Last night," she said in a small voice, "I really wasn't myself."

That was true enough.

"I met this man, and he dragged me to a bar on B Deck. I couldn't get in without him. And then he gave me a beer—I don't drink much, but I drank that, and then I couldn't keep my hands off him."

"But not before?" Windham asked.

Rikki shook her head. "He was dragging me around. I thought it pretty strange, but he had said he needed my help."

"To do what?"

She shrugged. "Something about putting one over on someone? I don't know. It's all pretty fuzzy."

"You think he put something in your beer?"

"Or he used one of those touch drops, you know, the aphrodisiacs?"

Windham raised her chin lightly. Touch drops were illegal in most sectors but that didn't stop their use. Their name reflected what they did: they changed behavior with a single touch.

"What makes you think that?" Windham asked.

"Two things." Rikki bit her lower lip, and winced at the slight pain. Okay, maybe she was taking this acting thing a bit too far. "The first are these."

She raised her hand to her collar and brought it down, just like she had done in the main part of security.

Windham didn't even look, which confirmed what Rikki already knew: that the woman had seen the bruises through that tiny drone and had decided to take on this incident herself.

"The second is…" Rikki let her voice trail off as if she was embarrassed. "I, um, saw him tonight, and I went up to him, thinking that maybe, you know, it would, I would, you know, feel the same way?"

The woman nodded. "But you didn't."

Rikki made a face. "We danced and I wanted him to stop touching me."

She was lying. It was surprisingly hard to lie about this part.

"And I kept telling him I wanted to stop, and he wouldn't, so finally, I just stopped, and then I got away from him as fast as I could."

"Did you have a physical reaction to him tonight?" Windham asked.

Oh, yeah, Rikki wanted to say. *Just as strong, just as thrilling as last night. Only I didn't let myself act on it.*

"Yes," she said with some emphasis. "But not what I expected. He disgusted me. I couldn't wait to get away from him."

Windham closed her eyes for just a brief moment, but that moment was enough. Rikki knew what it meant: Windham dealt with a lot of aphrodisiac-based crimes, and she thought this was another.

"I realize that you're not the police," Rikki said before Windham could speak up. "I know you can't do anything to him, and you probably don't want to, since he has a suite the size of your office—"

Windham looked like she was about to deny that was an issue, which she probably had to do to cover the ship's ass in some kind of legal proceeding, but Rikki didn't let the woman talk.

"—but I'm not sure he is who he says he is."

That caught Windham's attention. "What do you mean?"

"Like I said, it's all pretty hazy. But he said a few things. For one thing, he asked me to call him Misha, and I have no idea how you get from Rafael to Misha."

"That's not enough, ma'am."

"I *know*," Rikki said. "I remember laughing about something, about the way it took only so much money to get a ship to think you were really rich, but I'm not sure I dreamed it or what. And he said something about being rich giving you access—"

"We can't help you in a lawsuit against him, if that's what you're looking for," Windham said.

"No, I'm not," Rikki said. "It's just that I, um, haven't washed my hand, and I touched his face, and I'm pretty sure I have some of his DNA…"

Windham's gaze met Rikki's. It wasn't exactly legal for the ship to check DNA without suspicion of a crime. Rikki just hoped that she had presented enough information to give the ship cover.

Windham's gaze flitted to Rikki's neck again. Then Windham nodded as if she had made a decision.

"We'll do a swipe," she said. "Come with me."

Chapter 15

THE SQUARE LITTLE MAN WITH THE INJURED HAND HAD left the ballroom, and Rikki hadn't returned. Misha still leaned against the pole, a bit amazed at himself. He wasn't sure why he had thought she would come back. To apologize?

Not that she had anything to apologize for.

But it seemed odd to him that she was so angry at him, and yet she had clearly waited for him. The square little man had confirmed that.

So what had she wanted? To confront Misha? But why? They had had their confrontation that morning, and she should have left things alone.

He frowned, went over their interaction, and found it somewhat strange, but he couldn't quite tell why.

Maybe she had wanted him to follow her. But why would she want that? To take their disagreement into the corridor? To play some kind of sexual game he didn't entirely understand?

She certainly had been experienced and the square little man had thought she was some kind of professional.

Sometimes female assassins used all of their wiles to deal with their targets. She had certainly flirted with Testrial, but she hadn't gone to his room until the night she killed him.

So that didn't seem like it was the way she operated.

Still, Misha had been misjudging her from the start.

The waltzes continued. He was getting sick of them. *One* two three, *one* two three. If he wasn't careful, he was going to hear that rhythm in his head for days.

He pushed up his sleeve and checked his wrist screen. Rikki's icon remained motionless outside the side exit. She was just standing in the corridor.

He frowned, wondering if she had dumped her identicard. He caught himself thinking that she didn't know how to turn it off, but he couldn't make those assumptions now. She was smarter than he gave her credit for. He constantly underestimated her abilities and it had hurt him. He couldn't continue doing that.

So why was she just standing in that corridor?

He sighed. He could, he supposed, just stomp his way down that corridor and confront her. But where would that get him? He had done that just a few minutes ago, and she had walked away from him.

Then, as he watched, the icon moved down the corridor. After a moment, the icon moved inside the ladies room and stayed in the front part of the lounge for a good five minutes.

Now he was getting suspicious. She was up to something. Had she taken two jobs on this cruise? The ship was still in the NetherRealm. If she killed another person here, she would try to get away with that as well. And if it was an actual job, she might actually be right.

He glanced up. No one watched him. The dancers continued to turn, bright swirls of color against the room's black-and-silver background.

Yet he had been thinking so hard about Rikki that he had forgotten to keep track of his surroundings. Again.

That was why the woman was dangerous. She took away his concentration.

He certainly hadn't concentrated on anything but her the night before.

He glanced at his wrist screen. She had left the ladies' room now, and had found one of the lifts. It was heading to the main floor.

Something about that bothered him. She was up to something, but he didn't know what.

He tugged his sleeve over the screen, then circled the dance floor, staying at the edges. He remained in the shadows as much as possible, feeling a bit unsettled.

He had no idea if anyone was watching him. He even double-checked the chip in his hand to make sure it was off.

Then he slipped out the same door Rikki had used. He half-expected to find her in the corridor, waiting for him, arms crossed. It wouldn't have surprised him if she had slipped someone else her chip, and tried to see if Misha was following her.

But she wasn't there. The corridor, blazing white after the darkness of the ballroom, was empty.

He walked carefully in the direction she had gone, and then, as he got on the lift, he looked at his wrist screen again.

His breath caught.

She had gone to the security office.

Why would she go there? To turn him in for Testrial's murder? To confess?

He stopped the lift.

He needed to make a decision. He had no idea what she was telling the security office. He wanted to wait for her outside, but he wasn't sure how that would look, particularly if she told them that he had ordered the hit on Testrial.

Misha sighed.

He had no idea why she would report him. Or maybe she was going to report the square little man. Maybe the man had lied to Misha. Maybe he had tried to hurt Rikki.

A flash of anger ran through Misha. He didn't want anyone to hurt her, anyone to touch her.

But he knew she could handle herself.

He would talk to her later, after she left the office.

Until then, he would continue to imitate a passenger having a good time. The best way to do that would be to return to the lounge on B Deck. He would drink or, to be more accurate, pretend to drink, and continue to maintain his cover.

There was nothing else he could do.

Chapter 16

WINDHAM LED RIKKI TO ANOTHER PART OF SECURITY. This cubicle had lab equipment, which surprised Rikki. The ship had more sophisticated systems than it claimed to have. She would have to be careful not to get her own DNA mixed in here, because that might misidentify her as well—not as Rikki Bastogne, but not as Rachel Carter either.

Windham brought over a small device, shaped like a keypad. Rikki recognized it: a DNA coder.

"This won't tell us who he is, unless he's in one of the systems we have access to," Windham said. "But it's a start, anyway, and if he's not here, then we can check other systems when we get to port."

Rikki nodded. She had known that, but her alias Rachel hadn't. Or at least, that was how she decided to play it.

"What do I do?" Rikki asked.

"Which hand is it?" Windham asked.

Rikki did not hold up the hand she used to touch her collar. She had been very careful here.

"Touch it right there." Windham pointed to the tiny pad on the device.

Rikki touched it, and released Misha's skin cells from the pouch she had kept them in. Then she looked up. "Like that?"

"Like that," Windham said.

"What if my DNA gets mixed with his?" Rikki asked.

"It doesn't matter," Windham said. "I have it set to look at male DNA only."

Excellent. That was better than Rikki could have hoped for. That way Windham wouldn't know that none of Rikki's DNA got into the mix. Windham would have thought that odd.

"It'll only take a minute," Windham said.

Rikki nodded, hoping the gesture came off more nervous than knowing. She wondered if the ship had access to the Assassins Guild's member database. It wouldn't surprise her if the ship did have it; that would be one way to protect Guild members if there was a dicey incident far from any port.

"Well," Windham said.

Rikki looked at her. Windham was staring at the device. Rikki couldn't see the display, and she knew that had to be on purpose.

"You found something?" she asked, making her voice more breathless than usual.

"Yeah," Windham said, and in her slow speech, Rikki could hear Windham debating something, probably how much to tell this passenger who suspected she had been coerced into something she wouldn't have normally done.

"What?" Rikki asked.

Windham frowned a little. "You're right. He's not who he says he is. He's a member of the Assassins Guild. Have you angered anyone lately, Miss Carter?"

"N-No," Rikki said. She was beginning to wonder if this had been such a good idea after all. She hadn't thought that Windham might think her an interstellar criminal.

"I see nothing in your records that would indicate problems either," Windham said more to herself than to Rikki.

Rikki had to get her away from this line of thought. "Was I, like, um, a diversion or something?"

She made her voice sound small and frightened. She hunched as she spoke, as if she couldn't believe who had touched her.

"Possibly," Windham said. "It says here that his name is Mikael Yurinovich Orlinski."

Rikki looked up in alarm. Suddenly she was no longer acting. "What?"

"Mikael Yurinovich Orlinski." Windham looked up at her curiously. "Do you know him?"

Rikki's breath had left her body. She had to force herself to inhale. She felt ill.

She sank into one of the nearby chairs.

"Miss Carter?" Windham asked. "Are you all right?"

"No," Rikki said softly, and she wasn't lying.

"Then you do know him," Windham said.

"Not exactly," Rikki said.

"Then what is it?" Windham asked.

Rikki looked up at her and told her the absolute truth:

"Eighteen years ago," she said, "his mother murdered my father."

Chapter 17

WHAT SHE REMEMBERED ABOUT THAT NIGHT—THE night her father died—lived in flashes. Initially, she had no memory of it at all. She woke up in a hospital bed, burned and immobile and in more pain than she had ever been in in her life.

A nurse soothed her, told her to go back to sleep, she would be taken care of, really, and oh, she was lucky to have survived.

Survived what? she wanted to ask, but she drifted to sleep before she could form the words.

It took weeks to form the words. By then, she had had nanotreatments that had repaired every wound, and had prevented the worst of the scarring. Later she got more nanotreatments, these to permanently vanquish the scars.

(Which made her privately wonder as she told the story to Windham: why hadn't Misha gotten rid of his scars? The treatments were easy, harmless, and certainly not expensive for an assassin with the Guild.)

But as she sat in that security office on a cruise ship, eighteen years later, she found she couldn't explain how the memories came back or indeed, even what had happened.

She never talked about what had happened. She tried not to think about it, which of course meant she thought about it every single day.

About the flashes, and why they only came in flashes,

and why the memories were never complete, even after
the courts ordered a review, something that should have
brought the entire memory back. Her counselors and
therapists—and there were dozens—all said the power
of her mind kept those memories away, that as long as
she didn't want to remember, she never ever would, at
least not past the memories that she already had, that she
had permitted herself, because those memories were, apparently, the only safe ones.

Or at least the ones that weren't the most traumatic.
What she remembered was this:

—Her father's face, purple with anger, his
  eyes small and flashing, his voice lacerating:
  *You don't beg. You never beg. Begging gets
  you nowhere.*

—The barracks (she and her father had lived
  in barracks) burning orange against the
  night sky, the flames illuminating the entire
  neighborhood, families standing outside covered in blankets and wearing nothing else,
  one little girl crying, sobbing so hard that
  Rikki wanted to tell her to shut up, crying
  got you nowhere, crying certainly wouldn't
  rebuild a house or make the pain go away.
  Instead, Rikki stared at that little girl—blond,
  heavy—as if that little girl held the secret to
  the entire universe.

—The quiet inside the house, a movement in the
  shadows, Rikki's heart pounding so hard it
  sounded like it came from outside her rather
  than inside. She couldn't catch her breath,
  but she knew someone was here, someone

who didn't belong, someone was inside the house, someone else, someone stealthy and silent and oh, so very terrifying.

— And then, finally, a woman's face, embedded in Rikki's mind like a brand. The authorities had pulled that image. It had been predominant in Rikki's mind, and it had stayed that way, although eventually it was more than a harshly beautiful face, more than the close-cut white-blond hair, the pale ice-blue eyes.

Later, as the memories shifted, grew, returned ever so slightly, the woman spoke to Rikki: *Don't worry. We have not come for you. You will survive this. You will be Just Fine.*

Just Fine. Sure, she was Just Fine. Damaged, battered, bruised, unable to speak for weeks, unable to cry for even longer. Even now, she rarely cried, never saw the point really; tears were for weaklings after all, weaklings and chubby little blond girls who had lost their homes to sudden fires, but not their fathers, not their entire *lives*.

Rikki had not been blond or chubby. She had short brown hair, and had been so thin that the hospital staff kept encouraging her to eat, worried that she had forgotten how in her long sleep, worried that maybe — like some spacer families — she had never really learned how to eat solids, only how to absorb liquid nutrients just to stay alive.

She had eaten real food her entire life, but her family — her father — had never had money, so she hadn't eaten a lot of it. She hadn't done a lot of anything Before. That was how she thought of it all: Before and After.

She liked After better.

But the In-Between, as she healed and people kept asking questions, and they kept wanting to know exactly what happened and why, she had hated the In-Between.

Mostly because she hadn't known the answers. Only that the terrifying blond woman, whom they later identified from the image in Rikki's mind as Anna Ilyinichna Valentinov, better known as Halina Layla Orlinskaya, one of the most ruthless assassins in the galaxy. It was said she only killed for political gain and she never, ever left survivors, But later, Rikki learned that was not true, not in the years when Rikki's father died.

In those years, Orlinskaya had killed for money, and she had left dozens of survivors. In fact, she had become a wanted woman by her own government because she had refused to destroy an entire town, a town (it was said) that she had fallen in love with, a town that she notified of her government's intent to utterly demolish it, thus preventing the town's destruction, and saving thousands of lives.

After that, after that nonevent, Orlinskaya had killed at least a thousand people, but only those she was contracted for, leaving parents and siblings and casual bystanders alive.

Oh, and children as well. She left a lot of children, mentally scarred from what they had seen, but never, ever touched or bruised or physically damaged in any way.

The fire, the bruising, the battering that Rikki had undergone—those were the unusual things, things that didn't fit into Orlinskaya's usual pattern, things that made no sense, and ultimately made the investigation against her come to nothing.

But the authorities had her DNA on scene. They knew she had been there, that she was the only one who could have killed Rikki's father.

They simply hadn't known why.

Rikki couldn't tell the security official on the ship any of this. She wasn't sure exactly how she could tell Windham anything pertinent without blowing her cover. Rikki Bastogne was listed as an unregistered assassin in many databases, which could easily get her in trouble.

Yet she wanted to tell Windham how to look it up. She really wanted to. Because there, in the files, Windham would find pictures of Mikael Yurinovich Orlinski who, for the six years prior to the death of Rikki's father, traveled with his mother on every single kill. Sometimes, the authorities weren't certain if Orlinskaya had killed her victims herself or if she had sent Mikael to do so, like a female lion providing easy prey to train her cub in the art of survival.

For everyone agreed that Orlinskaya killed to survive. First she had killed at the behest of her government, and then, after decades and their decision to put a bounty on her head, she killed to protect herself (and her cub) and to put food on the table. Killing was all she had known.

It was all Rikki had known as well, but of course, she did not tell Windham this. She didn't mention how the testing had gone before the authorities put her in government care, how she had shown an incredible aptitude for death-dealing as well.

Death-dealers had thousands of professions. Various societies had learned to recognize death-dealers because ignoring them caused crime and baseless murders. Channeling death-dealers into the military or mercenary positions or, yes, as assassins for hire, enabled society to keep these dangerous people under control.

Rikki had always thought it ironic that the culture thought her dangerous.

Or she did until the first time she had snapped the neck of a man five times her size.

Then she understood what everyone had seen in her.

And it hadn't surprised her that this thing existed inside her. She remained calm, detached, oddly uncaring after those missions.

After all except Testrial, when she had lost herself in heat and warmth and sensation.

When she had lost herself in Halina Layla Orlinskaya's son.

Rikki's stomach turned. She had to swallow several times to keep herself from being ill.

When she had herself under control, she reached across the desk and grabbed Windham's arm.

"Please," Rikki said, the tremor in her voice very real, "you have to get me away from him. Somehow, you have to get me off this ship."

Chapter 18

THE LOUNGE IN B DECK DIDN'T SEEM NEARLY AS EXCITING as it had the night before. Yeah, the lovely windows were still there. Misha could see himself reflected in them. He looked like he belonged here, in his long topcoat and his brocade vest. He leaned against the bar, a beer in hand, watching a couple at the roulette table lose a fortune.

It didn't amuse him. Nothing did.

And it didn't help that the overhead music was mostly waltzes. What was that all about, anyway? Encouragement to go to the ballroom?

He clutched the glass in his right hand and ignored the woman pressing up against him. She had been angling for his attention for nearly an hour now. She was pretty in a slutty way, wearing a dress that opened all the way to her navel revealing the mounds of her breasts without showing the nipples.

He had found Rikki a lot sexier in a gown that covered everything.

The light changed in the windows' reflections. The door had opened again, and this time, voices hushed, leaving only the damn waltz music. Misha didn't turn. He knew what the silence meant even before he saw the security guards searching the room.

It couldn't be a coincidence that they were here, not with Rikki in the security office. What had she told them? She hadn't confessed, had she?

For the first time, he regretted not going to his room. He wasn't carrying all of his identification, which was something that usually helped when shipboard security tried to cause a problem in a place like the NetherRealm.

The guards came up on both sides of him. The guards didn't have to move the woman in the slutty dress. She had vamoosed to a table beside the bar the minute the guards entered. So either she wasn't supposed to be in the lounge, or she was working the room in the way that the square little guy had thought Rikki was working the ballroom.

"Mr. Orlinski?" one of the guards said softly, putting a hand on Misha's arm. "Come with us, please."

He bit back annoyance. They knew who he was. Rikki hadn't told them; she didn't know.

Or, at least, she hadn't known that morning.

But something was happening. Maybe they figured out Testrial was missing and had run DNA on all of the passengers. When a passenger purchased a ticket on this cruise line, the passenger gave up all rights to privacy in cases of an emergency.

Maybe this was one of those emergencies.

Misha did not speak to the guards. He had learned long ago that if he was playing a rich passenger on a ship, that was a cover he shouldn't drop, not even if the guards knew his real name.

He finished the beer without asking whether or not he could, and then he spun and walked to the door, trusting the guards to follow.

The other passengers watched him go, probably wondering what the hell it was that he had done.

He was wondering what the hell it was that he had done.

Although he would probably find out soon enough.

Chapter 19

Rikki was shaking. She hadn't lost control of herself like this since—well, since last night. But not in quite the same way. Her cheeks flushed.

She *slept* with him. Willingly. The man who murdered her father. And he probably laughed at her the entire time.

Bess Windham didn't look moved. She continued to look at the floating screens around her desk, the screens that were opaque from the back so that Rikki couldn't see them.

"There's no murder here," Windham said.

"What?" Rikki asked. "He's a member of the Assassins Guild, for God's sake. You just told me that."

Windham nodded. "By the laws of the various sectors, which he seems to be quite scrupulous in following, that means none of the deaths he was party to were murders. They were legal assassinations."

The heat in Rikki's cheeks rose. She felt unbelievably warm and cold at the same time, despite the fact that the environmental controls were set at comfortable. It was an emotional reaction. An emotional reaction only. She had to remember that.

"I know," Rikki said as calmly as she could. "This would have happened before—"

She stopped herself. Windham was looking for a murder connected to Rachel Carter, not one connected to Rikki Bastogne.

Did Rikki give up her name here for protection?

She thought about it for a brief second. It was an impossible choice. Either she gave up her real name, which meant she gave up her profession, which put her under even more suspicion, or she backed off and dealt with it on her own.

She blinked hard, surprised at how easy it was to fake tears.

"Never mind," she said. "Obviously, you don't want to help me."

She stood up, feigning outrage. Only she wasn't really feigning, not really. She was outraged, at herself, mostly, but at Misha too. Or at Mikael Orlinski. God, she had slept with him. Enjoyed him.

And all the time, he had laughed at her.

What amazing cruelty.

She staggered away, hand to her throat, to the pretend injuries from the pretend attack that seemed a lot less like pretend now. She wished she had been assaulted while under the influence of touch drops. That was a lot more acceptable than the fact that she had slept with her father's killer.

Misha—Mikael, she had to call him Mikael—had known about it too. He had repeatedly told her he knew who she was. Repeatedly, as if giving her a clue.

And he smiled at her. A lot.

Damn him for smiling.

"Miss," Windham said from behind her, "it's not that I don't believe you—"

"Oh, you don't," Rikki said, surprised to hear her voice wobble. "Just let me leave the ship when the time comes. Okay? Don't charge me extra, and let me get off by some side exit."

"It's not normal procedure," Windham said.

"Of course it's not," Rikki said and let herself out of the room. She tugged her dress up a bit, covering her neck and wiped at her eyes.

A hand banged against the door, so that it didn't close. Windham was following her.

"We can give you some protection. Does he know what room you're in?"

Rikki didn't think so, but she wouldn't put it past him. "I don't know."

"We'll give you a new identi-card and a different room," Windham said.

"What will that do?" Rikki said. "If he wants to kill me, he'll find me. That's how assassins work."

She thought it ironic that she was explaining this to Windham, because Windham had no idea who she was.

"We can solve this," Windham said.

"No, we can't," Rikki said. "I'll just let my family know that if I turn up dead, you're liable."

If she had any family. She didn't really, not blood family. Although she had Jack Hunter, her heart-brother. They'd been raised together in a government home for orphaned and abandoned children. She had taken care of him, and he had taken care of her.

He would care if she died.

But she couldn't even give his name to Windham because Windham would tell him about Rachel Carter, not Rikki Bastogne.

Did Windham think she couldn't get away from Misha—Mikael, *dammit*. Did she think he was that much smarter than she was?

Well, he had outsmarted her so far, but he had had information, information that she now had.

And, apparently, he went by the book. She rarely did. That would give her an advantage.

Windham grabbed her arm. Rikki whirled, ready to strike. No one grabbed her like that, particularly when she was upset.

"Let us help," Windham said.

"What the hell does she need help for?" a strange voice said from the front of the security office.

Rikki looked up. The pugnacious bulldog man stood there, clutching a bandaged right hand.

The hand he had tried to grab her with. The hand she had bent backwards.

That flush in her cheeks grew even hotter.

She had had a hunch this plan would backfire.

And now it had.

Chapter 20

"SHE DOESN'T NEED HELP," THE BULLDOG SAID. "SHE'S the one who attacked me."

He stood near the desk, with the same security official who had first greeted Rikki. That official was standing near the bulldog, looking a bit confused. The official took a step back, raised his hands as if he was the one being arrested, and glanced at Windham.

Rikki couldn't see Windham's response, but she felt it. Windham let go of her arm.

"What's this?" Windham asked from behind Rikki.

"That bi—woman," the bulldog said. "She broke my thumb."

He waved his injured hand around. If the thumb had been broken, then some medical bot had set it and wrapped it so he wouldn't use it while the heal-a-bone grafted over the break.

Rikki just stood in place, completely off balance. She usually knew how to flow with changes, but the realization of who Misha—Mikael, *dammit*—was had left her completely unable to form rapid thoughts.

"I just wanted a dance," the man said, "and she attacked me."

"I did not attack him," Rikki said. "He grabbed me. I stopped him."

She would have to stick with that story.

"So the man with the touch drops," Windham said, "you didn't hurt him?"

Rikki glared at her. This was over. She had the information she wanted, and she would deal with Misha—*damn, damn, damn*, Mikael—on her own.

"No wonder you warn people that they're on their own legally on these ships," Rikki snapped. "We really are. You not only have no jurisdiction, but you abdicate all effort of even trying to keep us secure. I'm sorry I came here."

She shoved past the bulldog, who stepped away from her as if she frightened him, then banged open the security door.

As she did, she nearly hit a group of people coming down the hall. She looked up and found herself face to face with Misha.

Mikael.

Whatever his name was.

His eyes widened, and he looked really, really sympathetic. "Are you okay?" he asked.

"You tell me," she snapped, her heart racing. She didn't want to be anywhere near him.

"Rik—"

She lifted a hand. "Don't say another word," she said and hurried past him.

The discomfort she'd been playing at when she first went into the security office was play no longer. Her breath was coming in small gasps. She had to get away from him, from them, hell, she wanted off this ship, and she wasn't sure quite how she wanted to do it.

But she would figure out a way.

She headed to the lift, Misha calling behind her, not using her name now, smart man.

"Wait," he said. "Just for a few minutes. Wait."

Yeah, right. The last thing she wanted to do was wait for this man. She never wanted to see him again, never wanted his fake sympathy. Never wanted him.

She got on the lift and closed her eyes.

How could he still be so attractive with all that she knew about him? Why was it so hard to resist his voice?

Did he know that about her?

She made herself take a deep breath as the lift took her to K Deck. She would barricade herself in her room. She would come up with a new plan.

She would get the hell off this ship.

She had to.

Chapter 21

SOMETHING WAS VERY WRONG. RIKKI HAD LOOKED AT him like she had never looked at him before. With bafflement and anger and… fear?… was that fear he saw? He couldn't be sure.

Misha stood in the hallway, the security guards around him, and he watched Rikki run to the lift. She no longer seemed like the confident goddess he had seen in the ballroom, but like a woman in trouble.

He frowned, then glanced at the security office. Had they figured out that she had killed Testrial?

"Mr. Orlinski?" one of the security guards said. "You're wanted inside."

He didn't move. He continued to stare at the lift. He could no longer see Rikki, but he had this sense that he should go after her, that he should find her.

He surreptitiously checked his tracker, saw that her icon was moving toward K Deck. He let out a small sigh. He would find her as soon as he was done here.

He turned away from the lift, nodded at the security officer still holding the door, and stepped inside. Then he stopped. That square little man, the one who claimed that Rikki had hurt him, stood near the door, clutching his bandaged hand.

Misha frowned. A woman standing in the corridor frowned back at him.

"Mr. Orlinski," she said in a businesslike voice. "A word, if you please."

"That bitch's been lying to them," the square little man whispered. "Claims she's the victim, not us."

Misha shot him a confused look. Misha hadn't thought of himself as a victim, and he suspected the square man got what he deserved. But he didn't say anything. Instead, he followed the security woman into the corridor.

She stopped a few yards from the door, near a group of other doors, but not inside any office.

"I've become aware of who you really are, Mr. Orlinski," she said in a formal tone. "You do know that assassins are supposed to register with us whenever they ride Mariposa Starlines. You did not do so. In fact, you used a false name."

What was Rikki up to? Why had she given him away? Had she told them about Testrial? Had she said he had killed Testrial?

Misha frowned, and forced himself to concentrate. "Actually, Ms.—"

He peered at her, but she didn't give him her name. So he continued.

"Assassins are not required to register with any starline unless we are following a high-profile target, and there is the possibility of a high-profile death. Even then, it's recommended that an assassin report to the starline *after* the death so as not to compromise the completion of the job."

The woman huffed, and her mouth became a thin line. "Recommended by the Guild, I suppose," she said.

He nodded.

"I don't like it, Mr. Orlinski. You should have contacted us."

She wasn't saying anything about Testrial. It felt odd.

"I'm sorry," he said. "I won't make that mistake again."

"See that you don't," she said, then nodded at him, as if she expected him to leave.

He turned and started to go, when she added,

"One more thing, Mr. Orlinski."

He stopped just like she wanted him to. But he didn't turn around. He was a paying passenger after all. A paying *wealthy* passenger. She didn't dare mess with him too much.

She said, "I understand that you might have been using touch drops last evening."

"What?" Now he did turn around, so fast that she actually backed up one step before catching herself.

"I'll have you know that we don't allow the use of touch drops on this ship. They're illegal most places and they're just plain nasty."

"I don't use touch drops," he said. "I've never used touch drops. Who told you that I did?"

But he knew the answer before he finished the question. Damn Rikki. What was she playing at? She knew that he hadn't used touch drops. There had been no aphrodisiac involved. Not a one, or the two of them would have loathed each other by the next morning.

"That's immaterial, Mr. Orlinski. Just realize that if I find out you use touch drops again on this ship, you will be banned from the Mariposa Starlines. You're on probation with us, sir."

His mouth was open. He had to force himself to shut it. He was oddly shocked. He had never been accused of anything like this in his entire life.

"Did Miss—" and it took him a minute to remember

Rikki's fake name "—Carter tell you that? Because what happened between us was completely consensual."

The woman crossed her arms. "Just behave from now on, Mr. Orlinski. Promise me that."

She wasn't going to tell him any more, but then, she didn't have to.

"I don't use touch drops," he said. "And be careful. I paid for your highest-class ticket on this ship, and you're treating me like a common criminal. I will complain to your board if I have to."

"Money doesn't protect you from all of the rules, sir," she said. But she sounded a little less sure of herself than she had before.

"Of course it doesn't," he said, "but it does protect me from the ones I didn't break."

Then he turned around and strode to the front of the security office. As he passed the square man, the man grinned at him.

"Touch drops," the man said. "Now why didn't I think of that?"

"You should stop thinking about it now," Misha said and pushed his way out of the room.

He didn't even stop in the corridor. He didn't need to. He knew where he was going.

He was headed for the lift. He was headed for Rikki.

He was going to find out what was going on, once and for all.

Chapter 22

RIKKI CAREFULLY FOLDED THE BEAUTIFUL SILK DRESS. She had changed into her usual loose tan pants and comfortable blouse. She had put on her weapons, just in case, and had set her identi-card on a nearby stand.

The little room seemed even littler than it had just hours ago. If she didn't know better, she would think the damn thing was shrinking.

Maybe it was. After all, the ship was designed to keep people out of the rooms and spending money. Maybe Windham, that stupid security officer, had pressed some button, bringing the walls in even closer, so that she could monitor Rikki better.

Blaming the victim. How nice that was.

Not that Rikki was a victim—at least right now. She had made that part up. But she had been a victim at one time.

She no longer felt bad about betraying Misha— *dammit*, Mikael—by going to the security office. She no longer felt bad about lying about their night together.

When she had gone in, she had thought she was betraying something special to save her own skin. By the time she came out, she realized just how big a betrayal he had perpetrated on her.

She was still shaking with anger. And something else, something that hurt her heart so badly, she couldn't even articulate what exactly it was.

She sighed heavily and looked at the clothes folded on the bed next to her rucksack. She was implementing her emergency plan. There was only one way off the ship now, unless she waited until they got to a port, and then she wasn't sure if the next port would take visitors from interstellar cruise ships. Sometimes the ships docked for supplies and left only an hour or two later.

She couldn't take that risk. She needed to get off this ship now.

She clutched the folded dress to her chest. She had loved that dress, and had imagined when she bought it that, when she wore it, she would have a spectacular night. She had promised herself that she wouldn't wear it when she had a target, so that she wouldn't ruin the silk by accidentally getting blood on it.

She hadn't gotten blood on it, but it would be forever tainted by the memories of this night and what had happened, what she had learned. She set the dress down on the dresser, next to her identi-card. Maybe someone could get better use out of the dress than she ever would.

Someone knocked on her door. She jumped. No one knocked here. The cleaners were bots that sent an electronic notice of when they would arrive.

"Who is it?" she asked.

"Misha."

His voice made her heart pound. She looked at the bed, then at the room itself, suddenly feeling cornered. He was good at systems. He could probably get in.

She could defend herself, but still, she didn't want it to come to that.

"What do you want?"

"Let's talk," he said.

She shook her head, then realized he couldn't see it. "There's nothing to say."

"I think there is," he said.

He wouldn't go away. What did he want with her? Why was she so important? He had said that it was because she had been interfering with his work, but then he had said that he knew who she was. So what was it?

Did he think she had been interfering with his work as revenge for her father's death?

She swallowed hard. "Meet me in the K Deck lounge."

He could see how the other half lived.

"No," he said. "I don't think you'll show up."

He knew her better than she wanted him to.

She glanced at her stuff. She had only needed an hour or so, and then she would be gone.

Of course he would get in the way of that. He had gotten in the way of everything.

"I'm not letting you in here," she said.

"Then talk to me in the hallway," he said. "Or better yet, we can walk to the lounge together."

With his arm around her shoulder, guiding her so that she couldn't get away like he had done before? No thank you.

She glanced at her equipment, which was still on the small side table. She had her weapons, but he would hold her tight so that she couldn't use them.

She could probably fight him, but given that little scene in the security office, Windham would take Misha's side. She made a small growling sound at herself. Not Misha. Mikael. Why couldn't she get that through her stupid head? Misha was a love name, and she didn't want to think of him that way ever again.

On impulse, she grabbed a small narcotic on a little sleeve that fit over her middle finger. The narcotic was strong, but not deadly. It just put anyone who used it to sleep quickly.

Then she squared her shoulders, opened the door, and slipped out of the room.

Chapter 23

HE LOOKED GORGEOUS. WHY DID HE ALWAYS LOOK gorgeous? And why couldn't Rikki just shut off that attraction to him? Maybe she should take touch drops, just so that she could have him repel her the next day. Except that would mean she would have to sleep with him again.

Such hardship.

Her cheeks warmed. It *was* a hardship. She had to remember that.

He had stepped to the far side of the corridor so that she could get out of the door, and let the door close behind her. He hadn't tried to rush her to get inside, something she had been prepared for.

He still wore the same coat and brocade vest he had worn in the ballroom, and that outfit still looked fantastic. She felt frumpy in her loose shirt and tan pants, then questioned why in the universe she would feel frumpy and, more importantly, why in the universe she should even care.

He looked like the man she had seen that first morning, vulnerable, softer, younger somehow. That morning when he had said his name was Misha, as if it meant something to her.

Had his eyes flashed at that point? Had he been hiding amusement?

She leaned against the door, keeping her hands at her sides. "What do you want?"

Her voice was cold.

"I thought we were going to the lounge…?" His words trailed off.

"This will only take a minute. I want you to leave me alone."

He frowned. "I know you're mad at me. I know I said a few things that were phrased wrong—"

"Phrased wrong?" she asked.

"That thing about control and finding you and the way that our businesses intersected. I shouldn't have startled you with that announcement that I was the one who hired you and I shouldn't have questioned your competence."

Her cheeks were so warm she wanted to put a hand against them. But she didn't dare because of the little narcotic she had on her right hand.

"*That's* what you think this is all about?" she asked, keeping her voice cold.

His frown grew. "Isn't it?"

It had been earlier in the night, when she wanted to find out who he was and whether or not he was lying to her again. But that seemed like years ago now.

"Not anymore," she said flatly.

"Then tell me, Rikki, what's going on? I want to work together, maybe figure out how we can get you into the Guild, and—"

"I told you," she snapped. "I don't join things."

"Well, then," he said, "maybe we could get you some proper training, and then—"

"I don't need training," she said tightly. "I'm not interested in your training. I would like you to go away."

He tilted his head slightly as if he didn't understand. Had no woman said that to him before? That might have been possible, considering how pretty he was. He wasn't the kind of man women said no to.

Which meant that he didn't know how to handle it when it happened.

"What were you doing in the security office?" he asked slowly, as if he was just starting to figure things out.

"I wanted to find out who you were," she said.

"I told you my name this morning."

"You said your name was Misha."

"Yes," he said, still looking vulnerable. In fact, looking even more vulnerable than he had looked before.

"As if you expected me to know who that was," she said.

He made a little gesture with his hands and shoulder, a combination nod and bob and yeah-so movement. As if he still expected her to know who that was.

She continued, "I took a little of your DNA tonight and—"

"Took it?" he asked. "When it was freely offered this morning?"

She held up her right hand, determined not to smile, and tapped her thumb against her index finger. If he was paying attention, he would have seen the transparent sleeve over her middle finger. But he wasn't paying attention, which was what she planned.

Fair warning, though. She couldn't do anything without fair warning.

Another side of herself that she wasn't all that fond of.

"I forgot to keep the samples," she said. "Had I known they would have been useful, I would have kept some."

He smiled just a little, and damn him, the smile was warm. "You could have asked and I would have assisted you in the collection. You didn't have to swipe some off me during that dance."

So he figured that much out, after her little hint.

"I didn't want to romp in your room," she said. "I was done with games. I wanted to know who you were."

"I told you—"

"You didn't tell me a goddamn thing." She couldn't keep her voice down any longer. "You said your name was Misha, but that didn't mean anything to me."

He winced. Was that a wince? Really? What was he playing at? He had no right to wince, not after what he had done to her.

"You didn't tell me your name was Mikael Yurinovich Orlinski," she said. "The man who murdered my father."

"What?" he said. And he looked surprised. Surprised. What gave him the right to look surprised? Or to wince. He had no right to any emotions in this. He had used her, and he didn't get to play act anymore.

"Now do you understand why I want you to stay the hell away from me?" she asked, more loudly than she had intended.

"Actually, no," he said. "I would have thought that you would remember me fondly. After all, I—"

"You *murdered* my father. You and your mother. I was in the hospital for weeks after that."

"Yes, I know," he said. "And—"

She let out a cry, part of her amazed at her own reaction. It was as if that part of her had separated out, and was watching from above. She lunged at him. He put up his hand as if to stop her, and she grabbed it with her right hand, pressing that finger into the flesh of his wrist, right over a vein.

"You think that murdering my father is something I should be grateful for?" she asked when she could finally manage words.

"Um, I didn't kill him, my mother did, and yes, I think…" he blinked at her, his pupils growing wide. "I think…"

He tilted his head again, then licked his lips. The narcotic created dry mouth. That was the only sign it had been used.

"Whatthehelldidyoudo?"

He mushed all the words together. His mouth clearly wasn't working properly anymore.

He had only a few seconds of consciousness yet.

"Nothing you won't recover from," she said, "which is more than we can say about me. What you did to me is unspeakable, Mikael."

She was proud of herself for getting his name right. He blinked. He wasn't unconscious yet.

He shook his head just a little. Then his eyes closed and he slumped against the wall.

She grabbed him around the waist and pulled him toward her. That body of his, even heavy, even dead-weight, felt great through his clothes. She still liked the feel of him after everything.

Better to avoid him altogether. Better to stay away. He had some kind of hold on her that she didn't entirely understand.

She half-carried him the few steps across the corridor to her door. Then she used her palm to slap the door open. She brought him inside, and closed the door.

The security camera would see it all, of course, but wouldn't know what happened. They had a conversation, they touched, and then she grabbed him and dragged him into the room. That was all the camera would see.

That was all it needed to see—at least for the next hour or two.

And by then, she would be gone.

Chapter 24

THE BED SMELLED OF RIKKI. MISHA TURNED HIS HEAD slightly and inhaled deeply from the pillow. Amazing that he could recognize the scent of her after such a short acquaintance. Such a short, *amazing* acquaintance. Such a short, amazing, *arousing* acquaintance.

He stretched—and hit his feet on something. That caught his attention. His bed didn't have a frame or anything near the feet. He sat up slightly and nearly hit his head on a shelf beside the bed.

Not his room.

Not a room he'd ever seen before.

A utilitarian, small room. An uncomfortable room. A room filled with people.

He frowned and realized he was a bit woozy. A woman peered over him and it wasn't Rikki. It took Misha a minute to realize that the woman was that security officer—what was her name? Windham. That was it.

"Welcome back to the land of the living, Mr. Orlinski," she said.

"What?" he said. Or rather, he croaked. The word came out as "waaa?" with no strong consonants.

He was woozy, he could barely talk, his mouth tasted of sweaty feet, and he felt weak.

She had drugged him.

Not this stupid Windham woman, but Rikki. Damn it. When she grabbed him.

He remembered now: that slight needle-like pain on his wrist, the way the corridor had gone all colors, like a bad light show in a bar, her face leaning over his, telling him something important—

"We're not sure what she gave you, Mr. Orlinski, so we can't give you an antidote. But we have some general scrubbers in the security office that should work for standard sleeping drugs and for alcohol. Let me help you sit up."

She was still leaning over him, and the idea of her trying to fit into the small space that this bed occupied—a space that made him uncomfortable with her—had him waving his hands to keep her back.

"You're going to have to come with us, Mr. Orlinski," the security woman, Windham, said. "We need to find out a few things."

He managed to scoot up in the bed, looked down, saw that she had left him clothed—and by *she*, he meant Rikki. He didn't want to think of the security woman as a "she" in the Rikki-sense, which meant in the sexual sense, which really meant in the desirable sense, which also meant in the infuriating sense—

And what had she given him? Whatever it was, it was still in his system.

He patted his pockets and heard sounds above him. He looked up to see the men behind Windham (How had they all fit into this tiny room?) holding weapons on him.

He pulled out an all-purpose scrubber which he trusted a lot more than their scrubber. Besides, based on the taste still lingering unpleasantly in his mouth, he had a hunch he knew what kind of narcotic Rikki had used on him.

He held out one hand, showed the scrubber with the other, and sprayed the damn stuff up his nose. Then, for good measure, he dry-swallowed a small pill that he kept in the scrubber bottle.

Then he blinked and felt his head clear. A little, anyway. Not entirely, but enough to formulate questions. Or at least, near-questions, with actual consonants.

"Rikki?"

The Windham woman looked confused. And because his head wasn't entirely clear, it took him a second to understand why she was confused.

"Rachel?" he said firmly as if the first time he had just mangled Rikki's name.

"Gone," the woman said.

"Gone?" he asked, trying to comprehend that. How did a passenger get gone from an interstellar cruise liner. He pushed his fuzzy brain. "Did we stop somewhere?"

"No," the woman said. "She stole an emergency lifeship. At least, there's one missing and she doesn't show up on any of our in-house sensors."

The woman was slapping an identi-card against her hand.

Misha nodded toward it. "Ri—Rachel's?"

"Yes." That was an admission of defeat. If she had been wearing an identi-chip like he had, the security people could have tracked her better. But the cards—designed to get more money out of the poorer passengers—only tracked someone when she carried it. "And someone tampered with the security cameras near a lifeship pod not far from here. The ship's been gone for hours."

Meaning they couldn't easily track it and they

certainly couldn't turn this behemoth ship around to catch her. This ship had to keep going to its destination and trust local authorities to find Rikki.

Only, if she had escaped in the NetherRealm, there was no one authority, and no one to contact.

Despite himself, he felt admiration for her. She was right: she didn't need his training. He would never have tried something so daring on his own. The Guild frowned on theft in the commission of a job, even if that theft wouldn't have had many consequences, because the theft added something illegal to something legal.

And there weren't a lot of consequences if she vanished into the NetherRealm. Even the stolen lifeship wasn't that serious. Interstellar cruisers had learned through their own disasters to have twice the number of emergency lifeships on board than they needed, ostensibly because one part of the ship might be impossible to reach. But in reality, they wanted to show that they had no liability should something go horribly, awfully wrong.

He swung his legs off the side of the bed, not caring that he nearly kicked the security woman, or that his movement had forced a third guard (whom he hadn't noticed until now) back into the corridor. Misha wasn't quite willing to think of Rikki being missing yet. She had said something to him, and he needed to remember what that was.

"If she's gone, and she clearly drugged me, then what are you doing here?" he asked. "I think this would count as a personal matter."

"It would, Mr. Orlinski, if not for one *little* thing." The Windham woman's emphasis on the word "little" didn't make the little thing sound so very little.

She had his attention whether he wanted to give it to her or not.

"And what would that be?" he asked.

"Well," she said, her gaze steely, "I thought I'd better ask the only assassin we had on board if he had ever heard of someone named Elio Testrial."

Misha resisted the urge to close his eyes in disgust. Damn that Rikki. She had pulled it off again. She had gotten Misha blamed for her work—and not in a good way.

"Yeah," he said. "I've heard of Elio Testrial. I suppose you're going to want to discuss this in the security office."

The Windham woman smiled for the first time since he met her. It was not a pleasant smile.

"Now you're catching on, Mr. Orlinski. We'd like you to come with us."

PART 2

Chapter 25

IT TOOK MOST OF A WEEK FOR RIKKI TO MAKE HER WAY to Krell, a grimy little space station at the end of no-where. First she had to get off the interstellar cruise ship, which proved easier than expected. The emergency life-ship she had scouted had enough provisions to get her to Centaar, a small planet at the edge of the NetherRealm.

She docked in low orbit around Centaar on a docking ring known for theft and graft. She was giving them a gift: they could dismantle the lifeship for parts, so long as the folks running the ring brought her down to Oyal, a city on the surface. And they did.

Rikki hadn't been to Oyal before, but she had heard about it, and the place was as corrupt as she expected. The rich were very rich here, and lived in a protected dome outside the city—not because the atmosphere was tough for humans to breathe, but because a dome was difficult for armed gangs to easily breach.

She carried enough cash on her to pay off muggers, and searched for a place that would rent a ship, no questions asked. Most places had a few questions or wanted a huge financial guarantee that she would bring the ship back.

She knew she'd never get her guarantee back, so she wanted to pay the smallest guarantee possible. She found a ship-rental place on a back alley in Oyal that made her skin crawl.

But the place let her inspect the ship, and while its interior was shoddy, its equipment was in top shape. Still, the interior would have made Rikki hate the ship, except for one thing: She knew she was heading to Krell. She needed a clean and relatively safe place to sleep while she was there.

Krell was a short distance back the way she had come from, in the NetherRealm, a place for people who didn't want to be noticed. Krell didn't ID anyone or question them or even track its arrivals and departures. Security was nonexistent, theft was rampant, and cleanliness—well, that had gone out the window as well.

It hadn't been her idea to come to Krell. She had set up a meeting with an old friend, and he had chosen the venue.

The fact that the venue was Krell either meant he was afraid of something or he had done something particularly horrible. And knowing Jack Hunter, it was probably both.

Rikki had met Jack in that fateful year after her father died. Jack was the long-term survivor of government child care. Jack pretended nothing mattered, but he had protected her, even though he was a scrawny kid, one year younger and not even close to his adult growth.

In fact, she still saw him that way, even though he wasn't scrawny anymore, and his adult growth had made him into one of those men who was too big for comfortable space travel.

Jack was six foot six, a bear of a man. He was trim for his size, but out here, in the realm of space stations and starships, his height made him a giant.

Most men—most people—who spent a lot of time in

space were lean and not much bigger than Rikki. Misha—
Mikael. Dammit. Mikael—was a case in point. Slender,
deceptively strong, and not that tall, but perfect—

And as usual, she had to wrench her thoughts from
him. She had no idea why she was so obsessed with him.
He wanted to hurt her—he *had* hurt her—he had used
her, and she was like those pathetic people who sometimes tried to hire her to kill the object of their obsession
just so that they wouldn't obsess any longer.

She refused those jobs, knowing that those people
were borderline bugfuck crazy. And now she felt borderline bugfuck crazy too.

Because she couldn't keep Misha (Mikael!!) out of
her head.

Even when she was looking at Jack.

Jack sat in the middle of what was ridiculously called
an "open-air" restaurant.

There were buildings inside the space station, although on most places, like a *planet*, these "buildings"
would more properly have been called "rooms." The
rooms were attached, like row houses, and they had
entrances, and some of them—again, ridiculously, she
thought—had windows that looked into the "open air."

The corridor between all of these "buildings," these
rooms, was the open-air part. It couldn't be leased. It belonged to the station itself, which sometimes granted permission for a restaurant or a store to spill into the corridor.

And the spill area was the place Jack had chosen. It
was part of a restaurant named Starcatcher, and Jack,
courageous man that he was, was actually eating something off the menu.

Rikki approached, opened the ridiculous little gate

that separated the "open-air" part of the restaurant from the rest of the corridor, and stopped beside Jack's table. Without saying a word, she picked up a spoon and looked at it in the dim light.

Something was caked onto the handle. She made a face and set the spoon down.

"I can't believe you're eating here," she said as she grabbed a cloth napkin and used it to wipe off the chair. Then she swiped a napkin from the table next to her and spread it across the chair's seat.

"I can't believe you're going to sit on that," he said, his voice so deep that it rumbled. The voice still surprised her. It suited him, but she had met him years before his voice changed. "I'm sure they wash the napkins less often than they wipe off the chairs."

Her stomach flipped, just like he knew it would. He knew everything about her a brother would know—how to twist her stomach, how to make her blush, how to make her laugh. He would defend her to the death and he would always ride to her rescue and he would love her forever.

Their relationship was so purely platonic, so deeply familial that whenever a friend would ask why the two of them didn't get together, they would grimace in unison, and one of them would say, "Last I checked, it's against the law to sleep with a family member."

That made people think they were related, and they left it that way. Because it felt like they were related, and it always would.

"Then I'm just going to stand," she said.

"Hover," he corrected, his mouth full. "You're just going to hover."

"Whatever." She almost wiped her hands on her black pants, and then changed her mind. The very thought of getting that crap on her clothes made her vaguely queasy. "You could be a gentleman and give me your jacket to sit on."

"My jacket has been staying in this hellhole for the past three days, waiting for her ladyship to arrive."

"Oh, gross," she said. Then she gave up and sat down. She would have to shower when she got back to the tiny ship anyway, and she had brought clothing that she would never ever ever wear when she was in Krell.

God knew what was in the air here. The environmental system supposedly filtered things, but this being Krell, the filters probably hadn't been changed in two centuries.

"Is there a reason we're here?" she asked Jack.

"Triple cheese bacon burger," he said, his mouth full. "The best in the sector."

She looked at the thing in his hand. It vaguely resembled a burger. The meat (if it was meat) was burned to a crisp, with something flat and bacon-shaped hanging off of it. The cheese was such a bright orange that it hurt her eyes.

"I don't even want to think about it," she said.

He burped, wiped a hand over his mouth, and then grinned at her. "You know, for a death-dealer, you are unbelievably fastidious."

She let out an exasperated sigh. He wasn't supposed to say that "death-dealer" thing. He had picked up that phrase after she had weaned him off "killer" and "assassinator." She was beginning to think "assassinator" was the best choice.

"Violent does not mean messy," she said to him for maybe the thousandth time.

"Yeah, yeah, yeah," he said. "If there wasn't a component of messy, you wouldn't have sent me that emergency message from wherever the hell you were. Oye? Oyick?"

"Oyal," she said. And technically, she hadn't been there yet when she contacted him. She had contacted him from the docking ring above Centaar. Apparently, the comm system on that ring masked its signature as Oyal. "You could've come to me."

"No," he said flatly. "I couldn't."

She glanced at him. She had been so involved in her own little adventure that she didn't even think about him. Was he here because of something he needed? Or because he thought she needed the privacy only Krell guaranteed?

"You want to tell me what scared you?" Jack asked.

"You mean besides that bacon cheese blackened thingie you're eating?" she asked. "Maybe the fact that you are actually eating it."

He took another bite just to irritate her and then he grinned, his mouth full. She had to look away.

He chewed very deliberately, swallowed, took a sip of the water the restaurant had provided in a dirty glass, and said, "You were scared when you contacted me."

"I've never been scared," she said, and she wasn't sure she was scared now. But she was angry, and she did feel betrayed, and she still felt off-balance.

Misha (Mikael. For God's sake) had seemed sympathetic and vulnerable in that corridor, and he didn't deny the murder of her father. Yet he seemed to think she wouldn't mind. Was that because he had thought she had no scruples? (Wonder who gave him that idea—or what part of the night they spent together convinced him of it.)

Jack gave Rikki a tender grin. They both knew she lied about never being scared. In that first year, she used to hide under his bed, as far back in the corner as she could get, and sleep there so no bad guys could find her.

"I've never been scared as an adult," she said through gritted teeth. "And I'm not scared now."

"That you're willing to acknowledge," Jack said. "Even to yourself."

She hated this kind of circular argument. He specialized in it, and she could never win it. He always started from a faulty premise, said she didn't agree with the premise consciously, and then argued with her as if she held that faulty premise close to her heart.

And that irritated her. He irritated her. But in a good way. She had missed him. She smiled at him, and he clearly recognized the fondness in her smile.

He took another bite, then shoved the burger toward her. "You really should try this."

"Have you ever wondered how they got meat out here? Or what kind it really is?"

"I don't think about my food," he said.

"You should," she said, annoyed that he kept foisting this thing on her. "Maybe I killed it."

That got him. She only took jobs involving humans.

"Ew," he said, putting the burger down. "Not fair."

He grabbed his napkin, looked at it, and set it back down again. Then he wiped his mouth with the back of his hand.

"You're the person who picked Krell," she said.

"Because you're the person who sounded like she was in trouble." He set his plate aside. "You want to tell me what's going on? We are the only ones in this restaurant."

"For obvious reasons," she said.

A servo-bot floated up to them, and displayed a drop down holographic menu that looked like it went on for pages.

Rikki waved a hand at it, and hoped it would go away, instead of nag her to pay for the seat by eating food.

It did.

Maybe there were some benefits to Krell after all.

Still, she looked around. The corridor was mostly empty, and no one sat in the other open-air restaurants. She was sure someone was recording this conversation, but she was equally sure that Jack carried some kind of jammer. He'd been carrying one since he was thirteen and learned how to build one on his own.

Rikki hadn't carried a jammer to this meeting because she knew Jack would have one. And two jammers would occasionally interact with each other, occasionally creating a high-pitched noise that was both obvious and painful. And that high-pitched noise defeated the purpose of the jammer.

"Are you still doing that investigative thing for the Rovers?" she asked.

The Rovers were a group of loosely affiliated assassins. They did not want to join the Guild, but they had discovered it was hard to work alone. So two decades before, some Rovers set up a floating office, and hired a few non-assassins to vet the jobs.

Jack did freelance vetting for them. Or he had the last time that Rikki checked.

"No," he said flatly. "I don't work for them anymore."

She looked at him in surprise. Not because he didn't work for the Rovers, but because he sounded so emphatic about it.

"What happened?"

"Politics," he said in a way that closed off further discussion.

"So you're not vetting clients?"

"For you, I'll vet. What happened? Did you get yourself in trouble?"

"Yeah," she said softly.

All the humor had left his face. Trouble, in her profession, could mean a lot of things. "Someone after you?"

She held up her hands. "I don't know, exactly."

"You ki—um, do, um… you know… take on the wrong guy?"

Yes, she had done the wrong guy, but not in the way that Jack meant. "On my last job, the target was legitimate."

And then she thought about it, thought about the way Jack might interpret that phrase.

"Or at least," she said, "the target was justifiable. I… don't feel bad about finishing the job."

Jack nodded. He was frowning. They both knew it had been a long time since she had been so inarticulate about a job.

"Then what happened?" he asked softly.

"There's a good chance *I* was targeted," she said.

He tilted his head. "Why would that happen? A disgruntled target family?"

He sounded confused. He knew that she had had problems before and they hadn't rattled her.

She was shaking her head even as he spoke. "It's not that. It's probably me."

"You're confusing me, Rik," he said.

"Yeah," she said. "I'm not happy about this myself."

He grabbed the plate, probably because he needed to do something with his hands. They migrated toward the remains of that burger. Normally, she would have made a comment, something to put him off the food again, but she was no longer in a bantering mood.

"I think this might have something to do with my dad," she said.

She didn't have to explain that to Jack. He had lived through the aftermath with her. He had only been eleven, but he tried to keep her together. He managed pretty well, considering.

"Good Lord," he said. "Are you sure?"

"The guy who hired me," she said, "is the son of the assassin who killed my father."

Jack nodded. He put his hands down, no longer fiddling with the plate. Now she had his full attention.

"He was on the ship, Jack. He hired me so that he could track me down, so that he could find me." Her voice shook. She hadn't expected her voice to shake.

"Did he know who you were?" Jack asked.

"He said he did. We were—" God, how much should she tell him? She couldn't decide. She'd been thinking about it the whole way here, and she couldn't decide. "—talking, and at one point, he said he knew who I was."

"Talking about what?" Jack asked. He had noticed her hesitation.

She shook her head. She couldn't admit how badly Misha had used her. She shook her head again.

"I just want to know," Jack said gently, "if he was referring to your job or your history."

He knew how upset she was. He was treading lightly. She swallowed hard.

"I don't know. It's a mess, Jack," she said, and then she told him everything. Or almost everything. As much as she dared tell her little brother, in a public place, about a man who still confused her. A man who wouldn't leave her thoughts, no matter how hard she tried to get rid of him.

Chapter 26

It took Misha nearly a week to track Rikki. He wouldn't have been able to find her at all—or at least, not quickly, if it weren't for one thing: She did steal a emergency lifeship from an interstellar space cruiser. There were very few places in this part of the sector that would not have reported her for that theft, and most of those places were at the edge of the NetherRealm, which unsurprisingly, was where she had disappeared.

While he searched for her, he had to grudgingly admit that he had completely misread her. She was more than competent. She was just different than he was.

Very different.

Willing to break rules and laws and cross ethical boundaries to get what she wanted.

Whatever Rikki had given him had put him under for six hours, and then he had been interrogated by that stupid security officer for another four. He would have gotten out of there quicker if it weren't for the fact that the sleeping drug had made his brain work intermittently. If he had had all of his faculties, he would have told the stupid security officer that she was the one who wasn't thinking clearly—which was what he said after four wasted hours.

He asked her to check Rikki's DNA, which the woman did. Then he said, quite calmly (even though he was furious), which assassin had .spent time with Elio

Testrial? Which one had lied from the beginning? And which one was no longer on the ship?

His argument so convinced the security officer that she quit questioning him at that moment, not thinking to ask why he was so involved with Rikki and why she had targeted him in particular.

But that explained why the security officer worked for a cruise line, and not for some private investigative agency.

By the time, he had gotten out of the stupid security office, he was ten hours behind Rikki, and ten hours, at the pace that the cruise ship traveled, was a hell of a distance.

He could have stolen a lifeship on his own and back-tracked, but the ship was near its next restocking stop, so he disembarked there—and got no protest at all from the incompetent security officer. In fact, he got free passage on Mariposa Starlines for his next few jobs, in apology.

Which he did find deliciously ironic.

He spent the time waiting on the ship charting the possible courses Rikki had taken and only found one good one.

He avoided the docking rings above Centaar because they were notorious for stripping ships for parts. If he had been Rikki, of course, he would have parked there and let whatever happened happen.

He assumed she did that. And then he went to Oyal, where he spent a few days tracking down all of the ask-no-question ship rental places. He figured when he was done with those, he would go to ask-no-question ship purchasing places.

Only he didn't have to. He found the rental place on his second day, talked to the owners, and worried when he discovered that he paid more for the information than Rikki had paid for the ship's deposit.

Which put him in a hell of a dilemma. Did he wait to see if she returned the ship? Or did he try to find out where she went? The rental agency probably had a tracker on its ship, and even if Rikki disabled the tracker, it still would have given him an idea of where she would have gone. Still, he would have to do a lot of digging to find her.

He wasn't even sure if finding her was worth it.

The woman clearly hated him. She had treated him badly for reasons he didn't entirely fathom, and she seemed to believe he had done something wrong on the night her father died. He thought his actions had been blameless, so he wasn't quite sure what that was all about.

But her actions recently weren't blameless at all, and they did get in the way of his work. Once again, he had to talk himself out of being blamed for one of her jobs — even if, technically, he was the one who had hired her.

Something was going on here, something he didn't entirely understand. And that sentence could refer to his relationship with Rikki as well as the interactions they had had over work. He simply didn't understand her or what she wanted or how he had become her target.

Nor did he understand why she had fled when she discovered his real identity.

If that was why she had fled.

He decided to go to a small restaurant across from the ship rental place to consider his options. The restaurant was small, but it had windows on all sides. He could see anyone who came out of the ship rental place. If Rikki came back here, she would have to leave by that door.

He ordered some soup and coffee. Then he checked

his network. No one had contacted him about a new job yet, and no one wanted him back at the Guild.

Although he would have to go there if he didn't get this resolved soon. He might need the help of the Guild's investigative wing, and he might have to talk with the Guild's director, Kerani Ammons. Kerani had been a mentor to him from the moment he arrived. She understood his special circumstances, and would give him an honest assessment.

He needed honesty at the moment.

The soup arrived. It had a thick tomato broth, and smelled of garlic and spices. He put a spoon in it, and the spoon stood up by itself.

Maybe he should just go back to the Guild, figure out what was going on with him, and then decide what to do about Rikki. After all, he was in no hurry.

Or rather, part of him was in a hurry. The part who had found her delicious and sexually exciting. The part who had bonded with her in a way he had never bonded with any woman before her.

"Mikael Yurinovich Orlinski."

For a minute, he thought he was imagining the voice. After all, he had just thought of the women he'd been involved with, and this voice belonged to Liora Olliver, the woman he'd once been serious about.

Then a waft of musky perfume washed over him, and he knew that Liora was there. She bounced into the seat across from him. Her black hair was cropped short, and there were new lines around her eyes. But she was still slight and muscular, as different from Rikki as she could get.

Liora's dark eyes flashed, and she gave him a grin

that didn't quite seem sincere. "What are you doing here? Chasing your little Rover?"

He frowned at her. Rover? What was she talking about? The Rovers were a loosely affiliated group of assassins who had somehow gotten it into their heads that they wanted to destroy the Guild.

"Are you following me, Liora?" he asked, rather than answer her question directly. He had learned never to answer Liora's questions exactly, if he could at all avoid it. Liora loved games, and she was good at them—better at them than he was.

He used to find that attractive about her. Which, come to think of it, might be some of the appeal with Rikki.

As soon as he had that thought, though, he dismissed it. He had been attracted to Rikki long before he realized that she had been toying with him. And the toying with him was just confusing him.

Liora smiled. "Following *you*? Don't flatter yourself."

She tossed her hair back, then grabbed his coffee as if she was entitled to it. He didn't protest. It was another game.

"I'm here because I just got done with a job," she said.

Assassins, even Guild assassins, rarely confided in each other about their work. It wasn't quite a rule, but it wasn't done much either.

He really didn't believe her about the job. So he said before he could stop himself, "You had a job here? In the NetherRealm?"

That was as unusual as an assassin admitting to her work.

She shrugged one shoulder. "I'm not between jobs, like you are. I work a lot."

How did she know that he was between jobs? What was going on?

"It sounds like you are following me," he said, wondering if that was admitting to not having work.

"I'm not following you." She finished his coffee, set the mug down, and pushed it to the edge of the table so that one of the bots would refill it. "Not like you're following that Rover."

"What Rover?" As soon as he asked the question, he cursed himself. This was how Liora always sucked him in.

"That hot piece of ass you've been following all over the sector. What's her name? Rikki something?"

How did Liora know about that? He felt a surge of irritation, then bit it back. But from the look of triumph on Liora's face, he realized he didn't tamp the irritation down quickly enough.

He could deny that Rikki was a Rover (and he wasn't sure about that, was he? What did he really know about her?) or he could deny that he was interested in her. Either would please Liora. Both answers meant he was deep in her game.

"What do you want, Liora?" he asked.

She frowned just a little. He had managed to irritate her now, which pleased him.

"Nothing," she said and stood. "I just figured you'd want to see a face from home."

"If I wanted to see a face from home," he said, "it wouldn't be yours."

Her eyes narrowed. "I keep forgetting that you hate me because I broke up with you."

"No, sweetie," he said, "I don't hate you. Hating you

implies passion, and the passion left our relationship about six months in. At least on my side."

"We were together for five years," she said, sounding surprised. He had told her for a long time that he no longer cared about her. Apparently, he had finally gotten through.

"Amazing what inertia will do," he said.

"You're mean," she said.

"No, Liora. I'm not the mean one here."

Her eyes narrowed, and for a moment, he had a sense of just how dangerous she could be. Then she made a sound of disgust, turned and left without the last word.

There was a first time for everything.

And like so many firsts, this one left him unsettled. He wasn't sure what had just happened, but he was glad it was over.

PART 3

Chapter 27

IT TOOK RIKKI ANOTHER WEEK TO GET HOME—NOT that she had a real home. But she had an apartment, a place for her things, a place where she (kinda) relaxed. Someone else would probably—more accurately—call it a bolt-hole, a hiding place, the equivalent of that space she shoved herself into under Jack's bed when they were children, a place she could huddle in the dark and ignore the dust bunnies and never ever leave if she never ever wanted to.

The apartment was in Lakota, a small and pretty city in the southern hemisphere of a planet called Unbey. She had discovered this place on one of her early jobs, and she had saved up for the apartment, buying it under a name she never used anywhere other than Lakota.

The apartment covered the top floor of an old complex in a part of the city that was being gentrified. She bought when no one else knew about that part of the city, except that it was crime-ridden and filled with derelict buildings. Over time, the buildings got fixed, the crime moved to another part of the city, and her apartment, once an anomaly, was the centerpiece of the complex. She bought a few of the other apartments below her, under different names, and kept them mostly as a buffer, so that no one could get one and attack her from below.

She didn't love the Lakota apartment, but she almost

did—and that was the most attached she had ever felt to some place she had lived.

She had dropped off the rental on Oyal, gotten her deposit back, which surprised her, and then traveled to Centaar's other major city, Nety. She had the uncomfortable feeling that she was being followed, but she never saw who was following her, if anyone was at all. For all she knew, she was under surveillance because she had gone to that cheap ship rental place or because she was newly arrived from Krell or (most likely) because she had arrived on Centaar in a stolen lifeship.

The feeling of being followed forced her to take several extra transport trips, and go very far out of her way before coming here. She took all of the trips under different names, and twice she changed her appearance.

On the last flight to Unbey, she returned to her "off" look, her real look, her mousy brown hair, her unspectacular brown eyes. She wore no makeup, and out-of-fashion clothes that made her look ten years older than she really was.

She transformed herself into one of those women who disappeared when people looked at them: too old to be attractive; too young to be interesting. She liked it that way—she liked it when people looked through her. The last thing she wanted was to be noticed.

She let herself into the apartment, closed the door, and then stopped like she always did and looked across the entry at the view. The view was her great risk because it made the public parts of the apartment vulnerable.

Windows on all sides, with the entry smack-dab in the middle. The entry faced the lake that stretched for miles into the distance. The lake views were what had revived this neighborhood, what had inspired the city, if truth be told. Lake Lakota was the largest lake in the hemisphere, so large it was almost a small fresh-water ocean. It colored life in Lakota and relaxed her whenever she saw it.

She let out a small sigh, then set down her rucksack and the one small bag she carried. Most everything she needed was here. The apartment had a layer of dust—she always bought new cleaning robots, destroying the previous bunch before she left. She had new cleaning robots in the bag. She had to assemble them, but it wouldn't take her long.

She always bought new robots. Robots could be re-programmed in her absence, and she didn't want that. She changed a lot of things that could be tampered with whenever she left, which cost her more money than she probably should have spent, but she saw that as the price of having a bolt-hole.

Especially one as beautiful as this.

First she took a few minutes to assemble the robots. She set them out to clean while she got settled. Then she went into the bedroom and opened her walk-in closet door. A wardrobe of comfortable clothes faced her. She had missed them. She stepped through the closet to the bathroom, took a quick shower, and then put on a soft shirt and pants set, leaving her feet bare.

Her bare feet told her that the robots were doing their job.

Once she was comfortable, she went to her office. It was not too far from the entrance, with a secret passage leading to that entrance. She had built it herself so that no one else would even know it existed. If someone was spying on her through the amazing windows, the office itself would look like the necessary four walls in the middle of the apartment, at least one of them a bearing wall.

Only someone who came inside would know that these walls were spaced just a little too far apart, that there had to be something inside them.

What was inside them was a windowless, soundproof room that doubled as a research station and an armory. She had more weapons in there than anywhere else—and she did have a few other bolt-holes, not nearly as nice as this one or as centrally located. The research station allowed her to check on her own jobs, to make certain she wasn't being hired to do the wrong kind of work.

She had followed Jack's instructions on how to set this all up, but not even Jack had seen this place. Jack knew it existed—just like she knew that he had bolt-holes all over the sector—but he didn't know where it was or how to find it.

But he did know how to contact her, and he would as soon as he finished digging into Misha's (Mikael's) background. Rikki trusted Jack, and she knew he would dig as deeply as he could to find out everything there was to discover.

She also knew that on the subject of Misha (Mikael, dammit, she couldn't stop thinking of him that way), she wasn't entirely rational. So she was relying on Jack to be rational for her.

Besides, she had work to do.

She slipped inside the office, and reinstated her own links.

Rikki traveled with a variety of linking devices, but never had any permanently attached to her body (although she owned several that looked like they were attached—because not having obvious attached links often was a sign of an assassin).

But her best links stayed here. For anyone who wanted to give her work, she set up a program that told the person she would get to them when she got to them, weeks, maybe months later.

In this era of instant communication, not carrying her best links automatically trimmed her jobs down to the ones that could wait for her or the ones that needed someone of her caliber.

She had other ways to check these links—the information sent to them got copied by a system she had set up, and remained in a holding web in this sector, something she could access from any sophisticated enough link—but she had learned not to do that unless she couldn't return here within a few months.

Too easy to track her whereabouts, something she didn't want.

Particularly now that Misha (Mikael...) was out there.

She made herself shake off the thought as she stepped deeper into the room. Of all the places she owned, this was the one that was most hers. Its dark walls were covered with retired versions of her favorite weapons. It had a teak bar/shelf which she usually kept clean and polished that went all the way around the room. Right now it had a bit of dust on it, but she didn't mind. The cleaning bots would get to it by the end of the day.

In the center of the room, she had placed a gigantic love seat made of a shiny leather-like substance. Real leather no longer existed (or so she was told) but human beings kept imitating it because it felt so very good to sit on. The love seat had two ottomans that snapped into place.

She had seen a lot of offices with desks. She saw no point in a desk, not when she worked on her wrist links or on a special tablet. Instead, she curled onto the love seat and sat comfortably beneath a beautifully designed light fixture that could give her every spectrum from sunlight to the perfect spotlight.

Right now, she had it on sunlight. She slipped onto the love seat, and spread out over the ottoman. Then she leaned her head back and sighed.

What a horrible last month. She hated all of it. She hated her impulsiveness and what she had become. She hated asking for help. But most of all, she hated that momentary fear she had felt in the security office.

Jack was right about that: it was unusual, and it colored her thinking. Just not in the way he assumed.

Maybe it was time to get out of the game. Try to live a real life somewhere.

But that frightened her too. She wasn't cut out for a life without some kind of purpose, a life that followed the same routine day after day. She didn't even drop into that here, where it would be easy during her off times.

She needed some kind of adrenaline high—she needed something to keep her occupied.

Plus, she needed money if she was going to retire. She had more than enough to take the next few years off (if she watched her spending), but she didn't have enough for the next eighty years or more, however long she was going to live.

And in the first few years of that, she would need mobility. She would have to be able to afford a ship rental and several transports like she had just done on this trip to see Jack. Because someone might come after her. Someone who actually thought revenge was viable.

She sighed, opened her eyes, and grabbed one of the tablets. She clicked it on. Fifteen messages. The first few were for jobs that had since vanished. She deleted those.

That left five requests for work. She double-tapped the screen. Five people that other people wanted dead. Five people whose deaths other people believed would be justified.

This moment in her job, when she looked at the faces of people she didn't know, people whose lives might intersect with hers in a very dramatic—and usually violent—way, always astonished her. She had no idea who these people were, so she didn't know what they had done.

They were just faces, pleasant faces primarily, and they peered at her from their various attached files, smiling softly as if they all held a secret.

Well, she held the secret. Someone wanted them dead.

And if she was just a bit less honorable, she could take one job, and then contact the other four. She could get money from them to reveal the person who contacted her.

Behavior like that was against Assassin Guild rules, and she understood why. But she also understood the temptation. She knew dozens of operatives who supplemented their incomes that way, making her job—and the jobs of other legitimate assassins—much harder.

Still, at moments like this, when they were just faces, people she could possibly empathize with, she thought about the different ways her life could go.

Imagine what would have happened to her if she had turned down the Testrial job.

She set the tablet aside and sighed. After the whole Testrial experience, she was going to have to do even better research on the people who might become her targets—and spectacular research on the people who wanted to hire her.

All the way back here, she was wondering if she should hook back up with the Rovers. That loose affiliation of rogue assassins provided all kinds of vetting services and some partnering services as well, so that she wouldn't be working alone.

Although the way Jack had looked at her when she asked if he was still with the Rovers bothered her. He had said he was no longer with them in a tone that brooked no further discussion.

And that meant she should have probed.

She sighed and went back to the tablet. Right now, she would just have to do a lot of extra research.

And if she chose the wrong target for the wrong client, the blame would be all hers.

Just like it had been with Testrial.

The blame would be all hers.

Chapter 28

MISHA HUNKERED IN THE APARTMENT TWO AND A HALF blocks away from Rikki's. He couldn't believe she had such a glamorous hiding spot. Not that hiding spot was the right word. Nothing about that apartment hid. It was on the top floor of an elegant building in a relatively upscale neighborhood.

Although he suspected the neighborhood hadn't been upscale not too long ago, considering the place he was sitting in. This apartment had ruined walls, a carpet that smelled like pee, and windows so filthy he wasn't even sure they would work for his nefarious purposes.

He managed to clean the windows, though, with some kind of nanosolution—he didn't need to hire exterior robot cleaners after all—and then he had set up.

He was going to spy on her for a few days and figure out what she was doing.

He realized he had set up this surveillance the way he would set up a hit, and somehow that disturbed him. He liked to think he was setting up this way because that was the only way he knew, but he also realized that wasn't true. He had other ways of conducting business.

Hell, he could just grab Rikki's arm and pull her into one of the many restaurants that overlooked the lake, have a conversation, and get it all over with.

Except that he didn't believe a single conversation would solve anything.

He had tracked her relatively easily, and that wasn't her fault. She was more than cautious enough. No one who had just started looking for her would find this particular hiding place.

He had to admit, she was very good about concealing herself and her identity.

Her big mistake, after stealing that lifeship, was going back to the ship rental on Oyal. She had returned the ship, gotten her deposit back (which had shocked her and him both; he wondered if it had happened because the owner knew that Misha had enquired about her), and then had traveled to Nety.

She seemed to sense him, and she looked over her shoulder more than once. But he used a variety of ways to track her, sometimes renting his own ship to trail a transport she was on.

She took an amazing number of transports, and a lesser assassin would have lost her. He had come close a couple of times. But he kept telling himself that it didn't matter, because he had access to her real name and several of her aliases. And he had yet another piece of information: He knew how to send her money—or at least one way to do so.

That conversation with Liora had bothered him, though. Not because Liora had shown up on Oyal (which bothered him in a different way) but because of her mention of the Rovers. Then he learned that Rikki had gone to Krell, of all places.

Everything the Guild had on a rogue organization of assassins called the Rovers said that they often used Krell as a base for their operations. So she had been reporting in to someone.

And that had made Misha angry.

But he had tried to keep his focus, working hard at tracking her. It almost got impossible, as she changed names and looks on each transport she took. But the one thing she didn't do was book passage with someone else. So he looked for a female of the right age and same general look, knowing she would occasionally wear lifts to make herself taller, pad her clothes to look heavier, change her hair and eye color, and alter the way she wore clothing.

The one thing she couldn't—or, to be more accurate, didn't—change was the way she moved. She probably hadn't even thought of it. That was one of the many drawbacks of not having formal training. He had learned quite early in his Guild classes that changing movement was as, if not more, important than any elaborate disguise.

So as he watched vids of the various transports, he mostly watched for a very familiar (and very attractive) walk.

A walk he was seeing now, just outside Rikki's building.

He had placed high-powered lenses over his irises. The lenses were thicker than most zoom lenses, which usually ran on nanotech, but that was because they were better than any other he had ever seen.

He had complete control over distance and could see something as small as a piece of gravel from six blocks away.

These weren't surveillance lenses; these lenses were specifically designed for snipers. He had never been a sniper—even if he had been a good enough shot, he didn't like killing from great distances—but he loved these lenses.

They allowed him to see the main entrance to Rikki's building, and the nearby ground transport stop. He had checked visual footage from around the building for the last year before he even set up here—that's how he knew this was her building. The building itself didn't save its footage (or at least, it didn't make the footage available to people like him), but several other nearby buildings did. Plus the Lakota Transport Authority was more than willing to help a police officer from a nearby town on a particularly vexing case. They showed him their footage for the past year, and that she appeared repeatedly.

Plus he had an entrée into the law enforcement echelons of Lakota society now, something that might come in handy on a future case.

He had known she would arrive here, since her last space transport ended up on Unbey, but he wasn't sure if she would come here directly. It seemed that she had, however, if that rather dumpy woman with Rikki's walk getting off the ground transport was any indication.

She carried the same rucksack she had carried onto her last space transport. He had seen that footage as well, then he had hired a speed cruiser to get him here ahead of the transport ship. He had had a week to prepare, which was almost not enough. She also had a small bag that he hadn't seen before.

He watched her stop in the middle of the sidewalk, and glance up at the building itself. It was that movement, more than anything, that convinced him he was looking at Rikki. The long graceful neck, the way her head arched. He remembered that movement from their night together.

Damn it, he remembered everything from their night together, every single detail.

He couldn't clear it from his mind.

He made himself focus on the sidewalk, two and a half blocks away. He had picked this apartment for the unobstructed view of her place on the upper level of that upscale building, not for the view of the sidewalk. He had a partially obstructed view of the sidewalk—he saw the transport stop and the entrance to Rikki's building, but there was a blind spot in between, caused by a chimney-like structure on a building one block over.

Rikki stepped forward, and the obstruction blocked Misha's view. He held his breath and then made himself stop holding his breath when he realized what he was doing.

He was worried that she was just going to vanish on him again, like she had done on the ship. And it bothered him. He almost took it personally.

Rikki reappeared, walking purposefully into the building. She used some kind of palm reader identification— maybe a DNA scanner—to get into the building.

This time, it didn't feel like she had disappeared, but that was partly because of the monitors he had set up.

He had gotten into the building through the basement entrance, which had fewer security protections than the main entrance. That was a sign of a building being rehabbed, not one with a full slate of tenants.

The building's owners needed maintenance people, robots, and equipment to get in and out easily, without a lot of restrictions. Misha had initially planned to pose as one of them, but his friends at the Lakota Transport had given him a better idea.

He had posed as a member of the Transport Authority, to see if there was any possible way to locate an interior stop in the basement of the building. The building's owners were thrilled, even though they knew it was a remote possibility.

But with an interior stop, they could attract a higher class of tenants, ones that wanted to stay invisible.

Like Rikki should have, but didn't.

Misha had tracking devices on almost every part of the building. He had cameras on the interior staircases, and two more inside each of the elevators. He had sound equipment outside Rikki's door, as well as some truly sophisticated cameras, some that no existing locating equipment could find.

He flicked a remote, shutting off the sniper lenses in his eyes for a moment, turning the lenses into clear material. Then he turned to one of the screens he had set up below the window, and watched Rikki climb the stairs.

She didn't get winded as she climbed. That was another sign it was her, and not some woman who looked like her.

The cameras gave him a better view of her. Her hair was back to its normal color, which he very much liked. It accented her high cheekbones and made her beautiful eyes seem wider. She looked prettier, less austerely lovely, like this, almost approachable.

Although that might have been the clothing as well. It was nothing special, just some dark pants and a loose top. Maybe too loose, almost frumpy, hiding the in-shape body beneath.

If anyone took a cursory glance at this woman, they

would see someone who let herself go, who didn't care about her appearance.

But a close look would reveal an athletic woman in comfortable clothing, with near-flawless skin, and eyes so sharp that they missed nothing. It was hard to ignore the intelligence in those eyes, even though he suspected people would try.

She reached the top floor and let herself into her apartment with an economy of movement that surprised him.

He would have thought it would take a lot more to open that door's security. In the two hours that he had given himself, he hadn't been able to break in. He hadn't even managed to figure out what kind of security system she had set up—and that irritated him.

He had hoped to place cameras inside her apartment as well, and he hadn't been able to.

Instead, he had to console himself with the fact that the apartment had nearly a 360-degree view of its interior. Only the bearing walls inside prevented him from seeing a very small part of it.

He switched back to his sniper lenses and looked directly through the windows. The lenses gave him a double vision—one of her heat signature, and another of her movements inside, despite the nonreflective material on the windows themselves.

She set her pack down on a chair, fiddled with the small bag, pulled out bots and worked on them for a few minutes. Then she went into the bedroom. She stepped into a closet and changed clothes. When she came out, she wore even looser clothing, but it was made of a lighter-weight material, and it seemed to fit better.

She padded from the bedroom back to the entry, probably to pick up that pack.

And then she vanished.

He blinked twice, wondering if the lenses had shut down. But he knew they hadn't. He could see the chair, the table beside it, the knickknacks in the living area, the dishes on the glassed-in cupboard in the kitchen.

He could see everything but Rikki.

She had fooled him again, and he wasn't exactly sure how.

Chapter 29

RIKKI WAS TIRED, SHE WAS HUNGRY, AND SHE REALLY, really didn't want to talk with anyone. She curled her bare feet under her on the love seat and set down the tablet, then stretched under the light.

That was the problem with transports. No matter how hard you tried to remain private, you couldn't—not quite. You always had to smile at a fellow passenger, or tell someone (politely) that a seat was taken even when it wasn't. You had to fend off the most overly solicitous men, hoping to get laid on this short journey between here and there—no strings, as if that was an attractive part of the trip—and sometimes you even had to fend off interested women.

The key was to do it calmly, evenly, and without being memorable. Not being memorable was the most important part.

And not being memorable was also hard work. No inadvertent rudeness, no cursing, no elbow to the gut of the man who thought it sexy to run his hand over the ass of a woman he didn't know.

It was tiring to be invisible, and now that she was here, in her hidey-hole, she didn't want to work for at least a day or two. She wanted to stay private and hidden.

She had thought she would venture back out, get some food tonight, and then in the morning, do a bit of shopping, stocking up her kitchen so she wouldn't have to venture out again.

She never did that before she got to a place—or rather, she didn't do it any longer. She'd walked into too many of her hiding places to find that someone else had been there or that someone else was still there. Once she tossed a bag of groceries at some man who got up from her couch, politely smiled at her, and started to introduce himself.

She never ever knew who he was, and she really wasn't curious.

All she knew was that she could never ever go back to that place—and she never ever had.

This afternoon, she shouldn't have gotten comfortable. She shouldn't have put on her favorite clothes and settled in her office. She should have scouted her place, and then she should have gone back out immediately and taken care of her food needs.

But she hadn't done that.

And, honestly, even going back out was a risk. Someone might see her. Someone might follow her. Someone might try something.

Of course, if she lived her life in a constant state of paranoia, she would die of hunger long before she ever started to feel lonely.

She sighed and got up from her spot. The best thing to do would be to order in. She would use a bot service rather than some human service. Those were her only choices. Many places just sent things through an interconnected automated network. When she first moved here, the neighborhood was too dangerous for that.

By the time the building wanted to add that service,

she was ready for them. She said no, and she could say no because she had owned her apartment long enough to be grandfathered into—or out of—any service that the building wanted to provide.

She didn't want anything she didn't authorize and couldn't monitor to have access to her apartment, not even an automated food service network.

Which left her with robotic servers. She'd used several in the past, and as she got out of the ground transport, she had noticed that one of the services still existed. It was only two doors down, and it served sandwiches, which would do for the evening. If she bought a big enough one, it might even double as breakfast.

She stepped out of the office, went into the kitchen, and used the built-in network to order, paying out of her building fund. Then she made herself some coffee from the imported grounds she had brought in from one of her many stops, and contemplated her next move.

She probably shouldn't be working yet. She probably should wait until she heard from Jack. Then she could have him vet her next jobs.

But just sitting around would drive her nuts. Hell, traveling here with no real purpose behind her had driven her nuts.

She had been alone in her head ever since she left the cruise ship and that was just too long.

She sipped the coffee, decided it was the right amount of bitter mixed with sweet, and took it back to the office.

She didn't have to do anything today. She could take her own sweet time vetting the targets. In fact, she could take extra time vetting someone to vet the targets. And then maybe find someone else to vet the clients.

Still, she wanted to keep busy. If she kept busy, she didn't have to think about Misha (Mikael), and if she wasn't thinking about Misha *(Mikael)*, then she didn't have to worry about what Jack would find.

Even though she was—both thinking of Mikael (Misha) and worrying about what Jack would find.

In fact, she was obsessing about them. Which was the last thing she wanted to do.

And the only way to stop obsessing that she knew, anyway, was to work hard.

So she took the coffee back to her office, leaving the door open so she could hear the slight ping from the robot delivery service.

The sandwich sounded good. The perfect way to cap her day, and to welcome herself to Lakota. She'd sit in the living room, look at the lake and force herself to decompress.

When the sandwich arrived.

Until then, she had targets to vet.

She sat down with the tablets and got back to work.

Chapter 30

RIKKI APPEARED SUDDENLY, IN THE AREA WHERE SHE had been standing when he lost her. Misha frowned. There was no way she could suddenly be at the entrance to her own apartment, but she was, standing just inside the door, near the chair where she had dropped the rucksack.

He sat in the apartment two and a half blocks away, the sniper lenses scraping his eyeballs as he squinted. He got as close to his windows as he could. He was frowning. That was making the sniper lenses hurt too.

She stood in that entry as if she had just come back into the apartment. Which she hadn't, so far as he knew.

But he had no idea what had happened to her. There was no way she could have disappeared as thoroughly as she had either. She had even dropped off his heat vision sensors, which was very strange. His equipment should have kept an eye on her, even when he couldn't see her.

And it hadn't.

She ran a hand through her hair, tugged up her loose pants, and made her way to the kitchen. She was acting like someone who did not know she was being watched.

He always thought he would have a sixth sense about it if he was being watched. But the Guild told him he wouldn't. They told him to always behave as if someone could see him, which made him just a bit too cautious, just a little to aware of his surroundings at all times.

Except that night with Rikki.

His cheeks warmed. God, he blushed every time he thought about it, which was just strange. He wanted to think that flush came from anger, but it didn't. It came from the intimacy of the memory.

As he watched her meander to the kitchen, he also studied those bearing walls.

She had appeared in front of one of them.

Which only meant one thing: she had some kind of hidden passage in there.

He knew she had bought nearby apartments under other names. He wasn't sure how many of the neighboring apartments she owned—he doubted he could track down all her aliases as fast as he wanted to—but he knew that she owned several of them.

Maybe she had built some kind of interior staircase that had taken her down to a different apartment, and maybe that staircase had been protected from all kinds of surveillance.

That was the only thing he could think of that would cause her to disappear like that.

Once she reached the kitchen, she walked to the building network. And ordered food. He could see the information on the screen: a delivery menu, although he couldn't make out the company's logo.

Delivery. That shocked the hell out of him. Ordering food for delivery—of any kind—meant that she was feeling comfortable. Truly comfortable, like a person who didn't believe she could be in any danger.

That thought made him rock back on his heels and frown. *Was* she in danger? From him?

He shook his head, then leaned forward again. As he

did, he tapped into the building network through a hack he had set up days ago.

She had ordered from a business called Robby's Heroes. It took an actual glance at the menu for Misha to realize that a hero was a kind of sandwich, one he had never heard of. But it made his stomach growl when he looked at the ingredients. The sandwiches were huge.

And they were delivered by robot—also a risk. Any assassin knew—or rather, any *good* assassin knew—that a robot could be reprogrammed to do anything a person wanted. Even to kill, if need be.

He wondered if she had something in the apartment that tested for poisons. He wouldn't trust outside food like that.

He never ate take-out or delivery or any food he didn't prepare himself, except when he was on the job and playing a role.

Again, a Guild rule.

She was so clearly not Guild.

And she was giving him an opportunity.

Robby's Heroes told her that she would get her food in fifteen minutes.

It would take Misha five to get to the apartment. She had finally given him a way inside, and he planned to take it.

Chapter 31

HALF AN HOUR LATER, THE DELIVERY SERVICE PINGED the network gateway near Rikki's apartment entrance. She had almost forgotten she was going to get food because she had gotten so deeply involved in her research.

Of the five targets she'd been given, one intrigued her the most—a woman with a severe but beautiful face, which displayed a calm, almost ethereal expression. Rikki figured she could either rule out the woman as a target early or the woman would be so intriguing that she would want to stay on this case.

So far she had just scratched the surface: the material the client had sent her said that this woman was responsible for the deaths of more than 10,000 people. The deaths hadn't come in one incident—not one that Rikki could find, anyway. She should have been able to find something about an incident that large, with an old image of the woman. But Rikki couldn't. Which meant that the deaths had come one by one, and somehow that seemed even more dastardly.

But she didn't know.

If receiving the faces of the possible targets was always disconcerting, the research phase always proved fascinating. She focused on the woman, setting the others aside. She left their images up on the various tablets, but she doubted she would investigate them until she was done with the woman.

But Rikki had been so deeply involved in her research that she suspected the little robotic server had pinged her twice before she even noticed.

She carried the tablet with her out of her office, and tapped the network. She wasn't about to open a door to a robotic server, even if she had vetted the restaurant, which she hadn't—at least, she hadn't vetted it since she had come back. Instead, she just instructed the server to leave the food on the floor outside the door.

Then she instructed the building to let her know where the robotic server was, and when it exited.

If she was truly prepared, she would have known not only when it left, but when it returned to Robby's Heroes. But she wasn't that prepared. She was taking a slight risk and she knew it.

However, no one had ever figured out that she had a hideaway. So she figured she had a little leeway, if she was cautious.

Which she was.

Plus, she had set up this building so that she knew whenever someone had come in or out. And right now, no one was inside except a few tenants on the first floor and the building manager in the basement.

She waited until the system pinged her a final time, letting her know that the robot had left. Then she stepped into her office for a brief moment, checked the building's external cameras, and watched the robot, a small round thing with a little baseball cap adorned with the restaurant's logo, float back to Robby's Heroes.

She didn't see any arms or legs on it, and figured it probably had a food storage pouch. Not that it mattered.

Her stomach growled. She checked all the building's

security systems, noted that no one had come in or gone out since the robot appeared. Then she checked the hall cameras. Nothing. No one in the hallway. The only heat signature was tiny.

It came from her sandwich, which was cooling on the stoop.

"The hell with it," she said, left the office, and stepped into the entry. One quick move, and she had dinner.

Tomorrow, she would set up all of her protections. Tomorrow she could eat without all the stupid cautions. Tonight she would have to put the sandwich in her kitchen protector, just to make sure there were no foreign substances. But tomorrow, she would buy some robotic servers of her own, some food prep materials, and she would check out the local restaurants.

Tomorrow, she would be more cautious.

But tonight, she was going to eat.

She pulled open the front door and crouched at the same time, so that she could grab the bag and pull it inward.

The bag had the Robby's logo and was topped with a baseball cap of its own. Nice twist. It made her smile. But it also made the bag hard to grasp quickly.

The hallway smelled of tomato sauce, garlic, and meatballs. She was starving.

She grabbed the bag, yanked it inside, and as she started to close the door, a hand got in her way.

It slammed the door backwards. The door hit the wall with a bang.

Rikki started to stand up, but she got knocked aside. She fell back, grabbed the small laser pistol she always carried, rolled inside, just as the door banged closed.

She looked up, and saw Misha looking down, pointing his own pistol at her.

He looked different, thinner, his cheeks pinched, his eyes an electric blue, his hair so blond that it seemed almost white. She had forgotten how blond he was. He wore a tight T-shirt and pants that moved with him, showing all those corded muscles.

"I really don't appreciate people who drug me, abandon me, and leave me to take the blame for their crimes," he said.

"And I don't appreciate people who trespass," she said.

She wanted to stand, but she didn't dare. She scooted back toward the wall until it braced her. Then she stood, using the wall and the muscles in her legs to lever herself upward without moving her hands at all.

He hadn't shot her yet. That was a good thing, because he had the advantage. He had surprise.

Her heart was pounding, and if she hadn't had a lot of training, she would have been breathing hard, showing her nervousness.

Screw that. Her fear.

She'd been afraid of this man ever since she found out who he was. Afraid and angry. Fear didn't help her.

Anger did.

"I could kill you now and no one would think twice about it," she said. "You invaded my home."

"Go ahead," he said. "If you think you're quick enough."

She should shoot. Jack would be angry at her for not shooting.

But Misha hadn't shot either, and he could have killed her as easily as he invaded her apartment.

"What the hell do you want?" she asked.

"I wanted to find out why you want to destroy me," he said.

She raised her eyebrows. The door to her office was open. She could go in there, get more weaponry, or she could barricade herself inside. She hadn't made a good secondary way to leave the office, though.

Stupid her, she hadn't thought she would need it. Not here.

Her mistake.

"Destroy you?" she asked, her voice level. She knew she appeared calm. Misha couldn't feel her rapidly beating heart. Oddly, though, she was almost calm, after that moment of surprise.

Almost, but not quite.

Besides, she needed time to think. She hadn't expected this. She hadn't expected Misha to show up here. Now.

She had learned long ago when she was ambushed or had the disadvantage to get the other person to talk. If they talked, she had time to assess. Time to think.

Time to plan.

"Don't play coy," he said. "You nearly got me in trouble for Testrial's death. It took some fast talking to get out of it. And, as we established earlier, that's not the first time you managed to get me to take the blame for everything you've done."

She raised her eyebrows. She had known she would make him angry. She hadn't realized he would track her down.

"So avoid me from now on," she said, sounding much calmer than she felt.

"If only that was an option," he said.

"The universe is big," she said. "I'm sure you can figure out how to stay out of my way."

His eyes narrowed. He looked dangerous. Maybe he wasn't tracking her to complain. Maybe he was tracking her to make her stop getting in his way once and for all.

And the only way assassins knew how to solve their problems was by plying their trade.

"You think I'm here to kill you, don't you?" he said, his voice level.

She started. He had echoed her thoughts. She wondered if she had lost her ability to hide her emotions with him.

She hoped she hadn't. Because in addition to the anger she was feeling, she couldn't stop thinking about how good he looked in that shirt, a flush on his own cheeks, his blue eyes just a bit too bright, his hair tousled over his forehead—

The very idea that she was still attracted to this son of a bitch really pissed her off.

"If you are thinking of killing me," she said, "then you're fucking up. Because you've had at least two chances in the last five minutes to take me out and you've blown both of them. Either you're not as good as you think you are, or you're not sure you want to pull that trigger."

"You could have shot me just as easily," he said. "In fact, you could have shot me from the ground and done some pretty serious damage. Like you said, no one would have thought twice about it. So why didn't you?"

"Because I need a few answers before I send you to the big Assassins Guild in the Sky," she said, using a phrase Jack used to use when they were kids.

"Answers?" Misha asked. His eyes suddenly sparkled, and she wasn't sure why. What did he find so amusing? That she had thought about him? That she had questions for him?

Or that she was prolonging this?

Maybe he was some kind of cat, who got off on playing with his prey before killing it.

"Yeah, answers," she said. "Why didn't you kill me the first time we met?"

A slight frown creased that beautiful forehead of his. Why did this man have to be so goddamn attractive? "Why would I have done that? You were doing a job for me."

"Which," she said, "was a convoluted way of meeting me. Once you confirmed that I was Reggie Bastogne's daughter, why the hell didn't you just kill me?"

Misha's frown had grown deeper. "What? Why would I do that?"

"Because something kicked in after eighteen years, didn't it? Because you needed to finish the job, get rid of the kid, and do it right."

"What the hell are you talking about?" he asked.

"You should have just killed me," she said, her voice going up despite her attempts to keep it under control. "But no. You had to sleep with me, didn't you? You had to humiliate me, use me, make me enjoy that, just so you could get a little more sadistic pleasure before you finished the job. And since you didn't finish it there, you should have finished it here, because I'm done with you, Misha. I've had it."

Her pistol was shaking, which meant her hand was shaking, which meant she was shaking, which meant she had no fucking control at all, and she needed control to do a good job.

He extended a hand, upright and flat, in the *stop* position, and he stuck his own pistol into a holster on his hip.

"Truce," he said in an odd voice.

"No truce," she said. "I don't need a truce. I really don't need a truce."

But she needed something to make the shaking stop and she couldn't quite do it. It was as if all her training had left her, all of her control had left her. She was a little girl again, in a house with strangers, and her father—her father screaming, *No, no, no, no…*

Misha took a step toward her, both hands extended now, palms up, hands empty.

"Rikki," he said in that same voice, the voice she'd heard that morning, the morning after, when he handed her that horrible drink, when he had said his own name for the first time. "Something's going on here—"

"Damn straight something's going on here," she said. "You broke into my house, you're trying to kill me, you're finishing the job, you son of a bitch, you murdered my father—"

"No," Misha said. His expression was open, plain, as vulnerable as it had been that night—in the middle of the night, when she touched him. "I told you before. I did not murder your father."

"Liar!"

"Rikki." He hadn't moved any closer. "Do you remember that night?"

"Of course I remember that night," she snapped. But now she was lying. Could he tell she was lying? She was usually good at lying, but at the moment, she didn't feel like she was good at anything.

She was usually good at holding a laser pistol too, but she wasn't doing that very well either.

"If you remember that night," he said softly, "then you know I didn't kill your father."

There had been a hand around her shoulder, pulling her close, another hand on her head, pressing her face against the soft fabric of a newly washed shirt. The smell of sandalwood and something else, something unusual, a gentle voice, a male voice—Misha's voice?—younger, a little more vulnerable, with just a bit of a break, saying, *Don't look, you don't need to look, it's better if you don't look—*

"What the hell," she said, shaking her head. "What do you want from me?"

He stepped forward. "I thought I knew," he said. "But I'm not so sure anymore. I'm not sure at all."

Chapter 32

SHE LOOKED LIKE A SCARED LITTLE KID. THAT'S WHAT startled him the most. Suddenly, somehow, in the middle of their conversation—if he could call pulling laser pistols on each other and snapping at each other a conversation—she transformed from a calm, self-possessed, highly trained assassin into a terrified little girl.

Her eyes got wider, her voice got higher, and most astonishingly, her hand started to shake. He wasn't sure she had even realized how badly she was shaking.

And that frightened him. He didn't worry about a pistol in the hands of a professional. But when a pistol was in the hands of an amateur anything could happen.

And she had just lost control of herself—or, at least, of her adult self. She had gone from a professional assassin of long standing to a terrified little girl who believed she faced her father's killer.

Misha wasn't even sure she saw him. He wasn't sure she was here, at least mentally.

He'd seen enough people who suffered post-traumatic shock to know that they could mentally time-travel back to the event that started it all. And he had sent her time-traveling.

Surprising him, really, because she shouldn't have this issue. There were treatments, ways to overcome it. She should have gotten treatment that night all those years ago.

He had given her to medical professionals, told them she was in shock, told them she needed help. And they had promised to give it. Had they failed? God, he would never have given her up that night if he had known they were going to fail her. He thought she was in good hands.

All he wanted to do was get her away from that burning house, and make sure she didn't see his mother again. His mother had done her job, but no child needed to see the person who killed her father. He knew that better than anyone.

That was why he had taken care of her.

She had been such a fragile, bruised, frightened little girl.

And she looked frightened now.

He gently took the laser pistol from her. He wasn't even sure she knew he had taken it from her hand. He disarmed it, and put it in his waistband so that she couldn't reach it.

He knew better than to touch her as she stood there, her back against the wall, unable to go anywhere.

"Come on," he said softly. "Let's get something to eat."

She frowned at him—she was slowly coming back to herself—and she said, "Why are you here?"

The lying was over, at least for now. If he had been angry with her—and he had been when he got here—he wasn't any longer.

If she thought, if she truly thought, he had *murdered* her father, not assassinated a very bad man, but murdered the man who had raised her, if she thought Misha was now coming after her for a reason she didn't understand, then she had been right to flee that ship any way she could. She had been trying to survive.

He mentally moved her from colleague, adult, competent assassin, to victim, survivor, someone who, in this one area, wasn't rational at all.

He might move her back to the other category soon, but at the moment, it was better to treat her gently.

"Come on," he said. "That sandwich smells good. Is there enough for two?"

Her eyes—their proper brown now—looked wild. And sad. And lost. She looked down at the bag with the very silly baseball cap, and took a deep breath.

"You didn't come here to eat with me," she said.

All right. Half victim, half competent professional. He was going to have to tread lightly here.

"No," he said. "I didn't. I came because I was mad, because I couldn't work without figuring out what the hell happened between us."

"You used me," she said. "You're toying with me."

"I'm not, Rikki," he said. "I didn't. I was as surprised by what happened between us as you were."

She raised her gaze to his. Her mouth was a thin line.

He had forgotten how beautiful she was, or maybe he hadn't really known. The chestnut hair, the green eyes, they truly hadn't suited her. Now she looked perfect, except for the expression on her face—an expression filled with such sadness that he wanted to take her in his arms.

He hadn't expected this. He hadn't really experienced tenderness before.

Except that was a lie.

He had experienced tenderness that night, all those years ago, watching a little girl whose world was collapsing, and she didn't even know why.

Apparently even then she had figured out a way to wrap her fingers around his heart.

"You were trying to kill me," she repeated.

"No," he said. "If I wanted to do that, I would have done it so fast, you wouldn't even have known I was there."

Her eyes teared up and she looked away. He saw the force of her will in her slight frown, in the way the tears receded. She took a deep breath.

"Then why did you come after me?" she said.

"I told you. You were hurting my business. Initially, I thought you were doing it because you didn't know any better. I thought you needed Guild training."

"You thought I was incompetent." And in her voice, he heard the beginnings of anger.

Good. He could work with anger. He couldn't work with the sad lost little girl, but he could work with the angry woman.

"Yes," he said.

"I'm not," she said.

"That's open for debate," he said.

He saw her adult self snap into place. She stood taller, her cheeks flushed, her eyes became sharp.

"I got in here," he said. "You made some rookie mistakes."

"You didn't show up on any sensor," she said. "I monitor everything in this building."

"I hacked into the system," he said.

"You weren't in this apartment," she said. "I would have known."

"True enough," he said. "This place is a fortress. Or it was, until you decided to get take-out."

She cursed. She had clearly known she had taken a risk, and she knew it hadn't paid off.

"Come on," he said again. "Let's eat."

"Why should I eat with you?" she snapped.

He gave her a shrug, and his most appealing smile. "Because I have your gun?"

"That's not a good enough reason," she said as if he had been completely serious.

"Because you're hungry," he said, "and so am I."

Her eyes narrowed.

"Come on, Rikki," he said. "We have a lot to talk about. You have questions, I have questions. If you don't like the conversation, then you can use one of the weapons you've hidden all over this apartment, and kill me where I stand. But let's see if we can talk to each other first."

"Talk's overrated," she said. But she scooped up the bag. "Give me my gun back."

He supposed he could be churlish and hold onto it. Or was that churlish? Maybe it was just prudent.

Either way, he had to trust her a little.

He handed her the laser pistol. She examined it without taking her gaze off him, then she flicked it back on.

"I could kill you where you stand," she said, pointing it at him. Her hand was no longer shaking.

He shrugged again, as if he didn't care, as if his pulse hadn't started to race. "Then you'll never find out what happened that night."

"I'm not going to find out now. You're going to lie to me."

"I wasn't planning on it," he said. "But I can if you want me to."

Her gaze met his. She was furious. Good. He'd have to keep her that way, just to keep her with him mentally, not to get lost in that night so far in her past.

After a moment, she shook her head and brought the gun down.

"God, you're an asshole," she said.

"I'm surprised you're just figuring that out," he said.

"Oh, hell, I knew it from the moment I met you," she said. "The question is, just exactly what kind of asshole are you? An annoying one? Or one that is so vile, so venal, that he toys with his prey before he kills it?"

"A venal man wouldn't return the gun," he said.

"Unless he poisoned the food," she said. She waved the bag at him. "Go to the kitchen."

"And turn my back on you?"

"Again," she said. "Annoying? Or venal? Annoying wouldn't worry about his back."

He smiled at her and walked somewhat sideways, so that he could see her and the hallway as he headed toward the kitchen.

"Anyone would watch his back around you, Rikki," he said.

"Are you saying you can't trust me?"

"Rik," he said, and she started at the shortening of her name. He wondered who else had called her that. "You kill people for a living."

"So do you, asshole," she said.

"Good point," he said. "Very, very good point."

Chapter 33

MISHA SLIPPED INTO THE KITCHEN AS IF HE HAD BEEN there before. And considering how easily he had come into the apartment, he had at least seen it. Dammit. She had loved these open windows. She probably was going to have to move after this, and she really didn't want to.

She followed him in, and stopped near the counter. She disarmed the pistol and shoved it in the waistband of her pants. He had already had a dozen opportunities to kill her. If he tried again, she would stop him with her bare fists if she needed to.

But he wasn't going to try. If he had wanted to try, he would have done it when she lost it a few minutes ago.

She had never lost it like that before—at least, not with someone she really didn't know, someone she certainly didn't trust. She had only lost it like that with Jack, and it had been years since that happened.

Since they were children.

She pulled the sandwich out of the bag, and put it on a plate. The sandwich was still warm, and the scent of meatballs, marinara, garlic, and fresh bread made her stomach growl again. When had she last eaten?

She couldn't remember.

She set the plate in the very expensive food analyzer. Then she leaned against the counter and crossed her arms.

Misha was standing only a few feet from her, watching

her every move. That tousled hair, his eyes—no longer piercing, but soft, compassionate—made him so attractive. She hated this pull she felt for him. She hated the way her body betrayed her.

And it had betrayed her since he came into the apartment—since she met him, really. She still wanted him, even though she was furious at him. Furious, confused, and beneath it all, terrified.

"You wanted to talk," she said. "So talk."

He ran a hand over his mouth, a nervous gesture that surprised her. Then he frowned.

"I'm not sure how to approach this," he said.

She waited. She wasn't about to help him.

He nodded, and then sighed. "First, I need to ask you something."

"So ask," she said. The food analyzer beeped behind her. She turned slightly. The list of ingredients ran across the analyzer's screen. Nothing artificial; spices were in order and in the right amounts.

She took the plate out, grabbed a knife, and cut the sandwich in half. Then she put that half on another plate and handed it to him.

"I thought you were going to ask me something," she said.

"Not when you have a knife in your hand," he said, and he wasn't joking.

"I'm going to have a knife while I eat this," she said. "It's too messy to eat with my hands."

He sucked in a breath. Then he said, "Let's at least go into the dining room."

She nodded. She grabbed silverware—and in deference to him, she grabbed a less nasty looking knife, and headed into the dining room that she almost never used. Usually she ate in her office or standing in the kitchen.

She sat down at the table, her back to the wall. She faced the kitchen door. He followed, holding matching silverware, his plate, and a glass of water. He sat across from her.

She cut up the sandwich. "So ask," she said.

He set his silverware down. He hadn't even started carving up the food. "Do you really not remember what happened that night?"

She stiffened. She didn't want to talk about that night. But she wasn't sure how she could avoid it.

"I remember it," she said.

"How much of it?" he asked.

Finally, the right question. She stabbed a bit of sandwich with her fork and ate. It was good: spicy, garlicky, with a strong after-bite. Better than she remembered.

"I remember that night," she said.

He tilted his head and took a bite of his own sandwich. "Then you remember me."

She was starting to shake again. She didn't remember him. She knew he had to be there because at the time, his mother rarely worked alone. At least according to all the available information about the woman.

And really, there wasn't a lot of available information. Halina Layla Orlinskaya had been an assassin, after all.

"Should I remember you?" Rikki asked.

"Yes," Misha said firmly. "You should. I got you out of the burning house."

Her cheeks grew warm. The fire— red and strong and hot, oh, so very hot and all the people silhouetted against it, that other little girl crying, the medical personnel—God. She didn't remember how she got out of the house at all.

How did he know that?

"After you killed my father," she said.

"I didn't kill him," Misha said. "My mother did."

Rikki took another bite, but this time, she didn't taste it.

"But let's focus for a second on what happened between us," Misha said.

She had trouble swallowing. "Nothing happened between us." Another lie. Everything was happening between them.

"That night," he said. "Let's focus on what happened that night."

She waited. She felt like she was made of glass and she could shatter at any moment. She *hated* that feeling. She had started this work, this profession, so she could learn how to take care of herself, how to prevent nights like that, to make sure if someone died, that someone was the right person, not a single father doing his best.

"I got you out of the house," Misha said.

So you say. She bit back the words. She didn't dare say them. She didn't want him to know how little she remembered.

"And then I waited with you until the authorities arrived. My mother dealt with law enforcement."

"They didn't even arrest her for the arson," Rikki said bitterly.

He didn't break eye contact, but something changed in his expression. Something slight. Something she couldn't read.

God, she didn't trust him, and yet part of her really wanted to trust him. Thought she could trust him. *Hoped* she could trust him.

"Again," he said in that patient tone, "we're just going to focus on you and me for the moment. We'll get to the other details in a minute."

"That fire's not a detail," Rikki snapped.

"And neither is your father's death." Misha sounded cautious. His hands were folded in front of his plate. "Just let me continue."

She waited.

"After I got you out of the burning house," he said, "I waited with you for the authorities. Do you remember that?"

She remembered standing outside. She remembered everyone leaving the buildings. She remembered how the front of her—the part of her facing the fire—was very hot, almost too hot, and how the back of her was freezing cold.

She shrugged. That was the only answer she was going to give him.

"First, the police arrived," he said when it became clear she wasn't going to say anything else. "My mother went to talk with them. Then the fire brigade showed up. The fire had spread awfully fast, but everyone got out."

"Everyone except my father," she said and heard the bitterness in her own voice, a bitterness that sounded almost alien to her.

He turned his head slightly, almost as if he didn't believe what he was hearing. But he kept that eye contact.

"Your father was already dead," he said softly.

"So you say," she said.

He picked up his fork and knife, and cut into his sandwich. He took a bite.

That made her remember hers. She ate faster than she usually did, but it gave her something to do.

He took a drink of water. Then he said, "After the fire brigade showed up, the medical team showed up. I took you to them. Do you remember that?"

"Stop asking me what I remember," she snapped, and immediately wished she hadn't. That was an admission she didn't remember.

He nodded, just once, as if agreeing to her terms. "When we reached the medical team, I asked them to take care of you. They took you in. You were horribly bruised, and you had some broken bones—"

"What did you do to me?"

He bit his lower lip. "I took you to them. And after I got you into their transport, I told them to make sure you got psychological treatment as well."

"Why?" she asked.

"Because of the trauma," he said. "I went through a similar trauma. It's better to have the counseling. But I guess they didn't give it to you. Did they?"

The nurse wouldn't talk to her. Rikki was in that hospital bed, under wraps of all kinds, and no one talked.

"I was burned," she said. "You didn't mention the burns."

"Only your right hand," he said. "You tried to open the door."

She made herself finish the sandwich. The only burn scar she had that she had trouble getting rid of was on her right hand. It took several treatments before the skin came back.

Her right hand.

But she thought she had been burned other places. Even though the doctors kept her sedated while they worked.

Bruised, he said. Broken bones, he said. The very thought of that made her head hurt.

"Did they treat you for post-traumatic stress?" His voice was very soft.

He was trying. Or so it seemed. He was trying to talk to her.

What would it hurt to tell him that she didn't remember? Except that he could exploit her hole-filled memory. But he was doing that already.

"They tried," she said. "They tried all kinds of treatment."

"And the post-traumatic stress remained?" he said.

She shook her head. "I thought I was fine. I didn't seem to have it."

Until I met you, she thought. *Until I thought you were back, to kill me, and then so much of that night returned—not in memory, but in emotion.*

"Then what were they working on?" His voice was so gentle. *He* seemed gentle.

But he killed people for a living.

Just like she did.

Just like his mother had.

"Apparently there are gaps," she said. Her cheeks were warm. She hadn't talked like this with anyone except Jack.

Jack, who would say she was being stupid to trust this man. Jack, who was investigating him even now, while she sat across the table from him, finishing a sandwich.

"Gaps in your memory?" Misha asked.

She nodded and her eyes flooded. She looked away

from him and blinked hard. This man brought out all the wrong emotions in her.

He had finished his sandwich. She hadn't seen him finish. She was so self-involved that she had missed details she would normally keep track of.

"I didn't know," he started, then shook his head. "I thought there were methods now to bridge those gaps."

"The wonders of science," she said wryly.

"Yes," he said.

She shrugged. "Apparently, if you have a strong enough mind, you can overcome those things."

At least, that was what the doctors told her. Which meant they didn't know why she couldn't remember. Maybe they thought she was lying, protecting someone, needing the attention, *something*. Jack believed she didn't want to remember and maybe there was truth to that too, given how she felt right now.

Misha made a soft sound.

She frowned at him.

He gave her a half smile. "I'm sorry. I almost asked you what you were blocking. But if you can't remember, then you don't know."

She stood and picked up her plate. There was still a bit of sandwich on it, but she was no longer hungry.

"Apparently, I blocked you," she said and went into the kitchen.

She set the plate down in the sink and spread her hands over it, trying to regain control. She was making rookie mistakes over and over again, mostly because of something that had happened eighteen years ago.

What was wrong with her? Why couldn't she take control of the memory, of herself, of this situation?

She should order him to leave.

She should force him to leave.

She should talk to him and find out what happened.

She should get away.

She should just plain give up and crawl under the bed with the dust bunnies.

She wished Jack was here. Jack would know what to do. But her heart-brother couldn't save her anymore.

She was going to have to save herself.

Chapter 34

APPARENTLY, I BLOCKED YOU.

Misha sat at Rikki's dining room table, the empty plate before him, the fork still in his left hand, those words rolling around in his mind.

Apparently, I blocked you.

That sentence had hurt. He wasn't quite sure why it had hurt, but it felt like she had taken her fork and stabbed him in the heart with it.

He swallowed, tasting the garlic. He reached in his pocket and got a mouth-cleaning strip, just so that he would have something to do.

Apparently, I blocked you.

Maybe that bothered him because he hadn't blocked her. There wasn't a day in his life when he hadn't thought about that night—not because he was obsessed with a little girl, but because he thought of that night as a turning point for him, just the way his father's murder had been a turning point.

His mother had told him to get the kid out of the house. And he had done things like that countless times before. But this time, he had grabbed the little girl, felt her tremble against him, and he had protected her. He had felt compassion for her, and some fear, and he wanted her to be all right.

He had felt so badly for her, even before he met her, as he watched her father brutalize her. Misha had known what was coming—the assassination, the changed circumstance—but he had wondered how it would feel to lose a horrible parent, the oppressor, the person who had ruined your life instead of saved it.

He would have thought she would be grateful. Maybe that was too strong a word. He would have thought she would be relieved to be free of her father.

And Misha had checked on her after it was all over. She was hospitalized—her wounds too bad to let her out immediately—and he made sure that she got into a high-ranked government program, one that provided excellent health care and education, one whose graduates (survivors?) went on to healthy, productive lives.

Someone could argue that her life was productive now. She had an approved job. She was good at it—or she seemed to be.

But she had gaps in her memory. Gaps that, it seemed, included him.

He sighed and stood. Then he grabbed his own plate and went into the kitchen.

She had been bending over the sink. For a moment, he wondered if she had been sick, but the air smelled of the sandwich, not of vomit. She stood when she heard him and turned so that her back wasn't to him any longer.

Her eyes didn't meet his as she took his plate and set it beside hers in the cleaner.

"I'm going to tell you exactly what happened," he said. "I don't know if this is prescribed or not, if it will help you or not. But you should know."

She remained in front of that sink, slightly hunched, as if her body could protect her from his words.

"My mother took contracts, like you do," Misha said.

"She worked alone more or less, but a lot of governments hired her. She used to be a spy for the Kazan System until they gave her a job she couldn't do."

"I know," Rikki said softly.

He nodded, acknowledging her, but not letting her throw him off his rhythm. "The Eyad government hired my mother to assassinate your father. The Eyad government had caught him selling secrets."

Her lips thinned. She crossed her arms. "He was military. He would never do that."

Misha sighed silently. He had decided to tell this story, so he was going to have to go through with it all.

"There was a hearing when it was all over. My mother remained on site. You know that, right? That she contacted the authorities and went with them."

"Because she started the fire," Rikki said.

"We'll get to that," Misha said. "But first, think about this. Because you know it, even if you don't remember it. Your father's death was justified."

"Don't—"

"Not justifiable," Misha said. "The legal term. It was justified. The authorities checked. And you know it because my mother was never prosecuted, nor was anyone else."

Rikki straightened just slightly.

"If you want, we can look this up. I know it's in the information stream."

He had checked after he saw her again, to make sure he was remembering everything properly. To make sure she really was that little girl who had trusted him with her life.

Rikki stared at him.

"Your father," Misha said, "had sold the wrong information."

The skin around her eyes tightened, forming slight lines.

"And so the Eyad government contracted with my mother. They paid her like you and I get paid, half to start the job, and half after the job was completed."

Rikki swallowed visibly. Her arms were crossed so tightly that he could see the strain on her muscles.

"We watched your place." He kept his voice even and calm. This was the voice he reserved for survivors, people who walked in on him after he had finished a job, people who didn't always understand what he was doing.

Rikki's eyes were wide. She watched him as if she expected him to grab her suddenly and hurt her.

"I was on leave from the Guild," he said. "I went to school there, and it was vacation. On the vacations, Mother always made me go with her on jobs. She wanted me to know how ugly the work could be. But she was very good at it, and usually she finished the job quickly and easily."

It was his turn to swallow. His mother had been the best at the work because she had been clinical, cold, efficient. Ruthless.

"But your father's job, that wasn't easy. Or quick."

Rikki shifted slightly.

"Honestly," Misha said, "it was exactly the kind of job Mother had wanted me to see. She figured if I was ever going to turn away from the work, a job like that would make me do it."

And he nearly did. If it hadn't been for Rikki herself,

he would have. But he had known that if his mother hadn't killed her father, Rikki wouldn't have survived the year.

That had gotten him through the Guild training, through his own first botched job, through all the tough nights. Remembering the hard face of a little girl, bravely taking the "punishment" her father dished out, and vowing to survive it. A little girl who was breaking on her own. Who would have broken—and died—at that man's hands, sometime in the next few months, as the stress made that man more and more violent, and made him care less and less.

"When the medical team arrived," Misha said softly, "they treated you for several broken bones, for deep, deep bruises, and for a burn on your right hand. One of those bruises was on your stomach. It turns out you were bleeding internally."

"You remember this how?" Her voice wasn't shaking. It was strong. "I mean, you've done, what?, a hundred jobs in your lifetime, two hundred? Plus the work you did with your mother. How do you remember me?"

"I never forgot you," he said.

She turned her face slightly, as if he had hit her. "Why?"

"Because," he said as plainly as he could. "You're the reason I do this job."

Chapter 35

HE WAS BULLSHITTING HER. HE HAD TO BE.

Rikki was pressed against the cabinets, the cool lip of the sink digging into her back. Her arms were crossed—one of the therapists from so long ago would have made her uncross those arms (*You can't hear with your arms crossed, dear. Your arms physically block the information*)—and her fingers were tucked into fists.

She was not the reason he had become an assassin. She couldn't be. That made no sense at all.

"Me?" she asked.

"You." His face was filled with compassion. "You probably don't remember. You might not believe me."

He seemed to be saying that last part more to himself than to her. She pushed even harder against that sink.

"Your bruises, those injuries, your broken bones," he said. "We watched them happen."

"Your mother did it," Rikki said, even though she didn't remember getting the bruises or broken bones. She remembered the doctors talking about them, the discussions in the case of how unusual they were. That was the reason Halina Layla Orlinskaya had been held an extra few days. The bruising. The broken bones.

And then Orlinskaya had been released.

Rikki knew that. But she remembered getting the burn. The worst burn, she thought. The horrible burn.

The one on her hand.

"My mother didn't do it," Misha said softly. "Your father caused those bruises."

That first memory: Her father's face, purple with anger, his eyes small and flashing, his voice lacerating: *You don't beg. You never beg. Begging gets you nowhere. Stop begging, you little bitch.*

Rikki closed her eyes against the memory, but it only became stronger. His hands, so big. His knuckles, so sharp as they connected with her cheek, the taste of blood in her mouth.

She opened her eyes, and saw Misha, watching her, as if everything depended on what she was going to say next.

"We watched him hurt you," Misha said. "And I wanted to do something. Mother said we would do something. We had to give it time. I didn't think we had time."

Rikki crossed her arms harder, feeling them press against her rib cage, feeling the strain in her shoulders, her back.

"We planned the job. We were going to go in, and Mother would… take care of your father, and I would get you out, then call the authorities."

The shadows, the movement inside the house, the feeling of someone who didn't belong. Then the harshly beautiful woman's face, the close-cut white-blond hair, the pale ice-blue eyes, suddenly appearing right beside Rikki, startling them both. The woman recovered first.

Don't worry. We have not come for you. You will survive this. You will be Just Fine.

The woman had spoken with a trace of an accent, and

her words hadn't been comforting. Then she had said, in a much harsher voice, *Misha. Do your job.*

Misha.

The movement in the shadows, the feeling of someone who didn't belong. Someone beside her, brushing against her.

Rikki remembered that, the way he had been there, beside her. But he wasn't beside her now. He was in front of her in her own kitchen. She stared at his face, so like his mother's. Harsh, beautiful. Blue, blue eyes, but no ice. White-blond hair, tousled, not cut too close. Masculine features, compassion. The woman had had no compassion, even though her words had.

"Mother made the mistake," he said. "Mother, who usually never made mistakes."

Rikki frowned. He was standing too close, but she couldn't back away. She was pressed against the sink.

"Mother startled you," he said, "and you let out the smallest of sounds. She spoke to you, and beckoned me to get you out, but that was just enough to warn your father. He was prepared for us. He knew someone was coming for him. Someone had probably warned him. Or maybe he was just that smart."

He was just that smart. Her father had been brilliant, everyone said so. But no one had liked him. She knew that too. That hadn't fled her memory. The therapists asked her over and over again why no one had adopted her, why no one had been close enough to their family to show her some compassion.

My daddy doesn't believe in friends, she would say, until finally one therapist challenged her.

What's wrong with friends? the woman asked.

They make you weak, Rikki had said.

Later, she had told that to Jack. Twelve-year-old Jack. He had gotten mad. *Do I make you weak?* he asked.

She shook her head—then and now.

Misha was watching. He didn't stop talking. Maybe he couldn't.

"Your father was prepared," Misha said. "He had some kind of laser weapon. He tried to talk my mother into leaving. Then he tried to bribe her. My mother wasn't the kind of woman who took a bribe."

The voices. Rikki remembered voices. And someone beside her, hand on her arm.

She willed herself to concentrate on Misha, on the here and now.

"Your father was the one who started the fire, Rikki," Misha said. "He shot into a starter pile."

The sharp smell of the house, the stuff he had put on the walls. She had hated it. It had given her a headache. *Why do we need it, Daddy?*

He hadn't answered her. He had simply told her to get out of the way.

Misha kept his gaze on hers. He wasn't breaking eye contact. So she couldn't either.

"He'd been prepared," Misha said. "He used the laser to ignite the building. He thought that would make my mother run. My mother never ran. Not from anything."

"Except the Kazan System," Rikki blurted.

That broke the moment. Misha smiled. It seemed like he smiled with relief. At her comment? Or relief that she was listening?

Or was she reading something else into it?

"Yeah," he said. "You're right. She ran from them,

to save her own life. Although she would have told you she quit and moved."

Rikki shrugged. Semantics. She could focus on semantics rather than on what he was saying.

Because what he was saying disturbed her. So deep that it made her head hurt. Memories flooded into her brain—and they came with a whoosh. Not their own sound, but the sound of that fire, igniting.

With a whoosh.

Then the boy beside her said, *Holy shit!* and grabbed her around the shoulders, pulling her against him, and her father, screaming *No, no, no*—the last *no* getting cut off in the middle, and the heat, surrounding them, enveloping them, the smoke rising, the boy saying, *Come on, come on, we have to get out of here. I'll get you out*, and pulling her forward. And she didn't scream—Daddy! Get out, Daddy!—because she didn't want to, she didn't want him to get out, she wanted him to die, that horrible, horrible man, because then he wouldn't touch her again, he wouldn't hit her and hurt her and tell her not to cry—

Her knees buckled. She uncrossed her arms and caught herself on the side of the sink.

Misha took a step forward as if he was going to catch her, and then he stopped himself, clearly uncertain about whether or not he should touch her.

The bruising, the broken bones, so unusual for an Orlinskaya job, hadn't been caused by Orlinskaya at all. But by Rikki's father.

But that wasn't what made Rikki block the memory. She hadn't hidden from herself what kind of man he had been.

She had talked about it with her therapists—how he

hadn't had friends, how he hadn't been very nice. (But he had been smart. A survivor, he said. *I'm going to teach you how to be a survivor, Rikarda* (that name she hated). *You will know how to live because of me*.)

She had blocked the memory because of that visceral hatred, that moment when she knew she should yell for him, protect him, get him out of there—and she hadn't.

She wanted him to die. She wanted him to die horribly. And she made sure of it. She made sure he couldn't escape.

She had killed him.

So of course, she went out and killed others. She was suited for the job because she knew how important it was.

Because she wasn't good enough to do any other work.

"Rikki?" Misha asked, taking another step toward her.

She stood up, moved away from the sink, took a deep breath, then nodded at him.

"I'm all right. Really," she said. "I'm Just Fine."

Chapter 36

OF COURSE, SHE WAS LYING. SHE WASN'T FINE. MISHA had never seen anyone look like she did, so pale and wide-eyed and terrified—at least, not without being physically injured.

And he knew she wasn't injured. She wasn't poisoned either. He had eaten the same sandwich, and there had been nothing wrong with it.

Physically, she was right: she was fine. But emotionally, she was barely staying together.

She no longer held onto the sink though, and her arms weren't crossed. Her eyes were actually clear—and they hadn't been at times when he was telling her what happened.

He could see when the memories took her and when she came back. She was back now.

"You remember," he said.

"You came to my room," she said, and it took him a minute to understand what she meant.

"In the hospital? Yeah, I did." And with that, his shoulders relaxed just a bit. If she remembered that, then she remembered him.

"You told me to stay strong, you said you had to leave. You said everything would be better."

He nodded. It relieved him that she remembered, finally. It was important to him that she remember.

"Was I right?" he asked, and he heard his younger

self in that question: vulnerable, worried, caring. When had he stopped caring about things?

She nodded. Then she bit her lower lip. And nodded again.

"Yesterday, I wouldn't have said so. Yesterday, I would have told you that nothing was better than living with my father."

"What changed?" he asked.

"I made it up." Her voice shook. "I made it all up. That's why I could never tell the therapists what life with my father was really like. Except better. I always said it was better, and then they'd ask how, and I'd shut up. Or leave. Or quit seeing them."

He smiled just a bit. Now he understood the powerful mind comment. The therapists would use techniques to break her denial, and she would refuse or rebuild.

She was strong, inside and out. He liked that.

He extended a hand. "I'm sorry about what happened. I'm sorry that I was a part of it."

She looked at his hand, but didn't take it. Instead, she shook her head. "You're sorry for killing him?"

"For causing such pain," he said.

She was still shaking her head. "But you didn't. You told me it would be better. And it was."

He kept his hand out for another minute, until he felt really silly doing so. He let his hand drop.

"So the way you left the ship," he said. "That wasn't a deliberate setup? You didn't have that planned from the beginning, did you?"

She tilted her head a little. "What do you mean, the beginning?"

His breath caught. "When you got on the ship."

"You forget," she said. "I didn't know you were on the ship."

He had forgotten that. "All right, then. From the moment you went into the security office. You didn't see me as an opportunity? Again?"

He sounded a bit breathless, and he didn't want to. That breathlessness showed his vulnerability.

"It started out as a setup," she said, and he froze. He didn't want it to be a setup. He didn't want her to decide to hurt him.

"I needed your DNA," she said.

She had told him this before, about needing his DNA, about trying to find out who he really was. He had mentally dismissed it, because she had been acting so strange, but her story wasn't changing.

"I gave you a lot of it," he said just like he had before.

"I really needed to plan better," she said. "The next time I sleep with someone, I'll make sure to keep a vial of bodily fluids."

He started, not liking the idea of her sleeping with anyone else. Then he realized she was joking. Which relieved the part of his brain worried about her emotional state, but threw the rest of him off balance.

Again. Dammit.

She made a slight shrugging gesture, opening her hands as well. Then she turned to the sink and got herself a glass of water. "I wanted to know who you were. Really were. And I didn't have the capability to figure that out, but I knew ship's security would have a database that tied into the Guild. Every ship does."

That was true.

"So…" she wasn't looking at him anymore. "I went to the security office and made up a story—"

"About touch drops."

Her shrug got bigger. "No one in security could press charges or do anything, besides you were one of the richest passengers on the ship. They weren't going to touch you."

"But they did," he said. "They interrogated me for hours."

"Not about the touch drops," she said, with her back to him. She knew exactly why they had interrogated him. If interrogated was truly the right word. He made it sound more dramatic than it really was.

"No," he said after a moment, "not about the touch drops. But you left me holding the bag for Testrial."

She shrugged again. "Killing Testrial was your idea."

"Rikki," he said softly.

She shook her head and turned around. "I had just found out who you were," she said. "I was improvising. I thought you were playing some horrible cat-and-mouse game with me. I had to get off that ship, and fast."

He understood it. If she thought he had murdered her father, then her actions were not just rational, they were brilliant. She had deliberately delayed Misha, and she had completed an effective escape.

He had to take a deep breath just to calm himself. "If you hadn't found out about your father, if you had just confirmed that I was a Guild member, then what? What would you have done next?"

She put a hand to her forehead. "I don't know," she said. "It seems like years ago."

He studied her. He wasn't sure he believed her.

"Rikki. You didn't know who I was. You got my DNA and you gave it to security. Who did you think I was?"

She rubbed her hand over her forehead like it hurt. Then she sighed and looked at him. He was always startled that they were the same height.

"I thought maybe you were tracking me for some other reason. Revenge, or something."

"For?"

"How do I know what for?" she said. "I've done a lot of work for a lot of people, and there are even more people who aren't happy with me. For all I knew, you were working for Testrial, were angry that I had killed him, and decided to have a little fun before you made me pay."

His breath caught. "That's the second time you've said that I had sex with you because I wanted to use you before killing or hurting you. Do you really believe what happened between us was that shallow?"

Her gaze met his. Her eyes looked bruised. "You came in here with a weapon, poised and ready to shoot. You obviously thought I wanted to harm you somehow. Did you think the sex was sincere when you woke up in my bed after being drugged?"

He hadn't. He had thought that she had used him. He had been convinced of it. And that was where his anger really rested. In the belief that she had used him.

Because he was careful with sex. He knew it was the most potent weapon humans had with each other. More deadly than guns or knives or poisons. Sex could taint everything.

And clearly it had here.

Neither of them had trusted each other. Both of them had felt used.

"No," he said. "I thought you used me. I thought you were laughing at me."

She nodded. "So we felt the same way about each other."

Her mouth was open slightly, her lips moist. His heart was pounding. He wanted to touch her. Not comfort her, not hold her close. He wanted to show her how very sincere he could be.

Her gaze flicked down to his mouth, then back to his eyes. Suddenly, he was aroused. He couldn't remember ever getting aroused that fast.

Except when he had danced with her in the lounge. Except when he had kissed her the first time. Except when he brushed against her when he decided to help with Testrial.

"It was sincere," he said, his voice husky. "At least for me."

She blinked. He could actually see her think. Maybe she was wondering if she should be honest. But her expression didn't seem calculating.

Instead, it seemed even more vulnerable than it had.

"It was for me too," she said.

He took one step—or was it two—and he slid his arms around her. She leaned into him, her hands finding the back of his neck, pulling his face toward hers.

The kiss was bruising, tasting of water and marinara and her. So much like her that he wondered how he could have gone without her for so long. He actually craved her. He held her tight, unable to tell where her lips started and his ended, his tongue finding hers, his entire body on fire.

He wanted her, and he wanted her now. He thought

he had remembered how it felt to hold her, to want her, to make love to her, but he hadn't remembered. What he felt was two hundred times more powerful than his strongest memory.

He grabbed her shirt, and hiked it up, slipping his hands underneath it. His fingers found skin, and then her bare breasts. He pulled the shirt over those breasts, and crouched enough to taste them.

Her hands found his shirt, unbuttoning it, forcing it open. She grabbed his chin and lifted his face up, so that she could press her damp breasts against his chest, her skin against his, igniting him. It took all his control to keep kissing her as he tried to get her pants off.

She reached for his, and then she froze.

Her entire body became rigid.

"Stop," she said against his mouth. "Stop."

He stopped. It was one of the hardest things he had ever done, but he stopped.

She reached into the waistband of his pants and removed his laser pistol. She took one step back and held the pistol between her thumb and forefinger.

"Are we done with these?" she asked, her voice calm. She wasn't that scared woman any longer. There was no trembling anywhere.

He would have thought she was unaffected by him if it weren't for two things: her swollen lips and the fact that her nipples were so hard they looked like little bullets—metal bullets. The old-fashioned kind.

The nipples drove him crazy. He had to look away, just to maintain his concentration on what she had said.

"It's probably wise to disarm first," he said. "All weapons."

She nodded, then set his laser pistol on the counter. She put hers beside his.

He pulled off his boots, removed his knife, and set it on the counter behind him. She took something the size of her thumb out of the pocket of her pants, and set that near the weapons on the counter beside her.

He didn't even know what kind of weapon that was.

"Any more weapons?" he asked her as if it had been his idea to remove them. Or at least, that was what he had been trying for. In actuality, he sounded a bit desperate, or at least like a man in a hurry.

Maybe because he was a man in a hurry. He wanted her like he had never wanted a woman before.

"You want me to check?" she asked.

"I'll check," he said and grabbed the waistband on her pants, sliding them down. She wasn't wearing anything underneath them either, and the sight of her naked—or nearly naked, with the pants pooled at her ankles and the shirt still hiked above her large breasts, inflamed him.

He cupped his hands over her buttocks, pulling her close, and as he did, she tugged her shirt all the way off, making her breasts bob free.

He caught one of them between his lips, the other with his left hand, his right still against her rear. He pulled her close so that she could feel how hard he was.

She stuffed her hands in his pants, her fingers finding him. His breath caught, because if he breathed, he would have come right into her palm.

She grinned at him, seeing that, and not wanting to let it go. She undid his pants. They slipped to his knees, trapping his legs. She straddled him, and then slid onto him, wet and warm and ready.

He moaned again, put his hands on her waist, and used them to raise her up and down just enough to create incredible friction. She buried her face in his neck, kissing him, then—suddenly—she arched, a flush running up her entire torso from her chest to her neck to her face.

It made her even more beautiful.

He could feel her pulse against him as she came. He would have joined her, but if he did, he might drop her. Instead, he gritted his teeth, holding her in place with his hands. He couldn't move—his pants were wrapped around his legs—and it was a testament to his strength that his knees didn't buckle as sensation covered him.

Her orgasm continued, her eyes wild, her breasts in his face. He leaned forward and feasted, until finally, spent and sweat-covered, she kissed him.

And kissed him. And kissed him.

And he couldn't wait any longer.

"Rikki, we need to—"

But he wasn't quite sure what they needed to do. He had had a thought, it was gone, and it was his turn to come. He did, hard, as if he hadn't had an orgasm in years. She wrapped herself even tighter around him— arms, legs, and then he realized she was coming too. Again, and that made him even crazier.

Only he couldn't do anything, except let the sensation run through him.

Finally, it ended, and his legs became rubber. He wasn't sure if he had ever had an orgasm standing up, a real orgasm, not one of those surprise ejaculations that happened to boys in puberty.

He didn't think so, and he was beginning to understand why. His legs no longer supported him. Them. Him. He shook, and she laughed.

Not a mean laugh. A joyous laugh. She leaned backwards, grabbed the counter with her hands, and braced herself, but didn't disengage from him.

"Shuffle this way," she said.

He could see the muscles in her arms, the only thing holding both of them up. She didn't let him collapse. Instead, she rubbed on him, using her hips and her arms together, and damn, if he didn't get hard again, just like a young man.

He shook just a little, and his pants finally fell the rest of the way. Then he stepped forward, out of the pants, moving with her, and grabbed her, putting his hands beneath her and hoisting her onto the counter.

She shoved the weapons aside, and he hoped they were all disarmed. But nothing happened. Nothing accidentally fired or started humming.

He forgot them then, climbing on the counter with her, and taking her right there, thrusting deeply, like he had wanted to do before, but couldn't because of the position they had been in.

He had never felt like this, as if he was actually caressing her inside, but with strength, each thrust carrying part of him into her. She clutched at him, then gripped the countertop itself, her hands shaking, and she came again, so powerfully this time, that she pulled something out of him, and he came too, thrusting until he couldn't any longer.

He wanted to collapse on top of her. He needed to do so, his arms were trembling so badly, but he didn't want to crush her with his weight.

"Good heavens, you're hurting yourself," she said and pulled him down, his slick torso against hers.

He was shaking and spent and he had never felt this good in his entire life. Or this exhausted.

"Sincere enough for you?" he asked softly.

And she laughed again. "What would you do if I said no?"

"I don't know," he said, his words sounding a bit muffled, even to him. "Try again?"

Chapter 37

HE DIDN'T LOOK LIKE A MAN WHO COULD TRY AGAIN. Rikki wrapped her legs around Misha, holding him in place. His hair was a tousled mess, falling over his face like bangs. His skin was flushed, his eyes so blue that they seemed lit from within.

She had never in her life beheld such a gorgeous man. And he had just made love to her.

Sincerely.

Earnestly.

With more passion than she had ever experienced in her life. Except for that one night on the ship. The night she couldn't get out of her mind.

He braced himself on one elbow and brought a hand forward to caress her face. His gaze was tender.

"You're unbelievably beautiful," he said.

"And you're quite the liar," she said.

"No," he said. "I'm not."

He kissed her, gently, his hand still cupping her cheek. Then he feathered kisses down her neck and onto her chest. He moved his hand down, and caressed her breast, bringing it forward, taking it in his mouth, and sucked.

Her skin was so sensitive that it almost hurt. And it felt good. No. It felt great. She shifted beneath him, aroused again.

"We're going to hurt each other," she said, her voice raspy.

"I don't care," he said, his breath light on her skin.

He slid down farther, his feet knocking something off the counter, feathering kisses along her belly, his hands on her hips. He brought her up to his mouth, and gently, ever so gently, kissed her.

Then his tongue was inside her, and she got crazy all over again. She reached for him, trying to pull him up so he could be inside her, but he held her, using his mouth to make her come—not once, not twice, but three times.

He made his way back up her torso, lingered on her breasts, and then put his mouth on hers. He tasted of her, which she wasn't sure she liked. But then she forgot it as he slipped inside her again, moving slowly, gently.

He braced himself on his elbows and looked at her, his gaze on hers, just like it had been when he told her that awful story of their past, when he made her remember everything she had forgotten.

His gaze held hers, and they watched each other as they reached one last climax—together.

Then he did collapse on her.

She could feel his heart racing. Or maybe that was her heart. Or both of theirs.

Either way, she was spent, and overly sensitive, and satisfied. For the moment, anyway.

"I didn't think I could do that," he said.

Be sincere? she almost joked, but she didn't. That was a precious statement, a statement she didn't want to make into anything funny.

His hand cupped her breast, his touch warm and soft. "I thought only young men could come that many times in a row."

"You're not young?" she asked in that light tone she heard in her head. "Could've fooled me."

He lifted his head and grinned at her. He really did look young now. And handsome. And perfect.

And God, she wanted him again. Or at least, she knew she would want him.

Right now, she was too tired.

And her back hurt.

Something was digging into her spine.

"I think we have to move," she said.

He shifted his hips. He was still inside her, even though he wasn't hard.

She grinned. "I was going to say 'Not that kind of move,' but you can continue as long as you like."

"If only I could," he said and slipped all the way out.

She felt a loss, as if he had taken something important with him. In her mind's eye, she saw herself reaching for him, so that he would stay with her like that forever.

And she immediately crushed that mental image: too needy, too vulnerable. She wasn't ever any of those things.

Although she had been this afternoon.

With this man whose mother had killed her father.

But even that no longer had the talismanic power it had had just a few hours earlier. She didn't hate him for that.

Especially since she could now acknowledge that she wanted her father dead—that Misha's mother had done her a favor that night, and Misha knew it.

Rikki knew it.

"Something's gouging my back," she said.

He levered himself off her. A flush still colored his pale skin. His body was amazing. She was impressed at the strength he had shown. Holding her up while having an orgasm, without leaning against anything.

She looked at those legs, the muscles in them, the muscles in his torso and arms and back.

She sat up, cupped his face, and kissed him. She didn't want to let him go, and that terrified her.

She had never felt like that about anyone before.

He put his arms around her and helped her off the counter. Then he looked at her back.

"There's a dent in the skin," he said. "You were on one of the forks, but tongs didn't break the surface. You'll probably be bruised."

She had been bruised from the last time they had made love, and she hadn't cared then. She didn't care now.

"I'll be all right," she said.

"I don't like hurting you," he said, and that sounded sincere too.

"You didn't hurt me," she said. "Believe me."

She touched that skin of his, so smooth and hard, over those amazing muscles. "How come I can't get enough of you?"

"It's not touch drops," he said, and there was a bit of irritation in his tone.

She looked at him. "I know."

He nodded, looked down, as if his own words had surprised him. "I think that offended me more than anything."

"That a man like you would need touch drops?"

He shook his head. He still wasn't looking at her. "That what we had that night could even be considered something artificial."

She swallowed. "What do we have?"

He lifted his head. "I don't know."

He tucked a strand of hair behind her ear. Then he kissed her, a light kiss, almost a benediction.

"But whatever it is," he said. "It's the most powerful thing I've ever experienced."

Powerful and out of control and addicting. Maybe that was why she had compared it to touch drops. She could get used to this man. Only that was the wrong way to put it.

She wanted to explore this man. She wanted to know every inch of him, everything he liked, everything that made him as wild as he had made her.

She could dedicate months to studying him, to figuring out what made his eyes that amazing blue, what could make him moan like he had, make him lose complete control.

She wanted to love him for days.

She kissed him, and then she stopped, frozen again. That word she had used. Over and over again — fortunately only inside her own mind.

Love.

She had made love with him. That was what she had thought. Twice, she'd had that thought. And now, she wanted to love him for days.

She never used that word. She didn't believe in that word.

She screwed men. She had sex with them. She had even fucked one or two.

But she had never made love before.

And if she had to guess what that felt like, she would have guessed that it felt like this.

He stuck a finger under her chin, and brought her head up so that she looked at him.

"You all right?" he asked.

Was she falling in love with him? Was she even capable of that? And, more importantly, could she stop it?

Because she couldn't love anyone. Any more than she could need anyone.

She was okay with craving him, okay with wanting him. Maybe even okay with obsessing about him.

But she couldn't tie herself to him in any way.

"I'm okay," she said, even though it might have been a lie. "Are you?"

"The best I've ever been," he said, his blue eyes twinkling. "Quite honestly—No. Make that quite sincerely, Rikki—this is the best I've ever been."

Chapter 38

SOMEWHERE IN THE MIDDLE OF THAT INCREDIBLE afternoon, Misha had decided he was going to be completely honest with her. He wasn't going to lie, he wasn't going to forget to tell her something. He was going to be as much of himself as he was capable of being.

He wasn't sure what that meant, but he was going to try.

Could this feeling, this desire for her that was so intense it almost hurt, be something he could get out of his system?

He wasn't sure.

And he wasn't sure he wanted to find out.

They ended up in her bathroom, showering together, playing with each other's bodies, but both clearly too tired to do much more. He dried her off, then dried himself off, and led her to bed.

The bedroom was as bright as the rest of the apartment, with floor-to-ceiling windows. It wasn't until he went in there, naked, holding her hand, that he realized they both were visible to the entire city—and had been throughout that incredible sexual marathon.

And what really surprised him was that he didn't care.

She hit some kind of button and the windows darkened. The bed was the only thing in the room besides the windows and two occasional tables. She pulled the covers down, and then got in bed, bringing him in.

For a moment, he thought she was going to start again. But she didn't. She just wrapped herself around him, nestled her head against his chest, and closed her eyes.

After a moment, he closed his eyes too.

He woke up hours later, hungrier than he ever remembered being. Rikki was still cradled in his arms, and he was hard against her. But his body ached, and even though the desire was there as strong as it had been earlier, he knew he might actually hurt them both if he started something so soon.

They needed to eat, not act like teenagers on a honeymoon. After they ate, they could resume their teenage-honeymoon behavior.

He smiled and stroked Rikki's hair. It was so soft. It cascaded around her, covering her. He loved the color — the real color. He kissed the crown of her head, then eased himself out. Gently. Slowly.

He didn't want to wake her. She had awakened him, twice, twitching and crying out with what had clearly been bad dreams. He wondered if her sleep was haunted by the death of her father, or if she was dreaming of other unpleasant things.

Still, he knew enough about brain science as it pertained to post-traumatic stress to know that sleep would help repair the emotional damage. It would link the connections, make the newly revived memories firmer, keep them easy to access.

And that was important, because she had to stop questioning herself.

He tucked her hair away from him, so that he wouldn't roll on it as he slid out of bed.

He was physically exhausted. He could only imagine how she felt—physically and emotionally exhausted.

Only really, he didn't have to imagine it.

He had gone through something similar at the Guild, back when they were testing him. They wanted to make certain he was becoming an assassin for the right reasons.

If revenge lurked in his past, in his trapped memories, then he could have lost control of his present—of himself—the way that Rikki had lost control when she found out who he was. When they had the discussion about that night, here in the apartment.

He hadn't gone through that—not outside of a supervised setting, not in the middle of a job—but that was only because the Guild had insisted on the psychological work up front. Probably because of some kind of experience that he knew nothing about.

He ran a hand through his hair, which was still damp from that shower. He had to find his clothes. And then he had to find a message board in the apartment. Because he knew there was no food here. He didn't want to risk delivery, not since he had compromised her security network. So he needed to bring back groceries. He had found a good place between his hideout and hers. He would come back and cook her something delicious, and then he would wake her up.

Most of his clothes were in the kitchen. His boots had gotten into the hallway, and he didn't remember that. In fact, the last thing he remembered about his boots was taking the knife out of its hiding place. He had been concentrating a lot more on her and their encounter than he had been on himself.

He also picked up the weapons, stopping for a moment to look at that small thing Rikki had taken from the seam of her pants. The thing wasn't much bigger than his thumb and it seemed to have a multipurpose. If he pressed it, a small sharp blade came out. But there was another button that he recognized. The small thing had a small laser as well.

It was an ingenious little weapon. He would have to ask her about it.

He left her weapons on the counter and took his, along with his clothes, into the bathroom. Once there, he dressed, and replaced the weapons. Then he found the message board built into the mirror, and recorded his plans. As he froze the frame in the entire mirror, so she would notice the message, he noted that he looked a little more flushed than usual, his lips as bruised as hers had been.

He smiled at the memory.

Then he finger-combed his hair, double-checked the weapons to make sure he hadn't done something stupid, and let himself out of the bathroom. He felt a bit muzzy-headed, not from any chemical, but from the complete shift in his perspective.

He had been furious with Rikki, and then he had felt compassion for her, and then that lust returned, even more powerful than before. And now that he was up and moving, the lust was there, in the background, but so was a tenderness he wasn't sure he had ever felt before.

He slipped silently down the hallway. The apartment looked different from the inside. It was pretty clear that those bearing walls were a bit longer than they needed to be, just a bit wider. The illusion only existed for someone looking into the apartment through the windows, not for someone walking past them.

As he got to the entrance, he stopped. Another door was open. It was probably the door leading to the steps that took Rikki to the apartments she owned on the lower level.

He was half-smiling as he peered inside, wanting to check his theory.

The view of the interior was so different from what he expected that he actually made a soft sound.

Usually he didn't go into places without having seen the schematics. He usually didn't have to guess what was behind one door because he knew.

He hadn't known here.

What he thought was a small staircase enclosure leading down a few flights was actually a workspace. Weapons covered the walls like decorations. There was a counter that went all the way around, drawers and cabinets, and, yes, an extra space toward the back that might indeed lead down to the lower apartments or might provide an excellent second hiding space.

In the center of the room was a large, soft couch-like thing that someone could stretch out on.

It was clear that Rikki had been doing just that when her food got delivered, hours ago. It seemed like it had been days ago, though, the way that he had changed, the way that she had changed. What they had discussed, what they had been through.

What they had *done*.

He smiled softly.

He was about to turn away from the room when he noticed five tablets on the couch-thing. They all had images on them, probably future targets.

And one of the images looked familiar.

He frowned, and walked inside. His heart was actually pounding. He knew this was a violation of the trust he wanted to build with Rikki, but he couldn't stop himself.

He would just double-check, make sure everything was fine, and then he would go get food.

His hand hovered over the tablet. His breath caught.

That face was familiar.

It belonged to Kerani Ammons, the director of the Assassins Guild.

Chapter 39

MISHA'S HEAD WAS SPINNING. THAT COULDN'T BE right. He couldn't be looking at Kerani Ammons's face. Because if he was looking at Kerani's face, then maybe Liora had been right. Maybe Rikki was with the Rovers.

His stomach twisted.

He picked up the tablet and it immediately shut off at the touch of his fingers. He cursed silently, then heard a slight sound behind him.

He turned to see the door closing.

He leapt for it, tablet still in hand, and managed to stop the door from sealing. He didn't want to have it close while he still had the tablet. He needed to re-jigger something so that he could put the tablet back down where he had found it, without getting trapped.

Dammit. What was this all about? Had Rikki been using him all along? Was she trying to get into the Guild by playing hard to get?

Because, after all, only a nonaffiliated assassin would have an excuse—a reason—to get into the Guild like this. And a nonaffiliated assassin would have to meet with Kerani before the final acceptance into the Guild.

Misha closed his eyes and rested his forehead on the door. Dammit, dammit, dammit. He didn't want to think like that. He didn't want to make that kind of assumption.

Dammit.

There was no proof that this tablet was anything other

than an informational device. He was the one who had assumed he was holding a target image.

He needed to get the tablet working.

He needed to fix the door, put the tablet back, and get breakfast.

He needed to trust.

That was what he had vowed to do. That was what he would do.

"What the hell do you think you're doing?" Rikki's voice. Low, menacing. He had never heard her sound like that.

He opened his eyes, raised his head, and looked into the hallway. She was standing near him, feet splayed, laser pistol pointed at him. Her hair was messed, her eyes shadowed, but she wasn't shaking. She looked strong.

She was also naked.

The way she had her arms, her hands holding that braced pistol, pushed up her spectacular breasts. He could see every muscle, every part of her, and dammit, he could feel himself growing hard.

"Okay," he said, trying to sound calm. "I know this looks bad."

Hell, it looked terrible. He was wedged between the door and the jam, the door vibrating as it continued its quest to shut. In his right hand—the hand in the hall-way—he held her tablet.

"It doesn't look bad," she said, her voice still low and ferocious. "It just proves that I should have listened to my doubts. You're a hell of a con man, Misha. I actually believed everything you said."

"I wasn't conning you," he said, but stopped himself before saying *I can explain this*. He could explain it, but he'd heard that sentence so many times from clearly guilty people or people whose guilt no longer mattered, who were going to die anyway, that he couldn't, in good conscience, say it himself.

"Then you want to tell me why I shouldn't shoot you?" she asked. Her face was impassive. He would have been happier if she had been angry.

He wondered if this was her professional face, the one countless people had last seen before they died.

"You'll damage your door," he said.

She shrugged, moving her breasts ever so slightly, which then made his breath catch. She was beautiful. Hair down, splendidly naked, gun in hand. He wasn't sure he had ever seen a more beautiful woman.

"You're already damaging my door," she said.

"I'd stop," he said, "but I can't move."

She looked at the door, then looked at his face, then looked at the exterior control panel. At least, he assumed that was the exterior control panel.

"Tell me what you were doing in there," she said. "And don't lie."

He licked his lips. "Did you see my message in the bathroom?"

"No," she said. "I heard the alarm, I grabbed my gun, I came here. I didn't have time to pee. And you know what? I would really like to pee. So get to the point."

He would have smiled at the irritation in her voice if it had been appropriate. But it wasn't. His heart started beating harder, and it wasn't just because the woman holding that gun on him was hot.

He was starting to get the feeling that she would pull that trigger if he gave her the slightest excuse.

"I was going to get us breakfast," he said. "I left you a message to that effect. Go check if you want. I'm not going anywhere."

Her eyes narrowed. "If I go, you'll figure out how to disentangle yourself and then you'll be gone before I get back."

Now that she had shown him where the entrance controls were with a single glance, she was probably right: he could do that. He could free himself and leave in the time it took to get to the bathroom and back.

But he didn't confirm her hypothesis.

He continued, "I came down the hallway and saw the open door. Honestly, I'd been wondering about these walls. I thought they were the wrong size to be simple bearing walls. I figured they were hiding a small staircase—"

He stopped himself before he added *to your other apartments*. In her mood, those words would probably not have the desired effect. She didn't need to know how thorough the background check he had done on her was.

"—or some other escape route from the apartment. I just wanted to if I was right."

Her expression didn't change. He couldn't tell if she had caught his near slipup or not. He couldn't tell what her emotion was.

And here he'd been thinking she wore every single emotion she ever had on her face. He had been very wrong about that.

"I looked in," he said, "and I was quite frankly surprised at the room itself."

"So you stepped in and started looking through my files."

He almost said *no*, which was ridiculous considering he was half in and half out, holding onto one of those files. It was just his instinct—and not a very good instinct—that made him want to deny it.

He smiled at her—his most charming smile, a sheepish smile, a forgive-me smile, one he had used in cons and preps for jobs.

The smile didn't seem to have any impact on her at all.

"I wouldn't have," he said, "except you had left these tablets scattered and I thought I recognized one of the people on them."

"Friend of yours?" she asked in a decidedly nasty tone.

"Actually, yes," he said, and he waved the tablet up toward her. "I know this woman. I know her really, really well."

Chapter 40

HE HAD SUCCEEDED IN DISTRACTING HER. DAMN HIM, he seemed to know exactly how to get to her.

Rikki stood across from him, feet planted, pistol braced. She was cold and probably covered with goose bumps, and she felt oddly exposed. Or maybe not so oddly, since she was naked, after all.

But she had learned a long time ago that she usually didn't feel naked when she was holding a weapon.

"You know her well, huh?" Rikki asked. "Who is she?"

"Get me out of here first," he said. "We have to talk."

She didn't like the way the door was groaning as it kept pressing on him. But she wasn't sure she could trust him either.

She moved the pistol to her left hand only and extended her right. "Give me the tablet."

His lips thinned. He didn't want to, which was interesting. Did he think he had some kind of advantage by holding it?

"I'm not getting you out of there until you do," she said.

He extended the tablet toward her. She took it and it automatically came back on. The tablet only worked when she touched it. If someone else held it, it went blank. It also sent her an alarm, warning her that someone else had picked up the tablet.

She glanced down at the image of the beautiful older woman, the one who had intrigued her.

"You going to let me out?" Misha asked.

He could have a weapon in his left hand. He could have one of a hundred weapons—all hers—in his left hand.

She would be foolish to just open that door.

She set the tablet down. "Tell me how you know this woman."

"You tell me why you have her image," he said.

She put both hands on the pistol. "No."

He lifted his right hand and slammed it against the wall behind him, coming amazingly close to the controls. Not that he would be able to open the door with a single flat palm against the panel.

"Do that again, and I will shoot you," she said.

She sounded convincing. But she was no longer convinced herself. She wanted to find out about that woman.

"Tell me how you know this woman," Rikki repeated.

He looked at her, and that expression had returned to his face, the one that closed him off from her. Even though she was angry at him, even though she no longer trusted him, she hated that sudden feeling of separation.

Which made her feel even odder that she had felt connected, even though she was both furious and betrayed.

"She's in the Guild," he said after a moment. And while he didn't seem to be lying, he didn't seem to be telling the entire truth either.

"What did you leave out?" Rikki asked.

"Nothing," he said.

"Oh, I think you left out a lot," she said.

He raised his chin just slightly. "And I don't think this door is going to work much longer."

It was making a slight whistling noise.

She had to give in now, whether she liked it or not.

With one hand, she picked up the tablet, double-tapped the screen with her thumb, and it moved away from the woman's image. The control panel appeared. She had backups and more backups all over the apartment so she wouldn't get trapped anywhere.

She tapped the door-open command, but made sure she hit the five-second delay.

Then she set the tablet down, put her hand back on the pistol, and braced herself in case he came out shooting.

He seemed to understand what she was thinking, because as the door eased off him, he raised both hands.

Both *empty* hands.

Keeping her gaze on him, she leaned over, double-tapped the tablet, and the door eased closed behind him.

"Come with me," she said. "I'm going to get dressed."

Chapter 41

RIKKI INDICATED WITH HER HEAD THAT MISHA SHOULD walk in front of her. She wanted to keep the gun on him.

He kept his hands up, like a man in some kind of old Earth vid.

"Maybe you should look at my message in the bathroom," he said.

"Maybe you should shut up," she snapped.

He took a few more steps, then stopped. "Are we going to the bedroom or to fetch your clothes from the kitchen?"

There was something suggestive in his tone. She didn't like it. She didn't like the reminder that she had slept with him yet again, and the next morning (Was it the next morning? She had no idea how long she'd slept) he had betrayed her once more.

How stupid was she? How often did she have to learn the same lesson? Misha couldn't be trusted no matter how sexy or handsome or unbelievably desirable he was.

He didn't know where the weapons were in the bedroom. She did. Even though he probably had put all of his weapons back, since he had all of his clothes on.

"Bedroom," she said.

He started walking again.

"Seriously," he said. "If you listen to the message—"

"I believe that you were going to get breakfast," she said. "I believe you got distracted when you realized you could get into my office. I am a bit surprised that you triggered the alarm. That was very unprofessional of you. But from that moment on, I don't believe a word you said."

He glanced over his shoulder at her when she said "unprofessional," so she knew he understood the dig. She kept her face impassive, but she was furious.

Furious at him for snooping.

Furious at herself for falling for him again.

What was wrong with her? It was like she had been hit with touch drops, even though she knew she hadn't.

So he wanted to find out what she was working on? Why? It made no sense, just like his being here made no sense. Not even that touchy-feely crap about needing to get her out of his system.

"Stand near the bed," she said.

She was half-tempted to make him undress and cuff himself. Then she would take advantage of him.

But she was too pissed to do that. Besides, that would make her as bad as he was.

She kept the pistol pointed at him, and backed up toward the closet. Once there, she grabbed a set of clothes. She didn't even look at them. But they would have to do.

His eyebrows went up. "You want me to help you dress?"

Because they both knew she couldn't dress without using both hands.

"There are laser cuffs on the table beside the bed," she said, making a decision. "Put them on."

He tilted his head sideways. "Rikki—"

"I said put them on."

He gave her a baleful look, and beneath it was such anger that it almost made her gasp. But he went to the table she indicated and pulled out the top pair of cuffs. He put them on loosely.

"Move your arms apart," she said.

His mouth got thin. If he moved his arms apart, then the cuffs would tighten. "Rikki, seriously—"

"I'm not screwing around, Misha. Move your arms apart."

He did, and winced as the cuffs tightened.

"Now, sit down," she said.

He shook his head once, but sat on the messed up sheets. Sheets she had slept so easily between not too long ago.

She glanced at the clothes she grabbed. Tan pants, white blouse. She hadn't done half-bad when she picked them blind. She set the gun on a shelf inside the closet, and dressed quickly, this time remembering undergarments and shoes.

Then she picked up the pistol again. Misha hadn't moved at all, except to watch appreciatively as she slid clothes over her body. Just the way he watched made her flush.

She picked up the pistol, keeping it pointed on him. She felt better dressed. Less vulnerable. Even more in control.

"The information I have says nothing about that woman being in the Guild," she said.

"It wouldn't," he said.

"Why not?" she asked.

"It's a target instruction, right? Would you want to go head-to-head with a Guild member?"

She shrugged one shoulder, then gave him a pointed look. "It doesn't seem so hard."

He grimaced. "You know what I mean."

"I don't, really," she said. "I don't understand any of it. You came to me, ready to shoot me—"

"I wasn't—"

"And then you somehow convinced me that we were pals—"

"I wouldn't say that what we did made us 'pals'—"

"And then you break into my office—"

"I didn't break in. The door was open—"

"And now you're lying to me about that woman."

"I'm not lying," he said.

"No," she said, "but you're leaving something out, and I'm not letting you out of this room until I know what it is."

He stood up, then sighed heavily, as if he was thinking about it. He didn't look friendly or charming or even amused anymore. His expression was hard.

"You do realize I could get out of here," he said.

She set her jaw. "Not without a fight."

"Someone would get hurt," he said, "and that someone wouldn't be me."

She laughed without any amusement. "You're so sure of yourself."

"Yes," he said. "I am."

"So," she said. "Is whatever you're hiding worth fighting over?"

"That's what I'm trying to figure out," he said. Then that harsh gaze of his met hers. She felt like he was assessing her, like he had no real idea who she was, and was trying to figure her out just with his eyes.

She waited, let him look. He had seen a lot of her. He had seen her vulnerable, and sad. He had seen how lost she felt because of her family. And he had seen her naked— not just naked, but in the middle of a deep passion.

But he had never seen what she could do, how ruthless she could be.

Although she wasn't exactly sure how ruthless she could be with him.

"Okay," he said after a moment. "I'm going to tell you this because I need some answers as well. Will I get them?"

"I'll make that decision after I've heard what you have to say."

He flipped his wrists upward, slammed them together, and the cuffs flared, then opened, and fell onto the floor with a clatter.

It took every bit of control she had not to show her surprise. She had no idea anyone could break out of laser cuffs.

"I'm going to tell you this," he said, his voice shaking with fury, "even though I'm not supposed to tell anyone, even though everyone in the Guild is sworn to secrecy. It's part of our code, which I actually believe in, as much as you like to make fun of it."

Her breath caught. His fury filled the room like a live thing, an extra presence.

But he hadn't moved away from the bed. He stood there, his arms at his sides, the cuffs lying useless on the floor beside his feet.

"That woman whose image you have there, the one you're clearly supposed to target, is the director of the Guild. She runs it. She never leaves Guild headquarters."

Now Rikki did let her mouth open slightly. She was surprised and she was willing to show it. She had no idea. More than that, she had no idea why she was supposed to target this woman or who had sent the contact.

"Clearly," Misha said, "your friends know this. And clearly they think you can get inside Guild head-quarters. Which makes me wonder whether or not all these coincidences when you ran into me, and then when you got in the way of my work, when you let me hire you to kill Elio Testrial, whether all of that was some elaborate ruse to get me to figure you need help, and the only help you can get is from the Guild. You let me make that offer so you could get close to our director."

Rikki stepped back as if he had slapped her. She made herself focus on his words rather than her (furious) reaction to them.

"If that was the case, I would have stayed and taken you up on the offer," she said.

He took a step toward her, that hard gaze still in his eyes. "That would have been too easy. I would have been suspicious, and you know it. Instead, you used that incredible body of yours to entice me, to muddle my thinking—"

"And that's why I fled?" she snapped. "So that you would follow me?"

"I'd be more likely to trust you if I thought you were reluctant," he said. "This morning, I was getting us breakfast for God's sake. I thought you were really vulnerable from your father's death—"

"Do *not* make light of that," she said, stepping closer to him. "Do *not*."

They stared at each other, the pistol between them. She had stayed far enough away so that he would have to struggle to reach the pistol. But he could do it if he moved quickly, and she knew that.

Then something shifted in his face. That hardness left his eyes. "Put the pistol down," he said.

She didn't move.

"You didn't know, did you?" he asked.

He could have been trying to fool her, to do—what, exactly? If he was telling the truth about the woman, then he only wanted truth from her. If he was lying, if he wanted something else, well, then that laser cuff trick showed her that he had a lot more experience with a lot of things than she ever did.

She lowered the pistol. He still didn't move. He was just looking at her.

"I had no idea who that woman was," she said softly. "And yes, she's a target. The only information I got was that she had killed tens of thousands of people."

His cheeks flushed. "She did not—"

Rikki raised a hand, stopping him. "If you think about it, that number makes sense. If she really does run the Guild—"

"She does," he said.

"—then you could say that all of the assassinations are on her shoulders."

Misha frowned ever so slightly. "Why would someone contact you?"

She shrugged a single shoulder. "There aren't a lot of unaffiliated assassins."

"Especially those who just got invited into the Guild," he said.

"Would you stop with that?" she asked. "I didn't tell anyone about it."

Except Jack. She had told Jack. But Jack wouldn't betray her. He was her best friend.

Misha's frown deepened. Had he seen that moment of doubt flicker across her face?

"You're still with the Rovers, though, right? You work with them?"

She started. How did he know about the Rovers? How did he know that she had once relied on them for vetting services, that she and Jack had used them for training?

Misha continued to stare at her. The Rovers thing was important to him, and she didn't quite know why.

"I haven't been affiliated with the Rovers in more than a decade," she said. "I told you. I don't join things."

He frowned just a little.

"Why is it important?" she asked.

"You went to Krell."

She felt the blood drain from her face. "How did you know that?"

"How do you think I found you?" he asked. "I tracked that lifeship and figured out you'd rented a terrible little ship on Oyal. I waited and examined the logs. You took it to Krell."

She wanted to hit her palm against her forehead. She had been so mesmerized by him that she hadn't asked how he found her. And if truth be told, she just figured he was good enough to track her. She no longer doubted that.

"So?" she asked, knowing that was a lame response.

"The Rovers sometimes use Krell as their base," he said.

She made a face. "*Everyone* in this part of the sector uses Krell as a base, particularly if they are a bit on the shady side. I'll bet you've used Krell."

The expression that flashed through his eyes confirmed that. Still, he didn't let up.

"But you've been part of their organization," he said.

"I'm not denying that," she said. "I told you: I don't join things. Where do you think I learned that I don't fit into an organization, even one that refuses to call itself an organization?"

He kept looking at her, as if he was trying to see through her. "You knew they're trying to destroy the Guild," he said.

The surprise made her take a step back. When she had been a Rover, they were just unaffiliated assassins, trying to help each other out. "What? No, I didn't know that."

"I want to believe you," Misha said, "but you see how hard it is? You were part of their group. They target Guild members. You targeted me."

"I did not," she said.

"Except on the ship," he said. "You left me to take the blame for Testrial."

Her eyes stung. She blinked hard. "When I found out who you were."

He looked at her intently, as if he was trying to see through her. "Tell me why I should trust you."

She shook her head. "I don't play games like that."

The statement made him wince as if she had said something that reminded him of something else.

"Games," he muttered, then frowned. And nodded once. "When did you get this?"

"Get what?" she asked, trying to follow the logic of the conversation. Half of it was taking place in his head.

"The information about Kerani," he said.

Ah, that made sense. He was trying to figure out a timeline. "Yesterday, just before you arrived," she said.

"So you haven't had time to research it," he said. Like that was important.

Maybe it was.

"I was going to research it after I had lunch," she said.

"Lunch." He smiled for the first time. His mood suddenly seemed lighter. "We need to eat."

"Yes," she said a bit stiffly. "We do."

He took three more steps toward her. It took all of her strength to hold her ground. He reached for her, slipped his hand along the side of her face, and kissed her.

Not a simple kiss, not a touch. But one of those kisses that made her hot all over. She wanted to lean into him, but she didn't. She wanted to melt into the kiss, lose herself in him like she had done the day before, but she held onto herself so tightly that she barely moved.

Although she kissed him back.

She couldn't stop herself from kissing him back.

He leaned back, and looked at her, his eyes that deep blue again. He ran a thumb along her face. "Let's work on this together."

"You think I'm with the Rovers," she said. "You think I'm targeting your precious Guild."

He shook his head just a little. "I think something strange is going on," he said. "I think you and I are both part of it, but not willingly."

She thought about Jack's strange expression, about the way he had spoken about the Rovers. There weren't many unaffiliated assassins anymore. Just her and a few others.

She had gotten out of the Rovers because they had started talking about rules. And dues. And organizing.

She hated organizations.

Her heartbeat had increased. She was probably flushed.

"What exactly do you want to work on?" she asked. "You don't want to target this woman, do you?"

"Of course not," he said. He let his hand drop. Then he tilted his head slightly. "You don't take every job you get, do you?"

"No," she said, a little offended that he would even think so.

"You research them first, right?"

"Yes," she said, feeling even more offended.

"So let's research who wants to hire you. There's got to be a reason behind this," Misha said.

She shrugged. "The mission seems easy to me. Someone wants to bring down the Guild."

He shook his head. "It's not that simple. Our last director was murdered. The Guild survived."

"You think this might be personal?" Rikki asked.

"I don't know what to think," Misha said. "Except that I think you and I can help each other, and we should."

It was a risk. It was a big risk. She was trusting him, and she hadn't trusted anyone in her life except Jack. And even then, she hadn't trusted Jack with everything.

"All right," she said after a minute. "But lunch first."

"And groceries," he said with a bit of grin. "How do you feel about working naked?"

"I have a hunch we'd get nothing done," she said.

"I think we'd get a lot done," he said. "But probably no work."

"No *probably* about it," she said and kissed him. Quickly. Without touching anything but his lips.

It wasn't like she had anything to steal. Not for someone from the Guild, anyway. Her risk had less to do with work than it did with her life. And he had had opportunities to hurt her, kill her, ruin her.

He hadn't taken them.

It was a risk, partnering with him on this.

But it was only a risk to her heart.

Chapter 42

THEY WORKED IN HER OFFICE, BECAUSE SHE HAD PROtected, encoded networks inside. He sprawled on her love seat as if it had been made for him. She sat in her usual spot, legs out. He had brought some of his own equipment from that hidey-hole he'd found two and a half blocks away.

She had gone up to that apartment with him, and wrinkled her nose at the smell. She had stayed in places like that on a job, but she hadn't enjoyed it.

She helped him carry most of his equipment back to her place, and what few changes of clothing he had brought.

She didn't exactly feel better about her choice to trust him—in fact, her heart fluttered every time she thought about it. But she wasn't sure if her heart fluttered because he was nearby or because she had decided to trust him or because she was worried about what might happen between them.

He had put his clothes in her closet, which felt odd. And he had put the groceries away in her kitchen, which felt even odder.

He had as many individual tablets as she did, plus some linked network devices, plus a few things she didn't recognize. She had shown him the other four tablets she had with information about targets. Misha said he didn't recognize those people. She wasn't sure she believed him, but she did think that those people weren't a priority.

She would work on them when this job—and that was how she was thinking of the Guild case—was done.

She piled the other tablets onto the side counter, and worked on two—the one with the image of the Guild's director, whose name was Kerani Ammons, and the other an unlinked device that she used to back-trace the contact.

The information Rikki had on Ammons included a false name—one Ammons had apparently used back when she was in the field—and some old information on Ammons's whereabouts. Misha hoped the information would show that this hit request was because of something Ammons had done in the past, not because of who she was now.

But the client trace was proving difficult. Rikki usually refused cases where she couldn't verify the client. A quick verification made the client seem legitimate, but no good assassin did a quick verification.

All of this made her nervous.

"I'm not finding much," she said.

Misha was lying on his stomach, three of the tablets on front of him. "What would you usually do in a case like this?" he asked.

"I'd turn it down," she said. "I need more client information."

"You wouldn't ask for that?"

"No," she said. "I'm not that hard up for work."

"And if you were?"

She looked at him. His hair was tousled like it had been the day before, his eyes a soft blue. His eyes fascinated her. They changed color with his moods. She had no idea there were so many shades of blue before.

"I'd still turn it down," she said. "The client seems dicey."

"You wouldn't hire a detective?"

She shook her head.

"Search more on your own?"

"No," she said. "That's all work with no pay. I don't work for free."

He nodded, then leaned back, as if considering her words. "I don't want to lose this commission. It's a lead to something I don't understand and letting go of it means someone else will do the job. Or will at least try the job."

Rikki shrugged. "Sometimes the client returns."

"That's a big risk," he said.

She nodded. "But we might have enough to trace the client with what we have here."

"I'm not much of a detective," Misha said.

She tucked her legs against his side, liking his warmth. "What do you do then, give it to some Guild investigator?"

"We do have divisions for everything," Misha said.

"Hmm," she said. "I could trace him, given time."

"And if you don't have time," Misha asked, "do you hire a detective?"

She thought about Jack. Then frowned just a little. He was still working for her on Misha.

"Not so much anymore," she said.

"But you used to?" Misha asked.

That was the first question he'd asked that made her uncomfortable. "Is it important?" she asked.

"I don't know." Misha wasn't looking at her. He was

looking at the information tablet in front of him. "I'm still not sure why you got this job."

"Which is another reason I'd turn it down." She ran a hand over his back, then let her fingers linger near his buttocks. She touched them lightly.

He rolled over, caught her hand, and kissed it. "Work, remember?"

"Hmm," she said, not really committing to anything.

He hadn't let go of her hand. She could sense his indecisiveness. He clearly wanted to throw the work aside as much as she did, but they both knew the quicker they finished, the more chance they had of tracking down the client.

"You know," she said, her voice slightly husky. "It would be better if I said no."

"To me?" Misha asked, then kissed her palm again.

She shook her head, suddenly not trusting her voice. She cleared her throat, and said, "No to the client. I'm wondering if this is some kind of test to see if I'll violate my own rules. I think it might be some kind of red flag if I do. There's enough here for you to notify your director and let your own people track this down."

He stared at her for a long moment. "I suppose. I don't like it though. I'd have to report back at the Guild. I can't just send this information through the networks."

"Let's just see what happens when I refuse the job," she said.

She sent a message back to the potential client, saying she did not feel this job was right for her.

"That's it?" Misha asked. "No explanation?"

"If they want an explanation, they'll ask," she said.

He pulled her close. She could feel his hardness against her stomach.

"And what if I want an explanation?" he asked.

"How about a demonstration instead?" she asked, taking her hand back so she could use it elsewhere.

"Oh, in that case," he said, his voice just a little strangled, his eyes turning that marvelous blue, "a demonstration will have to do."

Chapter 43

RIKKI SLEPT BESIDE HIM IN THAT BIG BED. SHE WAS beautiful, absolutely beautiful. And it broke his heart.

Misha hadn't even really realized he had one, not until he met Rikki. She made him feel more than anyone ever had—at least anyone in his memory. And the emotions were stronger than any he had ever felt, the anger more potent, the desire so powerful that at times he thought it was going to rip him apart.

He wasn't sure he ever wanted to be without her.

And this choice she'd made, the decision to let that client go, meant that he would have to leave her.

He ran a hand through his hair. His hands smelled of her. The faint scent aroused him all over again, but he was going to let her sleep. He needed to think.

He had to let the Guild know about the threat, and he couldn't bring her along. He would have to travel alone. At best, he could leave her in Prospera while he went to Guild headquarters, but even that might be too close.

He still didn't know how much he should trust her, even though he wanted to.

Trust wasn't something he was used to.

Maybe he should let the Guild know and then resign. He could quit the Guild, quit the business, and spend the rest of his life with Rikki. He had money set aside. She implied that she did as well.

She certainly owned a lot of property all over the sector. That was a sign of some kind of financial independence.

But if he wasn't with the Guild, if he didn't work, who was he? And what would she think of him?

He pulled the covers down just slightly so he could look at her body, her firm breasts, her powerful muscles, those legs that could hold him in place with just the strength of her thighs. He still didn't touch her, even though he wanted to. Even though he was ready to take her all over again.

It surprised him that he cared about her good opinion. He had never worried about anyone outside of the Guild before. He hadn't trusted anyone outside the Guild before.

Not that he trusted her.

But he almost did.

Finally, he couldn't wait any longer. He ran a hand down her side, then cupped her breast, lifting it to his mouth. He sucked on her nipple and she moaned, arching toward him. He slid the other hand between her legs. She was already wet.

He spread her legs gently, then slipped between them, going slowly. She moaned again, and moved with him, still not awake. He held her breasts, let her move, enjoying the friction, the dampness, the heat.

She came and that woke her up, her eyes fluttering open, her mouth falling back.

"I thought I was dreaming," she murmured.

"No dream," he said and continued the gentle movement. She came again, and he couldn't hold back his own orgasm. He had to move with her, thrust hard, and she shifted beneath him, taking him, controlling his thrusts, those legs he had fantasized about a moment before wrapped around him.

He cried out, surprising himself. He never lost that kind of control. And then he collapsed on her, his face pillowed against her breasts.

"Wow," she said. "I could do this forever."

"Me, too," he said. Then smiled at himself. "That was a lie, you know."

Her hand was in his hair. "I know. We'd need occasional rest periods."

He raised his head to kiss her, when something pinged.

"What's that?" he asked.

"I have a flag on certain incoming messages," she said, "particularly if they're ones I've been waiting for."

"Like our client?" he asked, then wondered if he should have used the word "our."

She didn't seem to notice.

"Yeah," she said. She shifted so she could open the drawer in the table beside the bed. That slight movement made desire flare through him. But for once, she didn't seem to notice.

"Something important?"

She was frowning. "Yeah. I need to deal with this."

"The client?"

She slipped out from underneath him. "No," she said. "It's Jack."

Chapter 44

RIKKI TAPPED A CODE ONTO THE TABLET SO THAT JACK would know she wasn't quite in a position to talk. Then she got out of bed, and carried the tablet with her, even though she wasn't going to use it to talk with Jack.

She didn't want Misha to look at it too closely.

Apparently she didn't trust him as much as she thought she did.

She grabbed a robe as she walked past the closet. Then she ran a hand through her hair. She stopped in the kitchen and got the device that Jack had given her long ago, something he called a "communicator for the assassinator." Or CFA for short.

It only connected the two of them, and was very hard to hack into.

She pressed the start button, but kept the visual to her face. She didn't want him to know exactly what she had been doing.

"Hey," she said. "I didn't think I'd hear from you so soon."

"It's been ten days, Rik," he said, his voice chiding. "Where are you?"

"Moving to my office," she said as she padded barefoot down the hall. Her clothes were strewn along the floor, mixing with Misha's clothing. She smiled at the memory.

"You sound odd," Jack said.

"It's been an eventful week." She stepped inside the office and pulled the door closed.

She wanted to be alone to hear this, whatever this was. She was almost afraid of what Jack would tell her.

Forget the qualifier. She *was* afraid. She was afraid he'd tell her that everything bad she suspected about Misha was true.

"Good thing you didn't run this down," Jack said.

"About Mikael Yurinovich Orlinski?" she asked.

"Yeah," he said. "Where *are* you? Are we going to do audio only?"

It was probably best, but it would be weird. She put the CFA into its little holder, and suddenly Jack appeared on her countertop—a small well-dressed version of Jack.

"What the hell?" he asked. "A robe? Isn't it the middle of the day where you are?"

"How do you know where I am?" she asked.

"You said your office. And you only have three, right?"

She smiled at him. "I'm not telling."

"It looks like there's a lot you're not telling me," Jack said. "You've got love bites on your neck."

Her hand flew to her throat.

He laughed. "Got ya."

She rolled her eyes. "Jeez, Jack. What are you, twelve?"

"If you recall, at twelve I had no idea what a love bite was."

She smiled in spite of herself. She remembered explaining some of the more interesting aspects of sex to him around that time. He hadn't believed her, until she showed him some holograms that would have gotten them kicked out of the government care facility if they had been caught.

"I hope he's good," Jack said.

"He was this afternoon," she said, wondering if Jack knew that the "he" in question was Misha.

"Okay," Jack said, "we're moving into the realm of too much information."

She grinned, then turned the conversation back to the reason he called. "You said it was a good thing that you looked into this, not me. Why?"

She wanted to sound tough, but she couldn't quite manage it. She needed to know, and she knew Jack would figure that out.

"Oh, Rik," he said. "I found all the reports. Police, base security, fire, medical personal, legal."

She was holding her breath. She made herself exhale. "Bad?"

Misha had been there to kill her father after all. He had lied to her. She sat down. She wasn't sure she wanted to know this now. She wanted to pretend everything was all right.

"The reports were, yeah," Jack said. "It's amazing you survived."

"I was in the hospital for a long time," she said.

"Weeks," he said. "And not from the fire like we thought. You were beaten within an inch of your life. If Mikael and his mother hadn't killed your father, Rik, you probably wouldn't have lived much longer. You were nearly dead. That's why you were in the hospital for so long. It took forever to fix you."

She closed her eyes. That was what Misha had said.

"Rik?" Jack sounded panicked.

She nodded, then made herself open her eyes. "What else?"

"This Mikael, he saved your life, Rik," Jack said. "Every account mentions that he got you out of that house, and his mother's testimony showed he had nothing to do with the death of your father. Which is too bad, really, because if I had run across your goddamn father, he would be dead too."

She was shaking, but she managed to find her voice. "You were a scrawny eleven-year-old."

Jack's features darkened. "You know what I mean."

He clearly wasn't up for the banter.

"Yeah," she said, feeling awkward. "I do."

"Look," Jack said. "So far as I can tell, this guy came after you not knowing who you were initially. He was protecting his turf. These Guild guys do that."

Misha hadn't lied to her. She was feeling giddy. He hadn't lied.

"He's like—some kind of straight arrow, for an assassin anyway. Everything he does is on the record, and by the book, and he doesn't seem to make a mistake. He had some years where he wandered and there's not as big a record about those, but then he came back to the Guild, and when he did, he's been influential in it. At least as far as I can tell. They're pretty secretive about the Guild stuff itself. But the legal stuff, the assassin stuff, he's damn near perfect."

She let out a small sigh. She hadn't expected that.

"But you really don't care now, do you?" Jack asked with a grin. "You got him out of your system?"

Only if you counted the fact that he wasn't inside her at the moment. But she didn't say that to her oldest friend. Some things were too personal even for people as close as they were.

"Not exactly," she said.

"He's not there, is he?" Jack asked.

She shrugged. "Not in the office."

"You didn't wait to hear from me?" Jack sounded offended.

"It's complicated," she said.

"It's not like you," Jack said.

"I know," she said. She almost added *I can't help myself*, but that sounded wrong, like she was under some kind of spell. Which was probably true in a way.

"You know, Rik," he said, "he seems legit, but I have the sudden urge to kick his ass."

"Jealous?" she asked.

"Hell, no." Then he made a face. "You know what I mean. It's just that he better treat you right. A man has to protect his family and you're all I got."

She smiled at him fondly. "I know. I promise I'll be careful."

"You better." He moved like he was about to sign off.

"Jack," she said. "One more question."

"Yeah?"

"You hear any rumblings about the Guild? About someone trying to bring it down?"

Jack looked odd for the first time since he contacted her. It was that same expression he'd had on Krell when she asked him about the Rovers.

"Did he get you into something?" Jack asked.

"No," she said. "It's just—I can't talk with you about it over any kind of net. But I was thinking, you know, with the Rovers—"

"I have nothing to do with them," Jack said curtly. "I have to go, Rik."

"Thanks," she said, but he had already severed the link.

That was strange. The same kind of response he had given her the last time she mentioned the Rovers. And it made him uncomfortable to discuss them on a link.

She sighed. She wanted to thank him. She wanted to pick his brain about this client. She wanted to let him know more about Misha.

But Jack clearly had issues of his own.

She picked up the CFA and stuck it into one of the more secure cabinets inside the office. Then she gathered up what few clothes they had scattered in here, and opened the door.

The air had been slightly stuffy. The other clothes were still strewn along the hallway, so Misha hadn't come out of the bedroom.

That was good, because an odd sense of joy coursed through her. He was who he said he was. He hadn't lied. He was a straight arrow, for an assassin. Exactly what he said he was.

She needed to apologize to him for failing to trust him. She needed to show him how sorry she was.

With every tool at her disposal.

Right now.

As creatively as she possibly could.

Chapter 45

JACK? SHE HAD NEVER MENTIONED SOMEONE NAMED JACK.

Misha remained alone in the big bed. He moved off the wet spot, out of the warmth made by their two bodies. He could hear her voice speaking softly as she moved down the hallway.

She didn't want him to hear a conversation with someone named Jack. And that made Misha feel odd.

He felt... jealous?

He had never been jealous before. Maybe it wasn't jealous. Maybe it was... proprietary. No. That was too close to jealous. But jealous was one of those dark emotions that got a man into trouble. Jealous made people act recklessly, kill recklessly. Jealous made people make fools of themselves.

He got out of bed and found some clothes. He wasn't going to listen in on the conversation. He had promised himself he would trust her.

But the temptation was great.

He really wanted to know who this Jack was.

Of course, Misha had to remind himself, he didn't know anything about her personal life. He knew how much money she had in certain accounts, he had found most of her property (he thought), and he knew how she made her living. But he had no idea who her friends were, if she even had any friends, and he had no idea how many lovers she'd had (clearly she'd had a few) and how many times she'd been married, if she had ever been.

Or even if she was married now.

He felt a chill despite his clothes. He was barefoot. He wanted to track down his boots, but they were in her comfortable office, and he suspected that was where she was talking to this Jack.

Whom Misha was determined not to be jealous of.

What an interesting emotion. It made him feel a little out of control and crazy, rather like he felt around Rikki herself.

Then Rikki slipped in the bedroom door. Her entire face was lit up, as if something had ignited inside her. Misha had never seen that expression before, he had never seen her look so... happy.

And she did. She looked ecstatic.

After talking with a man named Jack.

Whom she didn't want Misha to know anything about.

She grinned, then tweaked the collar of his shirt. "You're dressed."

"Not quite." He sounded surly. He felt surly.

"Well, I'm not," she said and untied her robe. She started to shake it off, but he caught her, put the robe back on her shoulders, and tied it shut.

Tight.

He didn't want to be distracted.

"Who is Jack?" he asked.

She raised her eyebrows, and then her grin got wider. "You're jealous."

"I am not," he said. "I just want to know who Jack is."

"You are actually jealous," she said with a laugh in her voice. "Wow."

"I am not jealous," he said, his voice flat. She was making him angry. "I don't believe in jealousy."

"A man who kills for a living who doesn't believe in jealousy. What happens, does the Guild screen all your potential hires? Half of my requests are because of some jealous lover somewhere."

"And you see that as a sign of love?" Misha asked, crossing his arms.

Her eyes were twinkling. There was no reason for her eyes to twinkle. No reason at all.

"No," she said. "It's not love. But it does mean you care."

He almost denied it. Then he stopped himself. He did care. That was part of the problem. He cared too much.

"I'm going to get us food," he said.

She put a hand on his arm, stopping him. The smile was gone from her face, although she still looked too happy for his tastes.

"I grew up with Jack," she said.

"You didn't have siblings," Misha said.

Her lips twisted just a little, as if she was holding back a smile. "I didn't. And it's amazing you know that."

"Mother and I had to learn everything about you and your father," he said primly. God, he sounded like a tight-assed little prick. He wanted to shake the mood, pretend he didn't care, but he did.

He did.

"And," she said, her entire expression serious now, "I met Jack after."

Misha's gaze met hers.

"He was younger than me. I used to beat up anyone who beat him up, not that you'd believe it if you saw him now."

Misha waited. Someone she had loved her entire adult life then. Someone called Jack.

"We're family, Jack and me," she said softly. "We're all we've ever had. And we're not lovers."

Misha's heart rose as she said that. He didn't want it to, but it did. He was relieved to hear it, even though he kept his expression calm. (He hoped he kept his expression calm.)

"I didn't say you were lovers," he said.

"But you thought it." Her grin had returned. "And it made you jealous."

He took a deep breath. He was going to ignore the jealousy thing. "It made me realize how little I know about you."

"You know all about me," she said.

He shook his head. "I don't know if you're in a relationship, I don't know if you've had children, I don't know who you associate with or what you're doing with your life, what your hopes and dreams are, whether or not you're happy with your work or if you feel you're not qualified for anything else…"

He made himself stop talking. His face flushed. He had revealed too much of himself already. And maybe he was jealous. Someone had spent years with her, years he could have spent with her.

What would their lives have been like if he had stayed with her in the hospital and refused to go with his mother, refused to go back to the Guild? Who would he have been then?

She was watching his face as if it told her something important.

"To answer your questions," she said softly, "I've

never been in a committed relationship. I don't have children, which I thought you would have figured out given how intimately you know part of me."

"Women do repair work now," he said.

She nodded. "Some women," she said. "I wouldn't be one of them. If I thought I was suited to having children. Which I am not. Children and this profession do not mix."

How well he knew that. His mother had no idea what to do with him once she became his guardian. She tried. He had to give her that. She did her very best. But she was cold, shut off, and not that interested in raising a child, particularly a boy who was angry and frightened and more than a little out of control.

"Let's see," Rikki said. "Your other questions. Mostly, I keep my own company. I have some friends, but not close ones, except Jack, who is, as I explained, family. Hopes? Dreams? They're for other people. And I like my work. Not all parts of it. But I feel like I'm doing something important, when I have the right target, someone who needs to go away forever. I'm rather passionate about the work, which takes most of my focus, even if I only take a few jobs per year."

He studied her face. She sounded like him. She sounded just like him.

"I don't know your hopes and dreams either, or if you even like the family business," Rikki said. "I know less about you than you do about me."

He shook his head. "No, you don't. You know my history."

"But not your present," she said.

He nodded once, took her hand, and cupped it in his.

"One serious relationship when I was too young to know better. It ended badly a decade ago. No children. I don't want them. If I tried to raise them, I'd be worse at it than my mother. And as hard as she tried, she sucked at parenting."

Rikki's gaze held his. The look of fascination in her dark eyes was mesmerizing.

"Hopes, dreams," he said, "I don't believe in them."

"Like you don't believe in jealousy?" she asked.

He shrugged. "But I love my work. And I love the Guild. It's my home, and my family. And I'm offended that it's being threatened."

"Only your leader is being threatened."

"If your Jack was being threatened, wouldn't you see that as a threat against you too?"

She frowned just a little as she considered this.

"Yes," she said simply, and in that moment, he knew just how deadly she could be. He could tell, just from the tone, that if someone harmed her good friend, she would hunt that person down and kill him brutally, with no remorse.

"So," he said. "That's me. That's all I am."

"And so much more," she said and leaned into him. "Except every time I come across you, you're wearing clothes."

She unbuttoned his shirt and slid it off his shoulders. Then she untied her robe. It fell open. She undid his pants, slowly, and took his already hard penis in her hand.

"You're not going anywhere," she said, "except with me."

Then she used his penis as if it were a leash, and led him back to bed.

"You make me crazy," he said softly as he took off his pants. Her hand still held him. She lay back, spread her legs, and pulled him—gently—inside her.

Then she grinned at him. "You make me crazy too," she said and proceeded to prove just how crazy she could get.

Chapter 46

MISHA WAS IN THE SHOWER WHEN THE NEXT PING occurred. Rikki was putting the finishing touches on lunch. She looked at a nearby tablet, thinking Jack was contacting her again. The conversation had ended badly, and he probably wanted to touch base.

But it wasn't Jack. The contact came from the client. She picked up the tablet and leaned on the counter, looking at the information the client had sent.

The information made her stomach turn—and would have, even if she hadn't known who the target was. On her own, without knowledge, Rikki would have turned this case down.

The client was too eager.

And she knew that because of only one thing:

The client didn't ask her why she had turned down the job. The client had presumed to know the reason. And the client had offered her five times the original fee.

She sighed. Jobs she had taken in the past that offered more than the original fee—without prompting by her—always caused trouble. And more than once would have gotten her in trouble with the laws of the various places she worked, if she hadn't been more cautious than usual with those jobs.

Her fingers itched. She wanted to turn this thing down.

But she set down the tablet and waited for Misha. Even though she knew what he was going to say. He was going to tell her to take the job so that they could track the client.

She set the tablet down. The question was one of ethics. Hers. Did she take a contract she had no intention of fulfilling? Did she help the Guild when she wasn't even sure if Misha was telling her the truth about this potential target?

But when had he lied to her? He hadn't. He hadn't been lying to her at all. Damn. This trust thing was hard. No. It was nearly impossible. She had never done it before and she didn't know how to do it now.

She turned back to the food prep. She had made a fruit salad and taken some of the freshly baked bread that one of the robots had brought back from the market. She carried plates into the dining room, and then brought in some iced tea.

By then, she heard the shower shut off.

She wished that ping had never come back. Because this would be a test of this fledgling relationship. She didn't want to hand control of her business over to anyone and yet if she went through with finding this client, she would lose control, at least in the short term.

Not that she needed another job. She had turned two of the others down as well, and told the other two to contact her again in six months if they hadn't found someone else to do the job. None of those jobs had looked interesting, and the two she had turned down had been—irony of ironies—jealousy-based relationship assassinations, something she always stayed far away from.

"You look thoughtful," Misha said.

She turned. He was standing in the doorway behind her. He was barefoot and his hair was still damp. He wore loose trousers and an open shirt. The unfinished look made him seem much younger, and very vulnerable.

"The client came back," she said.

"That was fast," he said. "Did he want to know why you had turned the job down?"

She shook her head. "He offered five times the original fee."

Misha straightened just a little. But that movement was enough to add years and professionalism to him. He no longer seemed young and vulnerable. Now he looked like a man no one ever messed with, a man no one got near when he got angry.

"How do you read that?" he asked in a tone that told her he already had an answer to his own question.

"If I were on my own, I wouldn't take the job," she said.

His eyes became steely. "Did you turn it down?"

"No," she said. "I didn't respond at all."

"Good," he said. "How long do you think you can string the client along?"

"Not long," she said. "It took him less than twenty-four hours to get back to me."

Misha nodded. He hadn't moved from his spot near the door. She was beginning to understand him. He kept his distance when they talked business so he could maintain his concentration.

He was as distracted by her as she was by him.

"You know what I'm going to ask, don't you?" he said.

Two days ago, she would have thought his tone cold. But it wasn't. It was cautious, as devoid of his personality as he could make it.

And she actually appreciated the professionalism. She wanted to keep the distance too right now.

(Actually, she wanted to strip off his clothes, and take him back to bed. But she forced that thought out of her mind. They could only make love so much. Right?)

"Rikki?" he asked.

She blinked, realizing that despite her best intentions, she was thinking about how she loved to run her hand along the muscles in his back, and made herself focus.

"You're going to ask me to take the job," she said, keeping her tone neutral as well.

"I don't want to interfere in your business," he said. "But this is important to the Guild."

"I thought we established that I don't care about the Guild," she said.

He nodded once. Then sighed. "All right," he said after a moment. "It's important to me."

She knew that. And this was where things got dicey for her. She had never made a choice like this. She had never been faced with one before.

In the past, she would have done what was best for her business and nothing more. She would have walked away from Misha, and forgotten all about him.

As if he was a man she could forget. He wasn't. Nor could she easily walk away.

But he was asking her to take a job she didn't plan to do. Asking her to risk her reputation for a cause she didn't believe in.

He was asking for her help because of their relationship.

Her gaze met his.

"I'd have you tell the client that I'll be doing the job, but if he checks on me, he'll see that I'm part of the Guild," Misha said. "I don't know any other way to do this."

"We could hand this over to your investigators and let them track him down," she said.

Misha shook his head. "Like I said, I'd have to take it to them in person. By then, he'll have hired someone else."

She sighed. He was right. And she didn't like it.

But what did it matter, really? This was a client she would never ever work for again—if this constituted working for him now. And the fact that she broke the contract—well, if she put the money in some kind of escrow, she could buy her way out of it.

No one expected rogue assassins to be ethical.

Except certain rogue assassins.

Like herself.

"How about this," she said. "How about I accept the job, and then I travel to the Guild."

He froze, as if she had just suggested she attack the Guild's director. This would be his test. She was having to trust him. In return, he needed to trust her.

"You and I together bring this information to the Guild," she said.

He was watching her warily. "Why?"

"Because it's my experience that clients like this one watch. They monitor to see when and how the job gets done. And if they have a lot of money, they might hire one or two or even three other people to do the same work, figuring that one of them will complete the job and the others are just the cost of doing business."

Misha rubbed a hand over his mouth. She caught the look of recognition in his eyes. He had had jobs like this as well.

"God," he said. "This is a risk."

"For me or you?" The question came out sharper than she intended.

He looked up at her. "For both of us."

She felt a fury building. She made herself breathe so that it wouldn't come out.

"I know what I'm risking," she said. "I'm risking my reputation by taking a job I never plan to do. But what are you risking? You already asked me to join the Guild, remember? Or is that out the window now that you know I've been contacted to kill your director?"

"It was out the window the minute you said you weren't interested in joining the Guild," he said. "We don't have visitors in the Guild. Only potential members."

She shrugged a shoulder. "So lie."

"I don't lie to the Guild," he said.

"Wow," she muttered. "You are a straight arrow."

"What?" Misha asked.

She shook her head. She wasn't going to explain that. "We have a stalemate. I'm not taking the job unless I can go with you to the Guild. No one will know what happens inside. Assassins get thwarted all the time. I keep my reputation, you give everyone the proper information, and we all win. Except the client, of course."

He was silent. That little frown he got when he was thinking had returned.

"You don't trust me, do you?" she said. She wasn't angry, exactly. She was disappointed. "Or rather, you do trust me. You believe I'll finish a job that I take on, no matter what the cost."

He looked at her. She could see the truth of her words in his gaze.

"It's your choice," she said and walked out of the room.

Chapter 47

HE STOOD IN THE DOORWAY TO THE CORRIDOR, FEELING awkward. She had gone through the kitchen door so she didn't have to pass him.

Two plates sat on the table, a beautiful fruit salad glistening between them. Two glasses of iced tea sweated on their coasters, the ice starting to melt.

It could have been a nice meal. It should have been a nice meal.

If they had been any other couple.

She was right: he didn't trust her. Not entirely.

And if he was wrong about her, he would be leading Kerani's killer right into the Guild, making the assassination easy. Particularly since Kerani wanted to meet all new prospects.

Rikki wouldn't have weapons, but she was good with her bare hands. He had seen that with Testrial. She had killed him in a matter of seconds.

It was safer not to trust her.

It was safer to go alone.

Except…

She was right about the client. Impatient rich clients often hired several people to do the same job. And in this case, that meant that others—maybe even someone inside the Guild—might try to kill Kerani.

He was going to lose precious time without Rikki.

But with Rikki…

Well, her presence might stall the impatient client, make him think that she was doing the job he had hired her for. A really smart client would have others as backup, so that they didn't interfere with each other's work.

Misha closed his eyes, then steeled himself. He had to apologize. He needed Rikki to do this job.

Besides, he didn't want to leave her. Not because he didn't trust her, but because he didn't like being away from her. He had hated being apart earlier, when she had betrayed him to the security officer.

He would hate it worse now.

Rather than getting Rikki out of his system, all of this time, all of this lovemaking, had embedded her firmly within him, making it seem like he couldn't be without her.

He opened his eyes. The ice was nearly melted now. The tea looked watery. He ran a hand through his hair, which was only slightly damp now, and he pivoted, stepping out of the room.

He found Rikki in her office, and thought it a good sign that she hadn't closed the door.

"I'm sorry," he said. "You're right. You have to go to the Guild, and you're right, that makes me uncomfortable. You're wrong about one thing, though."

She had her legs tucked under her as she sat on that love seat. She put her arm on the back of the love seat, pretending a relaxation that the tautness in her muscles belied.

"What would that be?" she asked coldly.

"It's still your choice." He held up a hand so that she didn't interrupt. "I know that on your own, you wouldn't take this job. But that's not the choice. The choice is between helping me and by extension, helping a woman you never met, or simply doing nothing. Not helping at all."

Rikki's expression seemed serene. He couldn't keep his gaze on her face. He watched those muscles, so tight, the only thing that gave an indication of how tense she actually was.

"And if I don't take the job?" she asked. "Then what?"

He shrugged. "Whatever you were planning to do."

"You would go to the Guild."

He nodded.

"Alone."

He nodded again. What could he say? "We could try to get as much information as possible here."

"We have nothing new."

For the first time, he noted another tablet beside her. So she had been checking on the client, trying to see if he had given more hints to his identity or whereabouts.

"The only way to get something new," she said, "is to start a money trail. And the only way to do that is to take the job."

Misha stared at her. He wasn't going to push her. He wanted her beside him. He wanted her to help him. Hell, he wanted her to have the exact same priorities he did, all the damn time, because he wanted to be with her.

But she didn't. Her refusal to be part of the Guild proved that.

"If I do this," she said, "you have to trust me. You have to let me into the Guild."

"Even if you decide not to join?" he asked.

"Even then," she said.

Such a risk. He would be betraying the Guild by bringing her in. But he might be betraying the Guild even more by refusing to act quickly on this threat to Kerani.

"All right," he said.

"All right?" she said, sounding surprised.

"All right," he said again. "We'll do it your way."

Until they got to the Guild. And then, whether she liked it or not, he would be in charge.

He would have to be.

Or Rikki might not get out alive.

PART 4

Chapter 48

THEY TRAVELED BACK TO PROSPERA ON THE MARIPOSA Starlines, only this time, Rikki got to be the wealthy traveler and Misha was her boy toy. They spent a lot of time in their expensive suite, and when they weren't doing what a wealthy woman and her boy toy usually did, they were trying to find out as much as they could about the client.

Rikki had never done most of her research naked before. She and Misha would make love, do a little work, and then venture onto the ship itself. She had bought a new wardrobe specifically for this—a lot of dresses, loose clothing, and expensive jewelry. She also wore some spectacular gowns, since she and Misha went to the ballroom almost every night.

They couldn't keep their hands off each other, and they didn't need to. She wanted the client to think she was using a man as cover. She even insisted that Misha not work that hard at hiding his identity. It gave her trip even more credence if she was seducing a member of the Assassins Guild.

And he willingly complied.

What little research they could do didn't yield much. Shortly after Rikki agreed to the contract, half the fee got deposited into the account she indicated. She couldn't track the money, which was unusual. She lost its trail in a different account each time she tried.

She finally decided that she had made enough attempts: any more and she would look really suspicious to the client, whose name she still didn't know. No matter how she tried to track him down, she couldn't find much.

But, like Misha, she wasn't an expert in investigation. They would leave the discovery to the Guild investigators. Instead, she "researched" the target.

The cover story that the client had set up for the target was surprisingly thin. She had to work hard not to puncture through it. She wasn't sure if she was supposed to.

Most of the deaths that the client had flagged as egregious had thin covers as well. They were usually people connected with the Rovers, which led Rikki to believe that her client was as well.

He had probably gotten her name through the Rovers or seen her work when she was with them.

This confirmed what Misha had said about the Rovers targeting the Guild. What better thing to do than put the Guild in disarray by killing its leader? Misha had said that the Guild had survived such a killing before, but Rikki suspected it had caused turmoil. And sometimes turmoil was all an outsider needed to gain access and control.

Maybe this plan was why Jack was so disgusted with the Rovers. But wouldn't he tell her if he knew? Although he didn't realize how deeply she was involved with Misha, so maybe Jack wouldn't have said a word.

She wondered what he'd think of her at the moment. Would he wonder if, indeed, she was working for the Rovers and didn't quite realize it? She wondered if she was. She wished she could check with Jack, but she had promised Misha that she would let his people handle the investigation once they delivered the information to the Guild.

The trip had gotten a bit strange, however. Even when she didn't think about the surreal part of actually living her cover.

She and Misha were in the ballroom, dancing a waltz, just like they had on their very first trip. So much was similar: apparently the ballrooms on the newer ships were exact replicas of each other. The huge room, the black and white and silver decor, the live orchestra.

Misha had protested the dancing at first, saying he didn't enjoy it. But she wanted them to be seen, and she figured that dancing was as good a way—if not a better way—than eating in all the various restaurants or frequenting the casino.

If she hadn't been attracted to Misha, she would have suggested the other venues, like she had with Testrial. The less she had to touch Testrial, the better off she had been.

But she loved touching Misha, and she loved dancing with him, particularly when he was dressed so perfectly. She had ostentatiously bought his clothes for him, having the ship's tailor make him several formal suits, all with long coats that went to his knees, flaring pants, and tight-fitting shirts with buttons that began in the middle of his chest.

If she was going to pay for a boy-toy's wardrobe, then he was going to look like a boy-toy, no matter how much it embarrassed him.

And she delighted in embarrassing him, sliding her hand down to his ass during the waltz, kissing him so passionately at the end of a tango that she almost took him beneath the stairs and had her way with him, climbing in his lap when they sat at a table, ostensibly to rest.

There wasn't a lot of rest when they were together, and usually she enjoyed that. But this night, in the middle of the waltz, Misha had suddenly become a distraction.

Because Rikki noticed something.

"See him?" she asked softly. She nodded toward a man standing near the orchestra. He was tall and thin, with a long face and an ill-fitting suit.

She spun Misha around so that he could look without being obvious.

"I'm supposed to lead," Misha said through gritted teeth.

"Archaic rule," she said. "Did you see him or do I have to move you again?"

"I saw him," Misha said. "He's following us."

"So you noticed," she said.

He smiled at her. "Regretfully, I do notice things other than you."

She smiled back. "You're very good at flattery."

"It's foreplay," he said.

"Oh, no," she said with a laugh. "If we go back to the room, I'll show you what foreplay is."

"You could show me here," Misha said, raising his eyebrows just a little. "And we could see just how intrepid our friend is."

"And we would make sure everyone on the ship remembered us," she said.

"I'm sure they will anyway," Misha said and this time, he spun her around.

She laughed from the sheer giddiness of it.

They continued to dance, and finally, as the music stopped, she brushed a strand of hair from her face. "Should we figure out who he is?"

"He's exactly what you think he is," Misha said.

"You've checked," she said, feeling a bit odd that he hadn't consulted her.

"It wasn't hard," Misha said. "He's not trying to hide. He's an investigator, and I assume he's from our friend."

"But you don't know," she said.

"And I'm not willing to find out. We don't want to cause trouble. And you're not supposed to be thinking about being followed. You're supposed to be thinking about your upcoming job."

She nodded, then smiled, put an arm around him, then slid her hand down his back and squeezed his ass again.

"I'd rather think about something else," she said.

He leaned over and kissed her, pulling her against him so she could feel how aroused he was. "It doesn't require thought."

"The room?" she said. "Or behind the stairs?"

"I'm too shy for behind the stairs," he said.

"It would be easy," she said. "I'm not wearing anything under this dress."

His eyes twinkled. "You drive a hard bargain," he said. "But I'm thinking of something quick, then something that takes time, and then, maybe, something quick. I'd rather have a bed for that kind of marathon."

"Who knew you were so traditional?" she said.

He put his arm around her shoulder, just like he had done when they met. He steered her out of the ballroom, and as he did, he said in her ear, "I can show you a few things that aren't traditional at all."

"Promises, promises," she said.

And then she held him to those promises when they got back to the room.

Chapter 49

THE MAN SHADOWED THEM ALL THE WAY TO PROSPERA. But when they got on the transport that would take them to the Guild, he was nowhere in sight.

Rikki almost missed him. She had gotten used to his glowering presence.

But she had more to focus on now that they were getting close to the Guild. Misha was getting nervous. She couldn't tell if he was having second thoughts.

Misha had taken her to the transport station on Prospera, then told her she would have to follow all of his instructions. There was a special way to the Guild that only members knew or people whom the Guild wanted to arrive.

They had to take a private transport. Misha hired it, and wouldn't let her near him as he did. So there were other things he had to do, things he didn't want her to see.

He sat quietly in the ground transport car he'd hired. Rikki sat close to him, hands folded in her lap. Because he wouldn't talk with her, she stared out the window at the scenery passing at five hundred miles per hour. Which meant, of course, that the scenery was just a blur of colors. She could tell she was going through a city because the colors changed from green and gold and red to dark blue and brown and black.

Otherwise there was no difference. The transport hadn't even slowed, because it was private. It just sped along the express track, going through every single station.

She had never traveled in a private transport on the planet Kordita. It felt odd. She'd been to the city of Prospera several times, but not outside it. So she didn't realize that the transport had taken a special turn toward the Guild until Misha told her the turn was unusual. It had been sharp and it made the windows in the transport become opaque.

Apparently, even if someone was cleared to hire a private transport to the Guild, that person wasn't allowed to see the way there.

The opaque windows gave an eerie light to the car, making the seats look like they were in some kind of shadow. She sat stiffly beside Misha, trying not to show her nerves.

But she was nervous, and she was beginning to think he was as well. He had gotten progressively more tense as the transport got farther away from Prospera. The gentle, sensual man she was coming to know had vanished as well. He was all hard edges and sharp lines now. His posture had become more and more rigid as they got closer to the Guild.

He had warned her that he wasn't quite certain what would happen when they arrived. He had never brought a guest before, and it had been decades since he was the newcomer. He had seen other newcomers enter the Guild, but he hadn't even been on security detail when they arrived.

He only knew in theory what would happen, and he only told her bits of that.

The transport took another sharp turn, and then came to an abrupt stop. Misha was braced, clearly ready for it, but he had to grab Rikki's arm to keep her from falling forward.

"Move with me," he said softly, keeping a grip on her.

He went to the door, slammed his hand against it, and then, as the door opened, pushed her out first.

She stumbled again, startled, and nearly fell on the three steps that led down to an empty platform.

It took her a moment to get her balance. She stood up, a bit startled at where she was.

· She was inside a station, with a small seating area, a bench, and several pillars. The station had no identification and no robotic guards that she could see.

For a moment, she thought she was the only one who had gotten off the transport, which made her stomach twist, as she wondered—fleetingly—what Misha had planned for her.

Then she saw him standing behind her, glancing around as if he was expecting someone. Maybe he was. He had told them he was bringing a friend, and he had sent her identification—her real identification. They both figured there was no reason to use an alias here since whoever hired her would know who she was, and might figure she was using her real identity to get into the Guild.

"Everything all right?" she asked softly.

He wasn't looking at her. He was scanning the area. "Let's just see how it goes," he said just as softly.

He put a hand on her arm, almost as if she was his prisoner. She wanted to shake him off, but that was because she was nervous. Still, she walked with a tension she hadn't had near Misha since she met him.

They stopped at the first pillar. A small window opened in its face.

"Weapons," he said.

He had prepared her for this, but she still didn't like

it. She had to surrender her weapons to the Guild. He swore she would get them back when she left.

If she left.

If this wasn't some kind of elaborate trick.

She made herself take a deep breath. She had to remind herself that she trusted Misha, that he had never lied to her (although he had occasionally left things out), and that he would want no harm to come to her.

Still, she couldn't get rid of the sense that she was walking naked into a pit of vipers.

She pulled out all of her weapons—her pistol, her backup pistol, and her tiny all-purpose weapon, the one she usually never removed. She had been half tempted to keep it, just to see what would happen, but she didn't.

She had agreed to this. She needed to go through with every step.

She set them all inside the window, and her heart sank as it closed, making a small sound as it whisked her weapons away.

Then it opened again, and Misha had to place his weapons inside—pistol, second pistol, and the knife he kept in his boot.

He looked as uncomfortable about this as she felt.

They moved to the next pillar. His grip remained tight on her arm. He was holding her so tightly it was almost painful. He was still looking around as if he expected something.

The window on the next pillar opened up slowly. She glanced over at Misha, uncertain what to do.

He glanced back, surprised for a moment, as if he thought she should know. And then he frowned just a little, and nodded toward the pillar.

"All identification," he said.

"All of it?" she asked.

"Legit and not," he said, and she could hear an attempt at a jaunty tone in his voice.

The attempt failed miserably.

She emptied out her identification into the window, but it didn't close.

"Any embedded identification too," he said.

"I'm not removing it," she said.

"You don't have to. We'll take care of that." He almost sounded annoyed, which made her feel annoyed. She didn't like the "we." It suddenly placed her against them.

Against him.

She extended her right hand and placed it in that little window, cringing as a warm beam of light touched her. Then she pulled back her right hand and extended her left. The same light touched it, making her tremble.

Misha felt that. He gave her his cool stare, but he didn't even try to reassure her. Maybe he had no reassurance to give.

The window closed. This little pillar didn't even make a sound as her identification got swept away.

Then the window reopened and Misha dumped all of his identification in it. He let the little scanner run over his left hand, the hand he was not holding her with.

The window closed, and Misha waited, almost as if he expected something else to happen. When it didn't, he took a deep breath.

"I guess we keep going," he said, sounding a bit confused.

He led her to the third pillar, which opened

completely, revealing a staircase leading into the darkness. His heart rate increased.

She wouldn't have noticed if she wasn't standing so close to him, if he didn't have such a firm grip on her arm that she could feel his heartbeat in his hand.

"Everything all right?" she asked as quietly as she could.

He didn't even move his lips as he replied, "This is almost too easy."

She wasn't sure what he meant: was it too easy to get into the Guild, which would be odd, since he came and went from here all the time.

Or was it too easy for her to enter?

She would ask for clarification when she could.

He started down the steps, but he kept a hand on her, holding her behind him, protecting her with his body. She kept glancing up the steps—or at least she did, until the pillar closed behind them.

Then a breeze started, caressing her face.

She stiffened at first, and finally understood what it was.

This was some kind of decontamination chamber. She hadn't ever encountered one outside of a ship or a port before. The air had that hot chemical smell that decontamination chambers always had.

Misha reached the bottom step, then looked both ways. The corridors themselves were arched, and wound in various directions. He waited in front of three of them before she reached the bottom step.

Then lights came on in a single corridor.

"Okay," he said again in an undertone, his lips still not moving. "This *is* weird."

He had told her that at some point they would separate. Clearly he had expected it before now.

"What should we do?" she asked, working to stay as
quiet as he was.

"Keep going," he said.

They walked through the lit corridor, and it wasn't
until they were almost through that she realized this was
the main part of the decontamination chamber. Then
they reached the end of it, and a single door opened,
leading into a dressing chamber.

"We have to leave our clothes too?" she asked, this
time in her regular voice.

"I warned you," he said.

"You didn't warn me about clothes," she muttered.
She stepped behind one of the dressing screens, not
because she wanted to hide herself from Misha, but
because she knew that some places like this monitored
the entries. Someone was probably watching, and there
might be laws that protected a newcomer's privacy.

At least, the privacy of their naked bodies. She was
certain her DNA had been scanned, her health monitored. Whoever ran this security system probably knew
about the carefully hidden burn scar on her hand, and
the mended bones in her body from that horrible night
so long ago.

The night she had met Misha.

She sighed and grabbed the only loose weave top that
fit her. The drawstring pants seemed to be one size, and
fortunately they were long enough for her. She slipped
the provided sandals on her feet.

Now there really was no way to hide a weapon, unless she had shoved one in a body cavity. And given

the kinds of searches the Guild tech had just given her, someone would have found that weapon too.

Rather than reassuring her, the huge search had made her even more nervous.

She emerged to find Misha waiting for her. He was wearing something similar, but on him, it looked natural. The clothing made him seem more relaxed, even though she could still feel the tension radiating off him.

His hair was tousled, like it often was in bed, and through the weave of the shirt, she could see his beautifully muscled chest. She wanted to run her hand along it, feel the contrast of the weave against the smoothness of his skin.

But then, she always wanted to touch him. It amazed her that this feeling never went away.

He took her hand and gave her a comforting smile.

"Ready for the Guild?" he asked.

"As ready as I'll ever be," she said. Fortunately he didn't ask how ready that was. Because she felt like a kid on her first day of school—terrified, out of her depth, and just a little bit trapped.

But she wasn't a kid. She was an adult, who could handle herself.

Even if, without her weapons, her clothing, and her identification, she felt more like a penitent than a person.

More like a prisoner than one of the best assassins in the sector.

"Then let's go," he said and led her out of the tiny room, and into the Guild proper.

Chapter 50

THEY STEPPED INTO A SUN-BAKED COURTYARD FILLED with greenery. The air was fresh, and it smelled of a dozen different kinds of flowers. Everywhere that Rikki looked, she could see green plants cascading over carefully manicured dirt paths. Benches were scattered throughout, and the plants themselves were structured so that they would cover an area, and reveal another.

The walls around her were tall enough that she couldn't see over them. They were made up of buildings that hooked together like row houses and they seemed to go on for miles. Some buildings appeared to stand alone. Arches made of stone and covered with ivy separated those buildings from some others, creating new paths off to the side.

She got the impression of a lot of space, a lot of land, and a lot of power.

There was also a timelessness here, as if time had stopped the moment she and Misha emerged in the courtyard.

"Wow." A voice came from one of the trees. A female voice, rich and throaty. "Did you sell your first-born, Misha?"

Misha frowned in the direction of the voice. He was looking down, so Rikki did too. A tiny woman stood between three trees, their leaves practically covering her. She came up to the middle of Rikki's chest, and she was so thin that Rikki could probably lift her with one hand.

"Shut up, Hazel," Misha said.

"I mean it, Mish. How'd you get a stranger in so deep?" The woman took a step out, her hands clasped behind her back.

Rikki could see the muscles in the woman's arms. She could also see the fondness that Misha had for her. It softened his features, made him almost smile.

"You know better than I do, Hazel," he said, "and don't pretend that you don't."

She grinned, then extended her hand to Rikki. "Hazel Sanchez."

Rikki took her hand. Hazel's grip was hard, her handshake so firm it nearly hurt. Rikki matched strength for strength.

"Rikki Bastogne," she said, feeling odd as she gave her real name. But they had to know it anyway.

"I hope you'll forgive me," Hazel said, "but I'm supposed to baby-sit while Misha explains why he brought a stranger here."

"See?" Misha said, more to Rikki than to Hazel. "I told you she knew."

Hazel's expression changed. She looked very serious. "I don't though. You have more upper level mojo than I thought, Mish."

"You think that's what it is?"

She shrugged. "I'm on probation, remember? They don't tell me nothing."

He laughed, probably because he was supposed to, since his laugh sounded a little odd. Rikki had never heard that laugh before. And she felt uncomfortable because he didn't explain anything to her.

He wouldn't tell her what Hazel Sanchez meant to

him, nor did he tell her what probation meant. Or why Hazel seemed so calm about that probation.

"Except you know where I'm supposed to go, right?" he asked Hazel.

"You know where you're going," she said with a grin.

Rikki watched, feeling separated from them both. She had never seen this side of Misha before. She was beginning to think she hadn't seen most sides of him, that he was a stranger to her.

"You know what I mean," Misha said to Hazel.

"You know what *I* mean," she said.

He made a face, but it was a pretend-exasperated face. He clearly liked this woman. He was flirting with her.

That jealousy that Rikki had teased Misha about a week or so back flared in her. He had had a relationship with Hazel, one that predated his with Rikki. She had a hunch they had never been lovers, but they had an easy friendship, one that spoke of history together, and she envied that.

Hazel stopped smiling first. Then she tilted her head to the left and said to Misha, "You're heading to the office. You need to explain yourself, my friend."

"Yeah, I figured," Misha said. Then, to Rikki's surprise, he put a hand on her shoulder and leaned into her, kissing her quickly on the lips.

It was casual, it was comfortable, and it calmed her.

"I'll be right back," he said and headed down one of the paths. "Be good."

Like she could be anything else. She was trapped inside a compound with people who didn't trust her.

It was pretty here. It smelled of flowers.

And it was about as close to hell as she had ever come.

Chapter 51

THE OFFICE WAS MISHA'S LEAST FAVORITE PLACE IN the Guild. The building itself was about half a mile from the spot where he had left Rikki, which was irritating in and of itself. He walked as fast as he could along the path; he would have jogged, but he thought it might make him look desperate.

He was feeling desperate. He didn't want to leave Rikki alone here, not even with Hazel. He had worked with Hazel for years, back when they were both apprentices. They had even partnered during their apprenticeship, helping each other on various jobs.

They'd been friends forever.

But he didn't trust her. She was a screwup. This was her fifth probation in ten years. She managed to work her way out of probation, usually by doing a spectacular job on something hard, but never could maintain that level of competence long.

Right now, he wanted Rikki beside him. He didn't want her in the hands of a screwup.

The office building was a square, five-story monstrosity. Someone had tried to design it like the other brown stone buildings of the Guild, but whoever that someone was had failed. The office looked exactly like it was—a building for bureaucrats, one that had no beauty and barely had any functionality.

The assassins who failed to survive in the outside

world worked here. They'd had the training, but for one reason or another, they couldn't handle the job itself. They "retired" inside the Guild and got to sit at desks, making life hell for everyone else.

Hazel should really have "retired" here. But she hated the office as much as Misha did, and was struggling to stay out of it as long as she possibly could.

Misha, on the other hand, had never been in danger of working here. He excelled at his job, and had from the moment he was certified.

Misha slipped in the main door, noting how much cooler the interior was than the garden. Some of that was the lack of light. This place had ceiling light so white that it seemed harsh.

Even so, they had tried to dress up the entry to make people comfortable. Tall green plants stood in corners, and blooming plants covered tables. The chairs had been both attractive and comfortable once upon a time, but were no longer. Too many nervous butts had fidgeted in those seats, too many worried people had rested their weight on their elbows on the upholstered arms.

He didn't sit. He had never sat down here. He made a point of that.

Instead, he stood near the desk, which wasn't a desk at all. It was a barrier separating the entry from the rest of the office complex.

He didn't recognize the woman behind it. She was doughy from sitting too much—that often happened to the office workers, because they were no longer required to physically train, just encouraged to. Her hair was gray, and so was her skin. Even her eyes were gray, and seemed just a bit faded.

"Mikael Yurinovich Orlinski," he said. "I had to come here to get my guest cleared."

She nodded, without saying anything. Then she handed him a tablet. "Sign in. We'll be with you when we can."

He signed his name, then looked theatrically around the entry. He was the only person here. He didn't want to tell her that he had another appointment after this. If he told the woman he was meeting with Kerani, she would think he was pulling rank, and might make him wait even longer.

But the woman ignored him, and he knew if he protested, this would take even longer than it already had.

He didn't pace because he'd once been told that pacing in the entry was annoying. He just stood between two chairs and leaned on the only empty bit of wall space.

He crossed his arms and closed his eyes most of the way, watching the room through his eyelashes.

It only took a minute.

"Mikael Yurinovich Orlinski," she said, as if she had a room full of people and had no idea which one he was.

He stood up, then met her gaze and smiled at her. She had opened a small door in that desk/barricade, and he walked through it.

"Room 53," she said, without giving him instructions.

He didn't need them. He'd been to Room 53 before. He had actually gotten lost looking for it the first time because he expected the room numbers to follow some sort of pattern.

Instead, they seemed to be random, and Room 53 was only a few yards from the front desk.

The person inside was his old sparring partner, Carl Rigley. Rigley still looked incredibly strong. He was a head taller than Misha and a bit broader. He sat on the edge of one of the biggest chairs in the room.

There were four others, as if someone was going to have a party.

Misha was surprised to see Rigley here. Rigley had been a great field operative, one of the best. He'd managed to flatten Misha half a dozen times after Misha thought his training was done.

Rigley must have seen Misha's surprise on his face, because Rigley slapped a hand against his leg.

"Distinctive limp," he said. "Too many visible scars that can no longer be covered up. An internal injury that we're not really going to discuss except to say that if you hit me wrong, I'll crater. No longer cleared for field duty. Just in case you were wondering."

Misha grabbed one of the chairs and sat across from him. "Sorry to hear it, Carl."

"Yeah, me too," Rigley said. "But theoretically this is cushy."

Misha understood the theoretically. He didn't want to leave the field either.

"You brought us a stranger," Rigley said.

Misha nodded. "And you let her inside the Guild. What's with that?"

"She's with you," Rigley said.

"Bullshit," Misha said. "She should've been stopped in one of the decon rooms if not in the station. What gives?"

"Special clearance," Rigley said. "Besides, you said this is a matter of some urgency."

Misha made a face. "You know who she is."

"Yeah," Rigley said. "Seems we had a warning about her. Someone inside the Guild wanted to see her up close and personal."

That made Misha even more nervous. "Kerani?"

Rigley shrugged. "I don't know. It's not my business."

Misha frowned. Kerani never let anyone in the Guild that easily. "Don't you find that odd?"

"My purpose is not to question my superiors but to enforce their directives." Rigley did not sound pleased. "I'm to find out what you and your lady friend need, and see if we can provide it."

"What do you mean?" Misha asked.

Rigley rolled his eyes. "Either I'm not good at bureaucratic speech yet or you aren't listening. Is she being recruited?"

"No," Misha said.

"Then why is she here?"

"To speak to our investigative branch. We have a possible threat to the Guild that needs someone with top-notch investigative skills to look into it."

"What kind of threat?" Rigley asked.

"Are you asking or is that a bureaucratic thing? Because I'd rather not discuss this too much." Misha didn't want to admit to anyone that Rikki had been hired to kill Kerani. That would cause more trouble than it solved.

Rigley leaned back in the chair, with a look of disappointment on his face. "It's just me," he said. "And mostly it's because there's no excitement here. Don't retire, Misha. There's no adrenaline inside these walls."

"I didn't think you retired," Misha said.

"Not voluntarily," Rigley said. "The injuries retired me. You stay clean."

"Yes, sir," Misha said.

The door opened, and the gray woman came in. She handed Misha a tablet. "This is where you may take your friend," she said. "Nowhere else. See that she leaves before the day is out."

Misha took the tablet but didn't look at it. Clearly the woman had been listening in.

Misha's gaze met Rigley's. "Nice chat between friends, huh?"

Rigley shrugged. "Between friends and friends of friends. Such is the way of the office."

Misha shook his head. "I don't envy you," he said as he stood up to leave.

Rigley sighed. "I don't see why anyone ever would," he said.

Chapter 52

THEY SAT ON A BENCH, WITH THEIR BACKS AGAINST THE rough stone wall, their feet extended on the large tiles that made up the sidewalk encircling the courtyard. Sunlight dappled through the trees here, and some of it warmed Rikki's feet.

She looked relaxed.

She didn't feel relaxed.

She wanted to get up and run out of this place.

"Misha kissed you," Hazel said, sounding like a teenager. A nosy teenager. "Misha doesn't touch people, let alone kiss them."

Misha touched Rikki all the time, in ways she didn't want to talk about. And that was the most chaste kiss he had ever given her.

Rikki shrugged.

"You're not going to tell me what's going on, are you?" Hazel said.

"I'll let Misha fill you in," Rikki said.

"Smart and cautious," Hazel said with a touch of annoyance in her voice.

"And she has big tits," said another voice. "Misha always liked big tits."

A petite woman with dark cropped hair stood just inside one of the doorways. As she stepped out, she tugged on the collar of her shirt which made her own breasts move.

They were large as well.

"Don't start, Liora," Hazel said.

"Oh, why not?" Liora said, looking at Rikki. "Does he spend a lot of time on them? Breasts are his favorite thing, after all."

Rikki's cheeks heated. She hadn't expected this. She was glad her face was in shadow.

"He does touch people, Hazel," Liora said. "When he fucks them."

"For God's sake, Liora," Hazel said. "You won the title of Bitch Queen of the Guild ten years ago. No one's fighting you for it this afternoon."

Liora smiled. She was pretty in a feral way. "I just wanted to see what Misha was dipping into these days. Athletic, pretty, but it's those breasts. And you're probably a bit cruel. He likes mean women because they remind him of his mother."

"Which explains why he was attracted to you," Hazel snapped. "But he realized you made his mother seem nice, so he broke up with you. *Years* ago. So lay off, Liora."

Years ago. Rikki didn't move. But she remembered what Misha had said: *One serious relationship when I was too young to know better. It ended badly a decade ago.*

This must have been it. And now Rikki understood why it ended badly.

"Oh, why should I?" Liora asked. "Misha brought her into our world. We can toy with her all we want. Tell me, does he bury his face in them, Miss Rikki Bastogne? Does he—"

"*I* don't want to hear this," Hazel said. "I like Misha,

but not that way, and you are putting images in my head that will never leave. So kindly shut up."

Rikki wasn't listening to Hazel. Or, at least, not listening closely. Because Liora had called her by name.

Now Rikki had put her identification into the system, but did that mean everyone had access to it? She would have to ask Misha. Because that seemed odd.

Rikki stretched her legs out and spread them just a little, making the movement suggestive.

"I could tell you all about our sex life if you want," she said calmly. "Detail by detail. It'll take a while. I don't mind, since it's clear you need something to jump-start yours."

Hazel made a small sound. It might have been amusement.

"Misha told me all about you," Rikki lied. "He called your relationship serious—"

"It was," Liora said. "Poor man. The end of it shattered him."

It was all Rikki could do to keep the contempt off her face. Instead, she decided to go for fake sympathy. And she lied.

"Actually, that's not what he said, exactly. He said the breakup was bad. He also said he wished he had been a little more honest with you. Because he says he can never ever love anyone. That lovely mother of his made sure of that as well."

Liora leaned her head back slightly, as if she had been slapped. Had she thought he loved her so long ago? Or had she thought that he loved Rikki, and she wanted to destroy that?

Either way, it didn't matter. Because Rikki was

telling her plainly, without going into detail, that her relationship with Misha was a purely sexual one, and that Liora could poke all she wanted, but she would never upset Rikki.

"And yes," Rikki said. "He does tend to focus on breasts."

"Oh, for God's sake," Hazel said. "I'm not allowed to leave. Can we stop this? The next thing you know, you'll both take off your shirts and compare."

"I wouldn't mind." Misha was standing at the edge of the path. His eyes were twinkling. "Although I do believe that Rikki's are not only bigger, they're also the original model with no enhancement. Which means, Liora, my dear, they have more sensation than yours ever did."

Liora glared at Misha with such hatred that Rikki's breath caught.

"You really are a son of a bitch," Liora said.

"Yes," he said calmly, "and you are, as Hazel said, the Bitch Queen of the Guild. I really don't think anyone is going to challenge you for that title."

"You heard that?" Hazel said, standing up. "You could have interrupted ten minutes ago. I had to listen to all this crap."

Misha's grin widened. "Me too." His gaze met Rikki's, so full of desire that she wished they had a private room. "I had no idea that Rikki was willing to share the details of our sex life."

Rikki grinned back at him. "I never had an interested audience before."

"I'm not interested," Liora said. "I just wanted you to know you're not that important."

Misha gave her a sideways glance that had no amusement in it. He seemed to be contemplating her, as if something she had said caught his attention.

But Liora was ignoring him. She had focused on Rikki, which annoyed Rikki to no end.

For a woman that no one considered important, Rikki sure was getting a lot of attention.

"Oh, I know I'm not important," Rikki said as blithely as she could. Misha turned toward her, and smiled at her, from his position just behind Liora. He knew Rikki had lied about what he had told her, and he didn't care. He seemed to be enjoying the discussion. "That's what made these last few weeks fun. They were about sex and nothing else. I'm sure you've had relationships like that too, Liora. Or do you call them relationships?"

She glanced at Hazel who threw her hands in the air and stood up.

"Am I excused now?" Hazel asked. "Because I was raised to keep my love life private—and I would if I had one. But I really, really don't like hearing about other people's."

"I'll take it from here," Misha said.

Hazel shook her head. "I'm sure you will," she said with an odd glance at Rikki. "C'mon, Liora. Let's leave these two alone."

"I'm not going with you," Liora said and pivoted. She headed down a side path, the branches of various plants rustling in her wake.

Rikki stood up. Misha walked toward her, and slipped his arm around her.

"That was fun," she said.

He kissed her behind her ear, sending a shiver

through her. "You know it's not impersonal for me," he whispered.

"I'm beginning to figure that out," she said.

He tugged on her earlobe gently with his teeth, and then pulled her close.

"Let's finish up here," he said softly, "and then go back to Prospera. I know a wonderful hotel with the best room service in the city."

"I have a hunch I'm not going to care about room service for several hours after we return," she said. "Provided there's other service."

"Oh, there will be," he said. "You can trust me on that."

Chapter 53

MISHA WANTED TO GET RIKKI OUT OF THE GUILD AS quickly as he could, partly because he had found that discussion so incredibly erotic, and partly because he couldn't get past the feeling that something was very wrong at the Guild, something he sensed but couldn't quite see.

It bothered him that Liora had found him on Oyal. It bothered him that she had known about Rikki then, and that she had known that Rikki went to Krell.

Now it bothered him that Rikki had gotten into the Guild so easily and that one of the first people she talked with was Liora.

Still, he had enjoyed watching Rikki best Liora verbally. Not many people could do that. He had been able to—that had been part of the attraction, the fights that they had—but it quickly wore thin, particularly when he realized that Liora was as empty emotionally as he was.

Rikki wasn't empty. She was fiery and passionate. But she could set it aside, which was probably something she had learned as a child. And when he was near her, he felt fiery and passionate, and not like himself at all.

His fingers had wandered to the side of her breast, probably because of the discussion about them. Liora had been right; he liked breasts. But more to the point, he liked Rikki's. He preferred them, and it drove him nuts that they were loose under the weave of that shirt. He wanted to capture them in his hands, and he didn't dare...

Nor did he dare continue with these thoughts when he needed to concentrate on being here. Rikki hadn't had any training. She didn't know what kind of people she had been talking to. Rikki was good, but he doubted she could take Liora in a fair fight.

And knowing Liora, the fight wouldn't be fair.

He walked with his arm around Rikki down the path. If someone had asked a few hours ago, he would have said he was doing this to maintain their cover story. But that wasn't really true. He wanted to continue touching her, and he wanted to protect her.

She didn't belong in the Guild, she wasn't a member, and the others were letting her know that. Even Hazel wanted to keep her distance, and that wasn't like her.

The office had only given him permission to take Rikki to the investigative unit, and then she had to leave. He didn't mind. He didn't want to stay either.

The investigative unit had its housing in the newest part of the Guild, not far from this part of the courtyard. The unit upgraded its technology whenever the Guild did, and finally the directors decided to put the unit as close to the new tech as it possibly could.

Strangely, though, the unit's building was open, with courtyards of its own, balconies on the second and third floors, and an open patio filled with tables and comfortable seating areas.

Kerani explained it to Misha once. She said that most members of the investigative unit never left the building, so they needed a comfortable place to work. The investigators who did their work on the fly, like he had always imagined investigators would, were the elite of the group—and the only ones with people skills.

He slipped in a side door, his arm still around Rikki. She didn't say anything, and moved as silently as she did.

He avoided the unit's reception area because he already had passes for both of them. Instead, he went to the forensic accounting division. He slid his arm down Rikki's side, and found her hand, wrapping his fingers in hers. Then he led her up a narrow flight of stairs to the second floor.

The forensic accounting division had one of those balconies. The doors were open, letting in the sunlight and the fresh breeze, which was good, because the division itself smelled of hot equipment, old food, and sweat.

Several accountants sat on various chairs, working on tablets, but only one sat at a desk, and he was the one Misha needed to talk to. He frowned. And of course, that person had to be Giles Fauchet.

Misha had known Fauchet as long as he had known Liora. In fact, Misha discovered after his breakup with Liora that she had been sleeping with Fauchet as well.

Fauchet had once had a rugged handsomeness, but that had gotten buried in his fleshy face. Or maybe Misha was just biased. Still, it pleased him to note that Fauchet was no longer the trim man he had been a decade ago. He had thickened out. And some of that thickness was not muscle.

"Well if it isn't Mikael Yurinovich Orlinski and the mystery woman." Fauchet leaned back in his chair. It actually groaned under his weight. "To what do I owe this honor?"

"It's not about you, Fauchet," Misha said. "I have something very serious here, and if you can't work with me, let's find someone who can."

Misha still held Rikki's hand, and he squeezed it. He wanted to reassure her that everything would be all right, but he didn't want to focus on her. Right now, he needed to concentrate on Fauchet and making sure this got done right.

Whatever bad he could say about Fauchet—and he could say a lot—there was one thing Misha knew: Fauchet was the best financial investigator that the Guild had.

"I don't even know what the problem is," Fauchet said. His gaze wandered to Rikki. She remained quiet beside Misha, clearly waiting for an opportunity to speak.

"Someone wants to kill Kerani," Misha said.

Fauchet shrugged. "And this is news how?"

When Misha had told Kerani of this near the office, she had reacted to the news the same way. She had barely thought it worth his time to report it.

Their meeting had only taken a minute, so short it could barely be counted as a meeting. She hadn't thought the threat important. She figured she was safe here. But she had been the one to give him permission to investigate the threat.

Apparently, she hadn't contacted the investigative unit, leaving it to him. Misha hated explaining this.

"They hired Rikki to kill Kerani."

Four people stood up. Another grabbed a weapon. Misha raised his hand to stop them all.

Rikki didn't move. He had warned her this would happen, and he had told her a lot would ride on her remaining nonaggressive.

So far, she was listening.

"Rikki turned the job down on her own," Misha

said. "She couldn't track the client, and that's important to her."

"Oh, a Rover with a conscience," someone said from beside the door. Misha couldn't see that person clearly, because he was in shadow.

"I'm not a Rover," Rikki said. Misha squeezed her hand. He didn't want her to talk. But she ignored him. "Not all independent assassins are affiliated with the Rovers."

"Anyway," Misha said over her. "I convinced her to take the job."

The person with the weapon turned it toward Misha.

He ignored it, and continued to focus on Fauchet, who looked fascinated.

"I wanted the client to pay her so that we had a money trail," Misha said.

Fauchet shrugged. "So why didn't you follow the trail?"

"We did," Misha said. "Whoever hired her is good. We kept losing the trail, and always in different ways. We need an expert to track it."

Fauchet grinned. "I'll take the compliment, even though I'm sure you didn't mean it."

"I did mean it," Misha said. He didn't add that he would have brought this to whoever was running the financial investigation division this afternoon. "This person is serious. He wants Kerani dead."

"So you bring the killer in here," said the person with the weapon.

Misha finally focused on him. He was young, clearly an in-the-field washout. Misha had never met him.

"Rikki didn't want the job," Misha said. "She's not going to do the job. But you can bet with the kind of money this client is throwing around, someone will."

"They won't be able to get into the Guild," Fauchet said. "And Kerani never leaves."

"Rikki got in," Misha said.

"With you vouching for her," Fauchet said.

"See how easy it is?" Rikki asked. She clearly didn't like Fauchet and she didn't have Misha's history with him. Misha squeezed her hand again, wishing she would shut up.

"Rafiq died inside the Guild," Misha said, reminding Fauchet that the previous director had been murdered.

"Because one of ours went off his nut," Fauchet said.

"Did one of ours go off his nut?" Misha asked. "Or was he hired?"

"We never found any money," Fauchet said.

"People can be paid in ways other than money," Misha said.

"Like sex," said the man with the gun.

Misha had had enough. "Sit down," he said to the man with the gun. "You're embarrassing yourself. I can disarm you in a nanosecond and you know it."

"But I'd still get a shot off," the man said.

"And you'd miss, the way you're holding the weapon," said Fauchet without turning around. "You're reflected in the door, my man, and believe me, it's a wonder you even made it through training."

The man glared at Misha, then looked at the others as if he expected them to back him. They didn't. He set the gun down on a nearby table, and sat, looking chastised.

"You made your point," Fauchet said. "Give me the information, and I'll see what I can find."

"You need to give Rikki a tablet," Misha said. "She'll open her accounts for you."

Misha said that with some import, because he wanted Fauchet to know that Rikki was making a sacrifice too.

But as Fauchet picked up a blank tablet, he didn't seem impressed. He handed it to Rikki.

"I'm sure you're smart enough to decouple the accounts from your personal information," he said to her, in a tone that implied she wasn't that smart at all.

Misha started to defend her, but this time, it was Rikki who squeezed his hand. She took the tablet with the other hand.

"Thank you for the reminder," she said sweetly as if she hadn't thought of it.

She squeezed Misha's hand a final time, then unhooked her fingers from his. Quickly, she put the account information into the tablet, then handed it to Fauchet.

"I've never used this account before," she said. "So all the contacts and all of the money in it have come from the client. I made a secondary file of all the passwords and names linked to the account so you can trace the information better. Misha and I didn't get far because this client knows what he's doing. He encrypted things in a way I've never seen before."

Her tone was careful, respectful, as if she had no idea how poorly Fauchet was treating her. Her entire behavior in the Guild had been a revelation to Misha.

No wonder people underestimated her. She lied easily, often playing dumb or downplaying something's importance, all the while fooling the people she was talking with.

Misha hated downgrading his own intelligence, even when he was playing a role. Yet Rikki used that technique to her advantage.

He had a lot to learn from her.

She smiled sweetly and handed the tablet back to Fauchet. He took it from her, his gaze running over her face as if he was trying to memorize it.

"I can contact you if I have questions?" he asked.

"Of course," she said. "You can reach me through Misha."

Fauchet still held the tablet. "You're a mystery, you know," he said. "I'm not sure I would give up five times my usual fee for love. Even if it is our Misha here."

Rikki smiled at him. "I never said I gave it up for love," she said. "I didn't like the client. He presumed that he could buy me, and I can't be bought."

Then she grabbed Misha's hand. Her grip was tight, but her palms were sweaty. He frowned at her.

"Can we leave now?" she asked.

He nodded. "Find this person," he said to Fauchet.

"Oh," Fauchet said, bending over the tablet. "I'm sure I will."

Chapter 54

RIKKI PRACTICALLY PULLED MISHA FROM THAT SECOND floor room. She knew she had to keep up appearances. She had to seem out of her depth, almost subservient, just so that no one would think she was conniving.

But she knew she wasn't the most conniving person in this compound. She wasn't even close.

She got Misha down the steps and the moment they stepped outside into the sunshine and the flowers, she said, "I don't like this."

"He has hated me for years," Misha said. "But he's good at his job. He—"

"I don't care about your past relationship," she said. "Two things happened this afternoon that shouldn't have."

"The Guild isn't the friendliest place to non—"

"Shut up and listen!" She raised her voice, then made herself take a deep breath. "Your friend Liora knew my name. I blew it off, figuring that I gave up my identification, but I didn't like it. Even your friend Hazel seemed surprised by it."

Misha frowned. She had his attention now.

"And upstairs, just a minute ago, that horrible man said that he wouldn't give up five times his usual fee for love."

"He wouldn't," Misha said. "He's not the kind of man to care about anyone but himself."

"You're so caught up in your past relationships with

these people that you're not thinking about what's actually going on," Rikki said, her voice even lower. She had no idea if this courtyard was bugged, if there were listening devices on the bushes beside her. "Pay attention to me, Misha. I never told him about the fee. There's nothing in my accounts that mentions the original fee that the client offered me. Only three people know that I got five times the original fee offered. You, me, and the client."

Misha froze. She could see all of the information filter through his brain, plus, she would wager, other pieces of information as well, things that happened that had clearly caught his attention, things she couldn't know because she didn't have the history. She watched him put things together, and she watched him become even more serious than he had been before.

"Come with me," he said, tugging on her hand.

"You said I can't go anywhere else," she said.

"If I leave you here," he said, "someone will probably kill you. That's what we're all trained for, remember?"

"I can defend myself," she said.

"Against five or six, maybe," he said. "Against dozens? No one's that good, Rikki. No one."

He had a point. He pulled her forward, and together they ran in a direction she hadn't gone before. Misha set a good pace and he had a great point about the risks to her life.

But she didn't like any of this. They had entered some kind of no-win situation from the moment she let herself get hired.

She should have realized it when Misha told her it had been too easy to get her inside the Guild. And then that horrible Liora woman had known her name. She hadn't taunted Rikki because she disliked Rikki or because she wanted Misha for herself.

She had taunted her to make her mad, to make her seem reckless to Hazel. But Rikki hadn't played along. And then Misha had arrived.

Liora hadn't left because she was angry. She had probably gone away to institute plan B—whatever that was.

Misha was running too quickly for Rikki to tell him this, and honestly, at this point, it was all supposition anyway. She had no idea where he was taking her. Maybe he was getting her out of the Guild.

That would be best for all of them.

Then they rounded a corner, and actually went through some greenery. It was a projection of some kind. The path sloped downward, and Rikki was so surprised at what she saw that she almost skidded to a stop.

Somehow, hidden among the buildings and the greenery, was an oasis of calm. A reflecting pool, surrounded by weeping willows. A woman sat on one of the benches with her feet tucked underneath it. She was elegant, wearing a deep blue sari.

She turned toward them, and Rikki gasped. It was the target. Only she was lovelier in person, with an angular face and hair so black it seemed to absorb light.

She stood when she saw them.

"Misha," she said. "What are you doing? You are not to bring this woman here—"

Something moved behind her.

Rikki shook her hand free of Misha's and ran toward the woman. Misha grabbed for her and missed.

The woman raised a small pistol and shot in a single movement. The shot hit Rikki, sending searing pain through her, but she didn't stop. She passed the woman, leapt onto the bench, and used it as leverage, so that her feet hit the intruder in the throat.

Rikki landed on her back, but she wasn't surprised to see Liora sprawled beside her.

Liora raised another pistol.

"You are so cooperative," she said and fired.

Chapter 55

LIORA'S SHOT MISSED, JUST LIKE RIKKI EXPECTED IT TO.

At least, it missed her. She hoped to hell it hadn't hit Kerani. Because Liora was holding Rikki's favorite pistol, and it wouldn't take much to make it look like Rikki had just completed the job she was paid for.

Despite the searing pain in her side, Rikki pushed off the ground and lunged for Liora. Liora let the gun drop, just like Rikki expected, and Rikki knew that the worst thing she could do at this moment was pick that gun up.

Instead, she went for Liora's throat.

Liora didn't expect it, but she managed to get her knees between them and tried to buck Rikki away. Rikki was bigger, but not stronger. Still, she had leverage.

She couldn't reach Liora's throat, so she grabbed her face on either side. Liora's eyes widened. Rikki pulled her head up just slightly so that it wasn't against the ground.

Liora kicked and thrashed, but Rikki held her down. Then Rikki twisted her head so hard to the right that she was sure everyone in the Guild heard the crack.

Liora went limp, her neck snapped, her eyes open.

Rikki let her go, then stood up, wiping her hands on those ridiculous loose weave pants. That pistol of hers looked mighty tempting, but she didn't grab it.

She hoped Misha would help her get out of here, but she wasn't sure he would, now that she had killed a woman he had once cared for, and had probably even loved.

No matter what the man said, he was capable of great emotion. And that emotion would probably be turned against her now.

She took a deep breath and turned around.

Both Misha and the director of the Guild stood behind her. The director's sari had a burn hole along the left side where that last laser shot had hit her.

Rikki's heart was pounding, and her own wound ached. But she knew better than to look at it. She didn't want to know how bad it was until she got out of here.

Misha looked at Liora, then at Rikki.

"I should have seen it," he said.

Rikki waited. Everything would depend on the next few minutes.

"She usually didn't even give me the time of day," he said. "And suddenly she was talking to me, acting jealous, trying to goad me. It fit."

Rikki blinked, feeling awkward, feeling very tired. The shock was setting in.

Misha wasn't talking about her. He was talking about Liora.

"We need medical attention," Kerani said. Still, she extended a hand to Rikki. "You saved my life today."

Rikki took a deep breath.

"My people missed it all," Kerani said, sounding both sad and surprised. "We'll need to investigate this."

"You better pick your investigators well," Rikki said. "I'm sure that Giles Fauchet's man is involved."

Kerani nodded. Very slowly. Too slowly. Rikki frowned. Why would someone nod slowly? It made no sense.

Just like the darkness covering the sun made no sense.

Oh, she was tired.

She closed her eyes, and thought she had better ease herself to the ground.

And that was the last thought she had for some time.

Chapter 56

SHE WOKE ON A COOL BED UNDER COOL SHEETS. SHE FELT like she had been sleeping for a long time. She recognized the muzzy feeling, the deep unsettled feeling of having lost consciousness against her will.

She expected to be in a hospital, but she wasn't. She was in a gorgeous hotel room, with paneled walls and windows overlooking the city of Prospera.

Shouldn't she be in a hospital? Or was that a long time ago? Way back in her past, in her childhood, when she had been in a hospital alone.

Only she hadn't been alone then, and she wasn't alone now.

Someone was holding her hand.

She turned her head.

Misha sat beside her. He looked haggard and too thin. When he saw her, he smiled.

"Welcome back, beautiful."

She frowned. "Back?" she whispered.

"You were unconscious for a while. Healing, the doctors said. But the wound wasn't serious. The doctors let me bring you here."

"Nonsense," she said, meeting his smile with her own. "You people didn't want me to stay in the Guild."

His smile widened. "That too."

The memory of that last day had come back. "Did your director make it?" Rikki asked.

"Barely," he said. "She nearly died. But as you guessed, we have good medical facilities in the Guild, and there was time."

She looked out the window at the city below. She rubbed her eyes, but the view didn't change. "I'm a bit surprised to be here."

"Why?" he asked.

"I figured someone would blame me," she said.

"Liora and Fauchet tried that. It didn't work."

"Still," she said. "I would have thought—"

"Kerani spoke up for you. She's the one who made sure everyone knew what had happened. She is amazed you fought for her, Rikki, when you didn't know her and weren't a Guild member."

"And had a past affiliation with the Rovers," Rikki said.

He nodded reluctantly. "That too," he said. "But that doesn't change the fact that you saved Kerani. You stopped a plot to overturn the Guild."

She licked her lips. They were dry. "I didn't stop any plot," she said. "We—you and I—we just revealed it."

"Whatever," he said and put his other hand on top of their clasped one. "Fauchet confessed. Liora's dead. And Kerani is still with us. Thanks to you."

"And you. Thanks to you." Rikki swallowed against a dry throat. "Thank you for getting me out of the Guild."

"My pleasure," he said. "I promised you a hotel room."

"You promised me room service," she said.

"I promised you a different kind of service," he said.

"Is that what you're here for?" she asked a little more seriously than she planned. "A bit of service, and then you'll return to the Guild."

"No," he said. "I'm staying with you. I'm not leaving your side. Ever."

"Even if I told you to go?" she asked.

He looked so fierce. "Even then."

She smiled. "Good. Because I want you here."

"Good," he said in the same tone. "Because I realized something these last few days, Rikki."

She had to turn her head to see him better. The tousled hair, the blue, blue eyes. She had come to trust that face. She had come to trust him.

"What's that?" she asked.

"I love you," he said. "You were right, what you said to Liora. I didn't think I could love anyone. But I love you."

Rikki felt warm, suddenly, and safe, for the first time, maybe ever. He had told her he loved her. So she could tell him how she felt too.

But wouldn't it sound like she was parroting him? Like she was just saying it?

Then she decided she didn't care how it sounded, because it was true.

"I love you too," she said. "I knew it in my apartment. But I didn't want to tell you."

"Because you didn't trust me," he said.

She shook her head. "Because I didn't trust myself."

He grinned, and the look made all the exhaustion leave his face. He was the most handsome man she had ever seen.

"You're extremely trustworthy, Rikki," he said.

"Yeah, that's why your friends targeted me."

"First," he said, "they weren't my friends. And secondly, they targeted you because I complained about you. You kept crossing my path. They figured they could use it to show that you were going after Kerani and you were using me to do so."

"Devious people," she muttered.

"Yeah," he said. "But no match for you."

"I'm devious?" She could be, she supposed. She preferred not to be, though.

"No," he said. "You're brilliant. And it was my mistake that I hadn't realized just how brilliant you are. Forgive me?"

"As long as you don't expect me to join the Guild." She sounded like a petulant child, but she didn't care. "I don't like it, Misha."

"I know," he said. "You don't have to join."

"Which means we can't be together," she said softly.

"Why not?" he asked.

"Because you can't leave," she said. "The Guild, it's part of you."

He nodded. "It is. It's where I grew up. But people leave home all the time, Rikki. And I want to be with you. If you'll have me."

Silly question. She smiled at him. "Only if you promise me one thing."

"What's that?" he asked, looking oh so serious.

"Room service."

He smoothed the hair off her forehead, and then he kissed her. Hard. Passionately. And that woke up all of her.

"Your wish is my command," he said and proceeded to fulfill his promise. Several times—and in a variety of fun and interesting ways.